THE HARBINGER BROKEN

THE HARBINGER BROKEN

ERIC N. LARD

The Harbinger Broken
Copyright © 2026 Eric N. Lard. All rights reserved.

Published By: 4 Horsemen Publications, Inc.

4 Horsemen Publications, Inc.
PO Box 419
Sylva, NC 28779
4horsemenpublications.com
info@4horsemenpublications.com

Cover by CD Corrigan
Typesetting by Autumn Skye
Edited by Joseph Mistretta

All rights to the work within are reserved to the author and publisher. No part of this publication may be reproduced, stored in a retrieval system, or transmitted in any form or by any means, electronic, mechanical, photocopying, recording, scanning, or otherwise, except as permitted under Section 107 or 108 of the 1976 International Copyright Act, without prior written permission except in brief quotations embodied in critical articles and reviews. Please contact either the Publisher or Author to gain permission.

All characters, organizations, and events portrayed in this novel are either products of the author's imagination or are used fictitiously.

All brands, quotes, and cited work respectfully belongs to the original rights holders and bear no affiliation to the authors or publisher.

Library of Congress Control Number: 2025949797

Paperback ISBN-13: 979-8-8232-1039-3
Hardcover ISBN-13: 979-8-8232-1040-9
Ebook ISBN-13: 979-8-8232-1041-6

DEDICATION

To the love of my life and mother of my wonderful boys who continues to put up with this ridiculous ambition of writing stories and selling them.

CONTENTS

Prologue ix
Chapter 1 1
Chapter 2 21
Chapter 3 45
Chapter 4 57
Chapter 5 84
Chapter 6 108
Chapter 7 128
Chapter 8 154
Chapter 9 175
Chapter 10 194
Chapter 11 219
Chapter 12 238
Chapter 13 259
Chapter 14 280
Book Club Questions 283
Author Bio 285

PROLOGUE

OFF-TIME

Realm Kirksfold, Dain Burrough
(The Dustbin), Badbriars

Present

She hadn't seen it coming.

Maddie Timms, or Madame Harbinger as some referred to her, Special Agent of Bureau Ekron, stared down in disbelief at the blood seeping between her fingers. The knife wound was in her stomach, just below the ribs.

Quaking legs struggled to carry her toward the dim haze of a streetlight haloed in mist. They faltered and she hit the ground, nails scrabbling on the bridge's slick cobblestone as she strained to stay upright.

I can't go out this way.

"Impressive," the man intoned casually, his voice smooth and rich as a well-aged Brythelund Barrow.

"Is it?" she managed between gasping breaths.

She blinked back tears as she held her breath, struggling to apply pressure to the wound with arms sapped by the onset of shock.

Dammit, it's deep. Mortal, she was sure. And, in this state, she was much too weak to bend time. Little good it would do her. The man before her could bend both time *and* space. She would die here in the slums of Realm Kirksfold.

Fitting, in a way. Some of her greatest work—and deepest regrets—lived here.

A distant foghorn split the silence. The man waited until its mournful wail receded and then stepped forward into the wan light, his meticulously polished wingtips clacking softly on the wet stone.

"Quite impressive. When did you figure out about the Operatrix?" he asked, referring to the headmistress of the Guild of Ways. His smile was warm. There was a twinkle in his eye, causing him to look very much like the tenured professor chatting over a pint with his star pupil.

"Just now," she rasped out as she sucked in another breath. Her stabilizing arm slipped, causing her to grind her teeth before gulping another breath. Each movement sent a jolt of icy fire through her. They crowded rational thought from her mind, leaving only a desperate desire to stay conscious. To spend one more minute on this familiar side of eternity.

Maddie cursed her weakness as warm tears flowed down her cheeks. After everything, chasing a phantom through time and *finally* uncovering the truth... She didn't want to give the bastard the satisfaction. Her mind darted from one outcome to the next, grasping at possibilities. Was someone coming to find her? No, they were all dead. Would a passerby confront him? No, they'd just die too, or he'd bend time to redo the moment. Also, it was the middle of the night in Kirksfold. Nobody cared.

"And what was it? Was it Raybold? No, no, it was Mankeer, wasn't it?" He drew out the fallen agent's name, as sudden understanding lit his eyes, erasing the modest wrinkles at their corners.

The response leaped from her throat, "Raybold. Mankeer. Jerse." She growled through gritted teeth, "Evesy, Lute... You killed them all to cover your tracks." *Erased them, really.* With that thought, she buried her chin in her chest and tried not to move or breathe.

This was it. He had to know he wasn't perfect. That despite his best efforts, she'd found them all. Or most of them, anyway. Names that should never have been removed from history.

Of course, she had still assumed he was acting with the help of others. It was impossible for one man to do it all, wasn't it? To shift the course of history without anyone suspecting a thing. Who knew what knowledge had been lost? What lies had become truth?

But now she understood. He *wasn't* a man. She didn't know *what* he was.

"Expand your mind, agent. This is much bigger than a handful of murders," he replied, staring down at her. It was an almost paternal admonishment. "So, it was Mankeer, then. That *was* sloppy. A moment but thricely," he said, shaking his head and clucking softly. "Very sloppy, indeed. I dare say I was sweating like a drunken deckhand by the third time-slip in so short a span. Agent Mankeer was sharp. He knew the second he saw me, of course. But he wasn't expecting me to bend the supposedly *immutable* laws of the temporal matrix and show up *off-time*."

He smiled, absently smoothing an eyebrow with his ring finger as he recalled the memory and then focused back on

Maddie. "Of course, I'm quite surprised you, of all people, didn't expect it either."

"Off-time?" Maddie blanched. That's how she'd been caught? She'd met him here, expecting to see the telltale flash of light when he bent space; to move in for the kill. It would be an awesome feat outside of a wayportal, but one she'd concluded must be within the killer's abilities. She'd planned for it. But when he appeared before her without warning...?

"That's right... I see the little gears turning. I've suspected for a long time that you could do it as well, you know. To bend time at will without having to wait on the hand of a clock to tell you when it was safe to cross the proverbial street, so to speak. And despite all your schooling telling you otherwise. You're really quite gifted. It's a shame."

Maddie fumbled for words, struggling to piece together how he could possibly know that one particular fact she'd worked so hard to keep hidden.

"Oh, enough of that. By now you must understand I've been watching your work with keen interest—guiding it, really. But enough about you. Back to me," he said, clapping his hands together. "Out of curiosity, when was it that you knew the killer was *just* one person? Not a clockie and a waysmith working together to manipulate temporal and spatial fabrics?" He asked this while wrapping a white silk scarf tightly around the knuckles of his left hand. He wiggled his fingers before making a fist and looking at it contemplatively.

When she failed to respond, he looked down. Maddie was struggling to maintain consciousness, but through a monumental effort of will, she lifted her chin and locked eyes with her killer in a final show of defiance. He nodded acknowledgment. And then his visage hardened. "So be it. I'll allow you to keep your little secret."

Then, stepping forward, his eyes gleaming with sadistic glee, he tightened his fist. "Carry it to the grave, shall you?"

He drew back his fist and before she could register the movement, she was lost to darkness.

CHAPTER 1

GHOSTS IN THE MIST

Realm Kirksfold, Dain Burrough
(The Dustbin), Southend on Selby

Four Days Prior

Holland Finnery stood alone in the predawn gloom, hands stuffed in the pockets of his heavy coat, staring absently at the mucky banks of an empty riverbed. A meager trickle flowed through its channels, but the muddy sand was dark with moisture from Realm Kirksfold's near-perpetual fog. He followed the stream toward the beach where the once-vigorous river had emptied into the Dains Bay.

Sadly, there was more of the same. Decades prior, the tide had gone out and never bothered to return, leaving only mud and the perpetual stench of low tide as a reminder. No reasonable explanation was ever provided by the authorities. Gravity and the hydrologic cycle appeared to be broken, and it was met with a collective shrug. How very Kirksfold.

Now it was the Dainsmire; miles of mist-shrouded and unnavigable muck. It provided a natural defense from over-aggressive neighbors, of which there was a seemingly endless supply, but it was hell on commerce.

Lost in thought, Holland gave it little attention as he turned right at the grassy dunes skirting the beach and trudged on. Dim spheres of light bloomed around streetlamps that stretched out into the gloom. Wind through the bamboo-like horsetail reeds hushed the dull thud of his boots as they beat their plodding mantra. A cold gust slipped a finger inside his collar. He shivered and burrowed deeper into his jacket before realizing he'd arrived at his destination.

A pier resting on tall, barren pilings disappeared out into the heavier fog of the Dainsmire. Beneath scattered lights, it looked like the ribcage of a massive snake; like the stretched-out bones of Ouroboros. He made his way along its broad-planked back until he reached the end.

"Must be dawn by now," he offered to the indifferent mist and then turned to look back the way he'd come. If the sun had bothered to come up, there wasn't the barest hint of it yet.

Holland turned and stared off into the darkness beyond the railing. A hundred yards farther on could be the chasm at the end of the world or the gleaming brilliance of Vantipolis, the pride of Realm Brythe itself, and he would never know it. Of course, Brythe was where the clockies were from. The seat of Bureau Ekron enjoyed a level of opulence unimaginable in Kirksfold.

Even Vellem, just beyond the portals in Dain Burrough's Hall of Ways, was orders of magnitude more affluent. Nothing good came from Vellem, but all things traveled through it. It was a tragic irony that Kirksfold—the place where all the waysmiths were born and without which the three realms would be nothing more than isolated islands of existence—was so destitute. But, as the saying goes, "Time *is* money." Especially when the past needed constant maintenance in order to stay the way you left it.

Holland searched the fog as troubled thoughts slipped beneath roiling seas of regret and remorse and, more than anything, futility.

Why couldn't it have been me?

His eyes lit on ghostly shapes shifting within the fog. Real or imagined, truth be told, he yearned to join them. Year after dismal year, the loneliness, the weight of life pressing down on him, crushed his soul into a thin, gossamer film. Soon, he figured it would just blow away. Or cease to be all together. He was ready for it.

He wallowed in the idea for long minutes and then grimaced before shaking his head in resignation. Holland unbuttoned his jacket with knobby fingers, stiff from years of working with his hands. Some of those years had been with the tools of a silversmith. But before that, they'd been the tools of a soldier—a maker of widows and orphans. And probably some of the very ghosts who haunted these mists. In fact, he was certain of it.

He removed his jacket, folding it and setting it down next to him on the bench. He untied his boots and removed his socks. His bare feet felt the rough planks of the pier. And then he did likewise with his shirt and slacks, feeling the bracing cold on his skin, but none of the exhilaration that should have come with it.

Could he just die of exposure? It'd be a decent way to go. No mess. No fuss.

He doubted it, though. It was cold, but not that kind of cold. He should have come out last winter. Then, he'd been in a bad way, and could barely muster the energy to get out of bed. *I am doing* so *much better now*, he thought ironically.

His eyes drifted down to the revolver he only half realized was in his lap, lying loosely in his hand. When had he grabbed it? Tiny droplets of moisture blistered the black metal.

Holland shivered hard against the cold. He was wearing nothing but boxers, old tattoos, and sinewy muscle under sagging skin. Today was his sixtieth birthday. And, of infinitely greater importance, the ten-year anniversary of the death of his wife of twenty-five years. A great hollowness bloomed inside of him.

He pulled back the hammer, watching in fascination as the cylinder revolved, bringing the solitary .32 caliber bullet into alignment with the pistol's snub-nose barrel. It settled into place, ready to do its work.

"Why shouldn't I?" he asked defiantly, his voice wavering and dropping away almost immediately in the enveloping fog. As expected, there was no response.

He stared back out into the depths. Water dripped from his hairline into his eyes and for a second, he could swear he saw her. The loaded pistol dropped to the bench as he frantically rubbed his eyes, desperate to catch a glimpse. But there was no one there. Just a trick of the fog and the light being devoured by it. The gun slid from its perch, hit the heavy planking, and went off like a thunderclap.

A dozen yards away, the railing splintered. Holland leaped to his feet, his attention darting from the smoking gun to the railing and then back out into the swirling mists. After a long beat, he shuddered, letting out a nervous, half-hearted laugh.

"Still looking out for me, Meri?"

He smiled momentarily before his laughter turned bitter and he was wiping tears from his eyes with the palms of his hands. He shivered again, harder this time, and shoved his numb fingers under his armpits and hugged himself close.

This was utter and complete foolishness.

There was no *easy* way out. If he ended it, wasn't it more likely he'd just be trading one hell for another? Besides, shouldn't she have moved on by now? It'd been a decade for Gadd's sake.

Of course she had. He was being a sentimental idiot. Meri had always been too good for this place.

His eyes dropped to the revolver. An idiot *and* a coward. As it was, there were things here in Kirksfold that still needed doing. If he couldn't help himself, at least he could help someone else, maybe. It was his penance. For not being there instead of her. And it seemed, in his mind at least, that she still wanted him to stay at it. *Very well.*

Holland stood there shivering for a while before reaching for his trousers. He was feeling the cold for real now. His teeth chattered as he fumbled with the zipper and buttons. He pulled on his shirt and jacket and finally his boots before reaching down and retrieving the now-cold revolver. Without giving it a second glance, he reared back and hucked it out into the mist. It was gone from view before it even reached the peak of its arc. He wouldn't be needing it and no one would find it out in the hundreds of square miles of mud.

Besides, he'd made up his mind about what to do next.

Over the last few months, he'd scraped together enough for another covert trip to St. Blair's in Vellem. He had a standing deal with the headmistress; she didn't ask where the kids came from, or how they got there, as long they had their implant ID, and their papers were in order. He didn't know what he'd been waiting for, but now was as good a time as any.

The civvy pack was the tough part. Transiting between realms was a highly regulated activity. All of it was overseen by the Operatrix and every waysmith was required to have their own implant ID to do it. But Holland was able to do it off books.

He was unique in this way, having a level of giftedness with waysmithing that allowed him to transit without the focusing element of a portal. A gift that, if discovered, would either mean his death, or his imprisonment for the rest of his life. The ability was much too dangerous a thing to be left in the hands of someone outside the system.

He didn't know if the Operatrix herself could do it. But she could sense the movements. That's why, even though he was generally an honest and upright citizen, he had to have a special smuggler's implant made to mask his activities.

And in order to keep his secret a secret, he tried to minimize how often he used his gift. But, if there was no point to his continued existence, he could at least do this in the meantime.

Still, the waysmithing was the easy part. The hard part was getting the implant installed and the documents that went along with it. That meant sneaking around the city after dark in some very sketchy parts of town. An old fool and a young kid would present easy targets. But he had ways...

First, he'd have to tell his apprentice not to come in today. Clients, he'd say. Supplies. Gone overnight. That'd do it.

Holland wiped his eyes once more and turned to walk back to his shop. In the eastern sky, there was a vague glow.

"You're late," he grumbled, before trudging in silence back to his humble workshop to make preparations.

Ghosts In The Mist

Realm Kirksfold, Dain Burrough
(The Dustbin), Old Fishmarket & Pendaring

Prentiss neared the end of the row of street vendors, twiddling thumbs and whistling a buoyant tune. He paid an inordinate amount of attention to the faded awning overhead while listening for ... wait for it—

"Hey? Where's my wallet? Hey! You there! Hey, kid!"

Prentiss spun on his heels as he reached the corner and pointed a finger at himself, mouthing the words, "Who, me?" and then chomped down on an apple.

The man and the vendor he'd been arguing with looked down to find only five of the half-dozen apples being purchased there. The two broke after the boy as he slipped around the corner and sprinted down the sidewalk in oversized boots that had probably not been re-soled in his lifetime.

He hazarded a glance over his shoulder right as the men burst into view from the market street. Perfect. He knew his cohorts were already filling their pockets with fruits and vegetables and now all he had to do was ditch these guys and go claim his share.

The vendor wouldn't be a problem; he was a blubber bucket. But the patron? The man in the brown pinstriped suit was high-steppin' like his pants were on fire. He must really want that wallet. *Time to pull a fast one.*

Prentiss hung a hard left and chucked his half-eaten apple. Yes, he'd been eating his apple as he ran. A stack of cans a little farther up the narrow street clattered loudly, confirming his aim, but he was already partway down an alley to his right, tucking in behind a stand of vertical pipes.

The pin-striped man blew past in a brown blur toward the sound of clattering refuse. The guy must have been some kind of athlete in his day. Prentiss could give him that much, at least.

As the sounds of pursuit faded, he breathed out a long pent-up sigh and stepped back out onto the street, headed the other way.

Bad timing. Two thick-skulled brutes by the names of Cheez and Sapp were skulking his way. They were a year or two from being full-blown Clan Karnal stooges. They weren't dealers or enforcers yet, but they practiced their own version of miscreant behavior every chance they got.

A devilish smile cracked across Sapp's face as he bumped the other teenager's shoulder. Cheez looked up, followed his gaze to Prentiss, and locked on like a pudgy barn owl eyeing an errant mouse. Prentiss was sure he'd never done anything to these two, but knew it didn't matter. He rabbited back into the alley and sprinted like his life depended on it, because maybe it did. Who was he kidding? He was a street rat in the Dustbin. Of course, it did.

The rough brick walls sped by and at the end of the long alley, he shot out like a scalded cat, smashing directly into a passerby. The two went down in a tangled mess in the middle of the muddy street.

"Oh, for Gadd's sake!" a familiar voice cried as the unlucky fellow struggled to stand while brushing muck off himself. Prentiss realized it was the brown-suit guy, just as Cheez and Sapp appeared from out of the alleyway. Prentiss stumbled back into a tiny three-wheeled truck idling in the street. The man sitting in it, nearly half of his body sticking out the driver's window, blared its tiny horn, causing everyone around to look.

Not good... too much attention.

"Get 'im!" Sapp growled as the brown-suited man made a lunge for Prentiss, but his diminutive size and prey animal quickness saved him. He darted between the man's legs and around the back of the truck. Pouring on the speed, Prentiss raced up the gutter, splashing greasy black water on everyone as he flew by.

People on the street keyed into the action and started grabbing at him as he ran. He was juking and dodging and leaping over carts when he heard a honk from another truck farther on, as it started off from an intersection.

He had an idea. He sprinted out in front of the truck, causing the driver to slam on his brakes and also lay on the horn. But before the man could get the truck moving again, Prentiss was around the fender, and underneath, holding onto the undercarriage.

There was plenty of ground clearance. But he was counting on the fact that downtown, no one could go very fast—the roads were strewn with potholes and much too narrow to accommodate people and vehicular traffic at the same time.

The flatbed truck lurched forward in a cloud of gray smoke, and he watched as his trio of followers came to a halt in the middle of the street, looking this way and that, and choking on exhaust.

Suckers.

Crowds and carts resumed their movement and soon his pursuers were gone from view.

Long minutes passed as the truck trundled along a circuitous path, up hills, down alleyways, and then speeding along a harrowingly narrow dike road. Prentiss's arms quivered. His stomach climbed into his throat as he envisioned hitting the cobbles and tumbling under one of the tires.

Just as he thought he couldn't hold on any longer, he heard the brakes squeal and the gears grind lower. The truck lurched to a stop.

Gadd's green goat!

He was about to drop to the ground and roll out of the way when it bucked into reverse, backing down into the middle of a two-bay loading dock. At least he was kind of out of sight.

He relaxed his arms, letting them extend fully but then the driver pulled the parking brake, jumped out, and started to unstrap his load. Prentiss yanked back up tight to the underbody with a silent groan, praying the man would be quick about it.

Another man greeted him from up on the dock, "Hey, Gurlish. This another one of them *special* shipments?"

"Best, you never mind 'bout that Humphreys," he said warningly. "You don't never want to know too much when it comes to Karnal's doings. Especially when it has to do with our mistress."

"Right, right. I could do without getting 'nowhered,' thank you very much. The Operatrix isn't the forgiving sort, is she?" he snorted.

"Heh. You're smarter than you look," the driver said, removing the last of the straps. He pulled himself up onto the dock. "Now, grab that cart so we can get these crates inside. Quickly. Live cargo, ya know."

"Shhh... I don't wanna know anything about any kiddos getting shipped off to Gadd knows where," the man said, laughing nervously. "Still, I should get a little something extra for my efforts, don't ya think?"

The driver, Gurlish, seemed to think about it for a second. "Yeah, why not? Lemme see, where'd I put that..."

There was a commotion. The other man groaned and dropped from the dock to the pavement. He landed right in front of Prentiss, smacking his face with a sickening thwack. Prentiss saw blood in the gray hair on the back of his head that didn't get there from the fall. The man was still alive. He groaned again, lifted his head, and locked bleary eyes with Prentiss as he struggled to speak. Prentiss worried he'd give him away, but the man called Gurlish jumped down and hit him with a heavy wrench and that was that.

Prentiss bit back the urge to cry out. He wanted to run but dared not reveal himself.

"Humphreys, you always was a dumbass. Now, I gotta box you up with the kids and let the lady deal with you. Guess yer gettin' nowhered after all."

Prentiss waited until the man opened the side of one of the crates and was struggling to load Humphreys' body inside before he made his move. Quickly and silently, he covered the distance to the back of the building. He turned back and saw it wasn't just the man in the crate, but another, smaller body shared the space. A kid, like they said. He shuddered to think who it might be, but knew better than to stick around to find out. Look what being nosy had done for poor old Humphreys…

Prentiss stepped into the darkened interior of the building and was confounded by flashes of blue light. He struggled to make heads or tails of his surroundings until, during a momentary pause, he caught a long line-up of what appeared to be open thresholds of various sizes. Dozens of portals stretched off to his right for a hundred yards or more. Larger ones stretched off to his left, roughly half that distance.

The Hall of Ways. Of course!

That's what they were doing with the crates. They weren't just sending the kids to another city; they were sending them to the other *realms*. He peeked around a column and took in the full length of the building. People, cargo, and their waysmith chaperones passed through one side of each portal, and then just that flash of light came out the other.

Except when someone was returning from the other realm. They popped in like nothing, no fanfare, just bloop—people.

He knew it was a lot more complicated than that but didn't know any of the details other than all of the portals for Realm Kirksfold were here and the Operatrix oversaw all of it. Oh, and that she had extra powers that helped her to keep everything straight and keep people from using the portals illegally. That's why they were so scared of her. She had the power to send people into the space between realms if they broke the rules. Nowhere or Elsewise or something like that. He repressed a shiver as he thought of it.

None of it mattered much in Prentiss's world. His life mostly revolved around his next meal. That and working for the old man. Which, truth be told, was more like standing around and watching him work as he tinkered on silver baubles and mumbled to himself. But the old man fed him when he was there, which meant Prentiss had a few fewer meals to worry about. Except on days like today, that was. He said he was going to be gone overnight, fetching supplies and meeting with a client. So, Prentiss was left to his own devices.

Prentiss's stomach grumbled. *Half an apple,* he thought bitterly. He needed to get back downtown and secure his share of what the other kids stole during his brilliant distraction maneuver. Knowing those knuckleheads, there wouldn't be much left by now.

His mind wandered as he surveyed the milling crowd for a potential mark when he remembered the wallet he'd nicked from the brown-suit guy. Prentiss patted his pockets and his momentary joy turned to irritation as he realized he must have lost it on his suicidal truck ride through town.

"Jonnes balls," he grumbled to himself.

He thought again of the dead man, Humphreys. He must have been a waysmith. And maybe Gurlish was, too, since he didn't seem too concerned about getting rid of him. And, since his little operation was so hush-hush, it made the most sense. But where would they be sending kids, anyway? And why? He didn't want to think too hard about it, but found he couldn't stop. *Not yer problem, Prentiss*, he scolded himself. But an uncomfortable hollow feeling came over him.

The Hall of Ways was one long, open building with all of those various-sized doors running down the middle separating the back-of-house area from the Queuing Corridor. He was at the freight end, with the largest portals and the lowest number of travelers. That meant fewer people to blend in with than farther up near the public entrance.

Bleak light leaked in through the windows of a full-length atrium high above as he made his way along the broad corridor. His mind was still reeling with questions.

He'd had friends who had disappeared. And had heard of others. Sometimes it was gang stuff. Sometimes it was creeps who had no business associating with kids, but most of the time it had to do with drugs. Something called sleet. Personally, he stayed away from the stuff. But he had one friend he was worried about. Barrett had been getting into a lot of trouble lately. Could she end up like those other kids?

Prentiss tried to put them out of his mind, but it flashed again on Humphreys's body getting stuffed into a crate with someone already in it. Maybe Barrett should get a civvy pack and skip town? That was the only way you could travel to the classier realm of Vellem and not get ported back. You had to have a chip identifying you as a resident.

Getting one the legal way was out of the question, but Prentiss had heard of a guy. Some sort of do-gooder who helped street kids get out of Kirksfold and into a decent orphanage or something like that. Not that he thought an orphanage sounded all that great, but Vellem was a far sight better than shitty Kirksfold.

Still, the whole thing sounded like an urban legend. Folks needed hope sometimes, even if it was a false one. But maybe he could check around...

"Nah. Why would I wanna leave all this?" Barrett asked, gesturing with a flourish to her shabby little nook in the stack of moldering pallets. Admittedly, it *was* high up on the stack and overlooked the muck extending into the misty oblivion of the Dainsmire just beyond the burned-down cannery. But still, there were limits to even Prentiss's imagination.

He didn't like that he detected the hint of a slur in her speech and her eyes moved in a way that might just be her waking up, or it could be something else. His gut told him it was something else.

"Cuz kids like us are gettin' nabbed," he said, grabbing his collar and yanking on it to emphasize the point. "I seen it." He did his best to look sincere without looking desperate. He didn't think it worked.

Barrett leaned in. "Nabbed? Like all cloak and dagger?" she asked conspiratorially. She leaned back again. "Who'd be stealing a bunch of skinny, lice-ridden beggars and pickpockets?" She absent-mindedly scratched behind her ear and then twirled a strand of blonde hair that somehow managed to shine in the flat light of the late-morning haze.

"I dunno. They said something about Clan Karnal. And the Operatrix."

"You think the *head* of the Guild of Ways would have anything to do with a mobster like Karnal? Pffft," she said, waving away the idea.

She sat up and yawned before rubbing her face. It didn't seem to achieve the desired result, so she patted it vigorously while staring contemplatively off into the distance. "Well, congratulations, Skinny Boy," she said, stretching luxuriously, "Now I'm awake ... and I am *hungry*."

Prentiss didn't much care for the nickname, but liked the fact that she called him by one. She was two years older and considered by all to be a pretty girl. He'd have had a crush on her too if he thought he had even the slightest chance. But she tended to fancy the older boys—hence her propensity for trouble.

"Well, you're in luck. Some guys owe me for a thing and they're more likely to pay up if you're there."

"And why's that?" she asked, batting her lashes and resting her chin on bridged fingers.

"Well, cuz everyone likes you," he said, rubbing the back of his neck and avoiding eye contact.

"Well ... there you go. Why would I wanna go and leave all this behind? Besides, this patron saint of the wayward street rat you're counting on is just a myth."

"Yeah, maybe so. But you should still be smart. I don't much care for some of the folks you've been running with."

Her eyes lit up with a dangerous fire. "Listen, Skinny Boy, I like you. But if you start pulling this same overprotective bullshit that Rynold's been laying down..."

"Rynold? Sapp?!? What's that no-good knuckle-dragger have to do with... Oh no. You're not—"

Barrett looked away and then looked back with an arched eyebrow and a devilish smile. "Maybe I am? What're you gonna do about it?"

Prentiss glowered, tried to say something, and then gave up, the wind completely deflated from his sails.

How could she? He felt betrayed, and he didn't even know why. She wasn't his girlfriend. She could date whomever she wanted.

Barrett rummaged for a short-sleeved shirt and Prentiss realized she intended to change into it with him standing there. He spun around quickly to look out over the picturesque remains of the blackened building and barren docks. He tried not to imagine in excruciating detail the activity going on just behind him, but the image played front and center in his mind's eye. His face, already flushing from anger, redoubled its efforts.

"What's the matter, Prentiss? We're just friends, right?"

What's the matter!?! The heat in his face spread to his ears. He was embarrassed and mad, and more than that, he was hurt. His vision blurred as his temper flared dangerously. This was what they meant by seeing red, a small part of his mind realized while the rest was swept by wildfire.

"You know what? I'll catch you later. Take care of yourself, Barrett." He hopped down the pallets and raced around the corner before she could call after him, or worse, catch up to him and see the stupid tears on his face.

"More kids missin' all the time. More shows up, and then more go away," Holland muttered, seemingly to himself. He scuffed through puddles as he made his way down the darkly glistening alley. A familiar combination of gloom and fog filled the spaces between buildings.

Holland squinted as he scrutinized his path. "Som'b'dy should do sumpthin 'bout this bloody weather," he continued to grumble as he walked. Of course, the weather wasn't bad by Dain Burrough standards. Always a variation on fog.

Sometimes mist, sometimes a driving mist. Sometimes rain. Right now, it was the kind of fog that left thick droplets on everything. He wiped his face with an irritated huff and adjusted the heavy rucksack hanging over his shoulder.

It looked like it was full to brimming with mannequin parts, which was a weird thing to be carrying around at night, but nothing anyone would fight him for. However, sometimes the bag moved oddly and contra to his own awkward gait. And, occasionally, the bag would fidget.

He turned a corner and a tall stone wall supporting the old thoroughfare of Tennyon Street loomed to one side. Opposite it, a gangly, three-story apartment crowded from the other side of the alley in an attempt to meet in the middle. Heavy boards spanned the gap between. Someone's noble attempt at sidestepping that eventuality. Probably stolen from some other structure being propped up against a similar such fate.

Unpleasant aromas from the alley competed with those wafting through fogged windows where they were cracked to let in the cool night air—the residents busily cooking their evening meals. For some working the skeleton crews, this would be the first and only meal of the day.

Dain Burrough—the Dustbin, as it was known—resembled an industrial-era slum that had never quite peeked through the haze of coal fire to glimpse the ever-glimmering utopia on the other side. Being the de facto capital of Realm Kirksfold, it did have its modern appurtenances, just never where something older was still able to be cobbled back together and the precious resources saved ... then stolen ... then squandered on vices. The Dustbin straddled many eras, but its dark side was transcendent. As ancient as mankind itself.

Holland looked both ways at an intersection of alleys and then chose the darker of the two when a couple of patrol-civil goons rounded a corner not far ahead. Their voices were boastful, deceptively casual. But these types were never above brutality while carrying out their duties. Even with regard to something as mundane as a weeknight curfew, one was playing with borrowed dice.

As a silversmith, Holland wore some of his own handiwork where teeth had been lost to similar entanglements. Luckily the replacements were not readily visible, otherwise he'd be at risk of losing them to the other thugs roaming the Dustbin at night.

Recently, Clan Karnal were the most prolific—easily identified by eye patches that were, for the most part, unnecessary but which mimicked their leader's imposing visage. Before them, had been the Cocks and before that, the Duinn St. Deadlies. There was always someone around to ensure the innocent bore the proper amount of misery.

Sounds of dripping water, the shuffling of small critters in the dark, and his own stuttering footsteps were all that greeted him as he walked past rotting trestle cross members and piles of refuse taller than himself. Somewhere a baby wailed without address, accompanied by a dog barking from farther on still.

Elsewhere shouting bloomed and then resolved faster than it should have. Likely that pair of goons had found a straggler who needed to comply with ordinances or provide suitable coin as recompense.

Holland had dodged a bullet there. He'd scraped up every penny for this current venture and couldn't afford to lose it. Not to mention the current recipient of his goodwill. He grumbled again to himself and shifted the bag. Its weight was biting into his shoulders and he'd had enough of the cloak and dagger for one night.

Moments later he came to a dimly lit wooden door and rapped three times. And then once more. He dropped the rucksack just outside the feeble cone of light, washing down from a gooseneck lamp mounted on the wall above.

"Ow!" came a muffled protest.

"Shaddup!" Holland scolded from the side of his mouth and kicked the bag, not hard but not softly either. This elicited a muffled, "Umph" followed by a string of grumbled expletives.

The sound of metal sliding on wood emanated from the door and yellow light cast through a fist-sized hole in the middle of it. A thin, well-worn wooden plank slid through the opening. Holland placed a small leather pouch upon it. The plank retreated with what amounted to a month's earnings.

"Civvy pack?" a baritone voice inquired from within.

"Yeh. Implant ID ... papers ... whole deal." Holland glowered.

"Another orphan for Vellem?"

He sighed but didn't respond, crossing his arms instead, and tapping his foot impatiently.

"Rates have gone up."

"Since last month?!?"

There was a pause. "Nah. Next month though. Come back tomorrow. Leave the bag."

"I'll be back in an hour and a half, and if the goods are damaged, you'll be the proprietor of a pile of ash."

"Ha!" the voice snorted. "Alright. Get lost, Finnery. You'll have what you're asking for."

The tension in Holland's shoulders slacked a little, and he nodded. "I'll be back at a quarter past."

"Don't push your luck!" the man inside scolded.

Holland nodded and shrugged, as much to himself as anyone. He turned, kicked the bag once more but softly this time, and while feigning to secure the knot on top, and whispered something to its contents before walking away in the opposite direction from which he'd come.

CHAPTER 2

A Poor Sort of Host

Holland sprang out of bed. The sounds of someone banging on the door downstairs and braying incessantly dislodged him from a most troubling dream. A dream of a place he'd sworn never to go back to.

"Master Finnery!" A pause, then banging, and then again more emphatically, "Master Finnery!"

"Go away!" Holland bellowed and paused for a moment, hoping the banging and yelling would cease. It did not.

He rolled out of bed and stretched his stiff muscles before stepping into worn leather boots, not bothering to change out of his billowing pajamas. He grabbed a woolen duckbill cap from the hook and disappeared down the narrow stairs leading from the silver crafter's loft.

"Follow me!" urged Prentiss, who happened to be his apprentice as well as the author of all the late-night racket. The boy was halfway down the uneven cobblestone street already, waving frantically for his aging, pajama-wearing companion to catch up.

"Keep yer britches on," he groused, but shuffled a little bit faster after the youth. Holland thought the boy was around eleven years old, though due to his size, it was hard to be sure. He didn't know if Prentiss had any idea either, to be honest. He was one of Dain Burrough's orphaned street kids.

A couple of minutes passed, and the two were blocks away, standing over the body of an attractive middle-aged woman in a crumpled heap. She wore a light wool trench coat that was soaked through and there was a dark stain, blood he assumed, on her front side about four buttons down.

"Yeh. Very sad," he said to the kid, patting him on the head as he walked past on his way back home. But Prentiss latched onto Holland's pajamas and wouldn't let go, skidding behind as he trudged back toward the shop and his warm bed. The boy shook his head furiously and pointed.

Holland looked over his shoulder and saw one slender hand shift ever so slightly. *Could be rigor mortis. The body does strange things after its spark's escaped*, he reasoned. But then it moved again, attempting weakly to reach out to the voices before collapsing back down.

"Jonnes balls," he sighed, eyes searching the mist-shrouded heavens above. Holland walked back to the body of the woman and scooped her up. She was light, though tall for a woman. He was also surprisingly strong for someone in the sixth decade of his miserable existence. Well, not all of it had been miserable. Just the last bit.

He proceeded to walk back the way they'd come. Prentiss tagged along, almost skipping with giddiness. Holland scowled at him, and the boy stopped, but only until he looked away again. Holland could hear the energetic scuffs of the boy's oversized boots and forged doggedly onward through his irritation. He was losing sleep. And now … he was entertaining company apparently.

A Poor Sort Of Host

Holland looked down at the woman's lightly tanned face, gone pale with shock and loss of blood. She looked familiar, but he couldn't place it. Alarm bells were clanging in the back of his mind, but he was still too groggy to listen properly. Truth be told, it was never one of his strong suits. If told one thing, he was twice as likely to do the other.

In the distance, a foghorn groaned. It was invisible within a blanket of mist that had ebbed away momentarily from town and was just now beginning to crowd the lights of the lower district.

"Fog's coming back in, but you can see all the way down to Sledge Pier," Prentiss said, as they walked along the hillside street leading back down to the flats where Holland's shop was located. He was right. The fog had retreated a fair amount back into the Dainsmire and with the resulting visibility, Holland was able to make out the skeletal shape of it under the lights.

He wasn't at all pleased to be reminded of the prior morning's events. Not because he was embarrassed, though that was a part of it. It was because he wasn't entirely convinced he wouldn't end up there again with the same desperate notion in his head.

As they walked, the fog rolled in, consuming the pier. He was glad to have it hidden from view. His thoughts returned to the dream from earlier. The place he'd found himself in, he called the Elsewhere. It wasn't in the three realms. Heck, he didn't even know if it was a real place except for the people, the Ephemera. He never saw them, but he knew they were there. It sounded crazy. But the real issue he was struggling with was the fact he'd sworn never to go there again. At least not intentionally.

It was because he'd shown someone once when he was a boy. But things didn't go well. He'd sworn off waysmithing entirely after that. Ran away and disappeared. It was probably why he had such a soft spot for the street kids. He'd been one of them.

Holland tried to stifle a yawn, but his hands were full carrying the injured woman. Instead, he was stuck with a deeply dissatisfying, yawnless moment. His irritation was holding fast. He looked down at the woman's face, nestled against his shoulder.

Damn, if she isn't familiar. A nagging sort of concern was growing in the back of his mind. Who knew what it would become when full-grown?

The following morning, Holland woke with a headache and a crick in his neck. He made his way down the narrow stairs, craning his head sideways, trying to tease the tightness out. It twinged again as he stooped through the doorway to his kitchen before taking his usual place at his workbench. Weak light cast through bleary panes onto a smattering of well-worn tools and a few small objects needing repair. Behind him was a small, cherry-sided woodstove with a stack of newspapers next to it. The most current one sat atop the heap and was drying out from the heavy morning mist.

On the floor, Holland's young apprentice sat with his chin resting on delicate fists, staring at the woman lying on a beggarly thin bed roll. Holland had checked on her several times during the night, and so was not surprised to see her covered in fever sweat. She muttered in protest to some phantom or other, visible only to her.

"How long she going to be like this?" the boy asked in a voice that seemed somehow smaller than it should. Holland didn't know when the boy had snuck in and stoked the woodstove, but was glad for its warmth. Especially on a morning like this when his body felt every year of his age and the rough use it'd been put through.

"Y'mean if she don't die? Reckon, day or two," answered the old man, while hunching over to scrutinize more intently a small locket, whose hinge had come undone. He rubbed the two-day-old growth of mostly white stubble on his face. Then he stretched his back and shoulders, the joints making loud cracking noises in the relative quiet of the modest shop. His attention fell back to the boy and the subject of his interest.

"Don't you think if she was going to die, she woulda done it by now?" the boy asked.

Holland snorted, "S'pose," not bothering to pause from his work.

"Nooo!" the woman bolted upright before crumpling back, moaning, and clutching her stomach with shaking hands.

Holland flashed to her side, speed belying years, and cradled her head as she rested back down, eyes damp with pain, her breathing ragged and fast.

"Wha...what...where am..." she labored out in a weak tumble of words.

"Looks as though you were on the wrong end of a robb'ry. Missed any vital organs, near as I can tell. But I'm no plumber," Holland reassured her.

"Oh..." she responded softly, the hand clutching his shirt sleeve wilting back. To Holland, she seemed oddly comforted by the revelation of having been mugged and stabbed. *As compared to what?* He had no idea.

He stroked her hair with a large, well-calloused hand and she faded back slowly into a world of slightly-less-troubled dreaming. But, as he brushed back the sweat-darkened strands of pale blonde hair, he caught a small metallic glint behind her ear.

"Boy," he said briskly. "We're done for the day. Go on home."

Prentiss's eyes widened, and he was gone in a flash, the shop door slamming back, bouncing off the strike without latching. A cold draft blew in through the gap as Holland's hand stretched to the stack of drying papers.

He drew back the topmost one. Pulled it up within inches of his nose, and then let it drift back until it resolved into focus. A skeptical eyebrow rose as his eyes found the headline.

> "Missing Ekron Agent Fingered in
> Series of Murders Spanning Centuries!"

He mouthed the words silently as he read them, doubting the absurd statement out of hand. But then tired blue eyes drifted toward the woman's face and his lips pursed in thought. He let her head rest on the pillow and then stepped to the workbench, returning with a small, tweezer-like instrument with a knurled brass dial on the side for fine adjustment. Holland gently brushed her hair out of the way again to reveal the integrated memory storage device, or memplant, as they were called.

It was similar in appearance to his own modified waysmithing unit, which normally would have acted as an access key and ID tag for using the portals, but it acted more like a location scrambler. The woman's implant was built to store selected memories. It was something the clockies used to keep their history straight because time healed itself and sometimes they would begin to remember things differently than how they experienced them. He didn't understand the intricacies because it was actually quite complicated. But, he knew for certain, the physics of this world were much more pliable than anyone was led to believe.

For instance, the rules said a waysmith needed an implant to use the focusing component of a portal. That part was true, but what they left out was the fact that some people didn't need a portal at all. Well, Holland didn't, anyway. It was a fact he kept hidden. Going so far as to not even use his abilities for years after the incident with the Elsewhere when he was a child. His eyes drifted to the woman's face again. He scowled, itching at a memory that just wouldn't be satisfied.

Another fact that wasn't really a fact was that portals couldn't be made. At least not anymore. But he'd created his own portal in his cellar. To his knowledge, no one but the Operatrix herself had their own. And she couldn't transit without it.

Holland scrutinized the device behind the woman's ear. He hadn't seen one like this since his years of service after the war. They could be highly useful for gathering intel if you had the right machine to decrypt the coding. And those machines were in short supply in Kirksfold. But there were ways. There were always ways...

He removed the kernel of it with a faint snick and brought it up for closer examination. His lips pursed again as he looked at the woman one last time. "What sort of trouble's found you, miss?" he whispered before disappearing up the narrow stairs.

Minutes later he emerged, wearing a worn and ill-fitting tan suit with a fur-lined tank commander's cap, ear flaps flopping loosely at its sides. He checked the woman's bandaged stomach and covered her with a knit blanket to go with her wool one. She'd need to be covered now that her fever had diminished.

THE HARBINGER BROKEN

The space was tight with the injured woman flopped down in the middle of it. He bumped a chair which then bumped a tall, narrow curio cabinet. The contents rattled and a picture frame toppled off the top shelf. He snagged it out of the air without even thinking. Old habits...

His fingers shook as he brushed dust off the glass and tarnished frame. The picture was of four people, two couples. They were smiling, struggling to contain their mirth at some inside joke. Moments passed, the silence only broken by the woman's long, slow breaths. She moaned softly, breaking him from his spell.

Holland jabbed the picture frame absently at the shelf before finally placing it face down and sliding it safely away from the edge. His attention was on all the empty space inside his shop. Specks of dust floated in air that suddenly felt cold despite the efforts of the wood stove. He swallowed, rubbed his tired face with hands that'd seen a lifetime of hard use before returning his attention to the woman.

She'd managed to uncover herself again in her fitful sleep. He pulled up her blankets once more, framing a face that tickled at the edge of a gaping hole in his memory. It was a face he would have remembered, he was sure. Before exiting the front door, he flipped the open sign to closed and locked it as he went. She'd be okay for an hour or two.

The sky was a faintly glowing gloom as feeble sunlight failed to penetrate the thick layer of what was either low clouds or high fog—a distinction which really didn't matter much. Wet refuse clogged the gutters in piles, forcing runnels of dingy water to pool up and skirt around the sides.

Similarly, Holland moved through the streets of the ironically named Dustbin. He slipped between clots of people and the occasional cart, carriage, or even the odd, tri-wheeled Bulger truck. He despised the latter the most. Their cabs were tiny, and the minuscule single-piston engines were vastly underpowered. It seemed to him that they were as often pushed as driven.

He much preferred to walk and endure the dour weather than to suffer the indignity of cramming himself into one of those ill-conceived abominations. Besides, being inside one always reminded him of things he preferred to keep in his deep—and as oft as possible—undisturbed memories.

Repeated honking and the braying of an ass drew Holland's attention back to his path. There was always a ream of activity around the winding, climbing, and plunging Gudgel's Ferry Road and its various arteries. Though, an outsider might be hard-pressed to divine a purpose to all the bustle. No one seemed particularly urgent in their endeavors. More inclined to argue about a knot of congestion at an intersection than take turns navigating around it.

Tromping directly through a broad gully of greasy run-off, he wondered if it had always been like this—one interminable season of miserable overcast. He thought he remembered it differently as a child. Indeed, the town's own nickname seemed to imply otherwise—Dustbin.

Soon, Holland stood before a dilapidated shop fronting the thoroughfare. It was mere blocks from what used to be the bay, but now was just a point where a polluted river trickled off into miles of misty bog.

Fogged windows suggested bodies inside, though the painted signage gave up little, stating only Ciller's in a fanciful, peeling gold cursive. Below that was the slightly less faded word Still where wood-carved letters protecting the original paint for decades had finally succumbed to the elements and to gravity. Holland could sympathize.

The Harbinger Broken

He approached the entrance but drew up short. Turning to leave, he stopped himself again, took a deep breath, and after another long pause, pushed through the door.

The clamoring of voices and clinking glassware from behind the bar didn't cease entirely, but there was a perceptible hiccup as he entered. Eyes probed and then returned to their prior interests as cards were folded with curses, drinks slurped, and returned sloshing to tables.

Smoke hung in lazy, striated layers, curled by passersby or the lone waitstaff as he made his less-than-urgent rounds between tables, booths, and back-of-house.

Holland eyed the one booth he was looking for. He darted a sidelong glance at the bar but managed to forge a direct path to the booth rather than order a bottle and a glass, as he'd done nearly every other time in the last forty years.

"By Jonnes... he lives," a bleary-eyed man close to Holland's age wearing dingy gray coveralls and matching headgear proclaimed, though unenthusiastically. He scratched at a greasy mess of salt-and-pepper chest hair, exposed by a tarnished brass zipper that looked as though it'd never made it fully up its path of travel. Draining his shot glass, he refilled it to overflowing from a mostly clear bottle, with an even clearer liquid, and slid it to the empty space before him.

Another shot glass flew at him from somewhere to his left and he caught it, filled it, and raised it all in one fluid motion. The wonders of muscle memory at work. He belched and raised a glass,

"To Holland! None of us would be 'ere ... without 'im," he exclaimed, this time with a little too much enthusiasm, and drained his glass, slamming it with a thud on the tabletop. Echoing thuds rattled around the establishment, either preceded or followed by grumbles of grudging agreement.

Though none rebutted the veracity of the statement, not all seemed too pleased with the reality of it. Whether that ire was at Holland's laud or to their own continued existence was up for speculation.

Holland looked around at the various patrons. Almost to a man, they were wearing the headgear of one or another branch of the DDF—the Dainlanz Defenciary Force—but most wore something similar to his own. This was unsurprising as all residents of the city-state of Dain Burrough traded a nine-year enlistment in the Defenciary for citizenship and its so-called benefits: namely, not being turned out into the mist-bound wastes for acts of treason. None but one or two looked up from their pursuits. He nodded to the ones that did and then returned his attention to the man at the booth.

"Have a seat, friend, Holland." The man motioned to the place across from him where the proffered glass remained untouched.

Holland waved his hands and scrunched up his face in disapproval. "Ya know I don't touch the stuff 'nymore, Malph." He grimaced and shook his head, but his eyes still lingered on the glass, overfilled with something akin to aviation fuel.

The man tilted his head in a "suit yourself" manner, leaned back, and crossed his arms across his chest. "Whadya want then, hero, Holland?"

Holland eased into the booth and slid the drink to the side with the back of his hand. "You hold a helluva grudge, ya know?"

The man's rheumy stare was unwavering and bore the weight of a tank track. He said nothing.

"Look. I've ... come into something. Some sorta ... trouble. Need it looked at," he provided, eyes scanning the entry and exits as old habits resurfaced, summoned by the growing sense of peril slinking into his idle thoughts. Thoughts that had grown complacent in the years since he'd last worn this hat and kept this company.

Still no response. The man appeared frozen, as if he were a forgotten exhibit in some depressing wax museum.

Holland sucked in air through his teeth. His hand moved from holding his own chin, slid to the side of his face, and then to the back of his neck. Then it settled on the table where he rubbed an empty space on his ring finger where a now-absent band had left a permanent indentation in the flesh. He darted a stealthy glance around the room and then leaned forward, speaking softly, "I need ta speak to our mutual friend..."

"Ya, of course, you do," the man said, but dropped his gaze for the first time in the labored conversation.

"Where can I find her these days?" Holland pressed.

"You know, Nelv. She'll prob'ly find you first," Malph spat out, smiling. But it was strained and the smile quickly slid back into the grimace infinitely more comfortable there.

"Yeh. Prob'ly so," Holland acknowledged, nodding soberly. "But I had to come, didn't I?"

There was a well-marbled silence that marinated in the space for several long minutes. Holland felt as uncomfortable as Malphius looked. Neither man was willing to do anything more. Yet both were hesitant to sever the exchange, knowing it'd likely be decades, if ever, before there'd be another chance at mending things.

Apparently sick of the game of verbal chicken, Malph spoke up,

"Yah, well don't let it 'it you in the arse on the way out..." he said, draining his drink and then reaching for the previously offered glass, and draining it as well. He whipped the empty glass at the bar. The solitary waitstaff, while passing between two tables, caught it, dried it with a dingy wash rag, and placed it on a table with an identical one that magically appeared in his hands. Newcomers sat down at the table while Holland took his leave.

Holland was halfway home and still shaking. It was a dirty trick for Malphius to pour him a glass of Ciller's signature gin. Downright mean-spirited. But Holland couldn't hold it against him. He knew he was just hurt. He hadn't shown his face at the Still for near-on eight years. Hadn't touched a drink in all that time, either. And he, sure as Jonnes, couldn't let something like friendship get in the way of his sobriety now.

Truth be told, his thoughts were so clear now, he almost couldn't recognize humanity when he saw it. As difficult as it'd been to sit with Malph, watching the man wage war on his liver, there was a certain warmth in the man's wrath. A tiny jolt of life sitting in proximity to his decades-long friend. Holland felt as though he was a comet on the return leg of some ridiculous elliptic, sneaking in the back door from the loneliest edges of the cosmos to greet humanity again.

Holland's long strides skirted a hill nowhere near the shortest path back to his shop. With his mind preoccupied, his old, weathered boots must have been on autopilot. He wouldn't have come here himself. Holland placed one foot in front of the other, but didn't dare get too close to the disorderly stairs leading to the top of the hill.

Instead, he passed by the wrought-iron arbor guarding the cemetery beyond and didn't spare a second glance in its direction. *This is close enough*, he thought, breathing out a ragged sigh and feeling a wonder of success as though he'd traversed a minefield while walking backward and juggling chainsaws and badgers.

Between the tavern and the graveyard lay a thousand deaths for his tenuous peace of mind. Holland shoved his hands in the pockets of his suit jacket and pushed on. Far off to his right, he knew, lay the rusting hulks of Bolsko-Cherjk siege works erected in a near-successful attempt to seize Dain Burrough thirty-some-odd-years prior. He knew bodies lay about those skeletal, sail-less windmills, imperfectly preserved in the bog in sludge-filled trench lines. He knew he should have been one of them.

The glow of a lantern beckoned from deep within the obscured bank and was either real or imagined. It mattered little either way. What business did the living have with ghosts? He struggled for a full breath, couldn't steal one from between what lay restlessly in the cemetery on the hill and the horrors perpetrated in that sense-robbing mist of the Dainsmire.

A block later, still lost in his thoughts, he was startled by a street urchin. The kid bounced off him and erupted into a slew of profanities, ending simply with, "Watch it, bag o' bones!" Then the boy ran off laughing and cursing words even Holland, long of tooth as he was, hadn't heard strung together before.

He'd have liked to have cuffed the kid for his insolence, but he was gone and somehow, he just didn't have it in him to be angry. He returned his hands to his pockets and found a device bearing a resemblance to an old steam pressure gauge but with a digital display built-in underneath the glass. The display had an address and a time, and as he stared at it in disbelief, it went blank. He shook the device, but it didn't come back to life. Quickly, he tried to recall what he'd seen:

A Poor Sort Of Host

10 Penny on Daring—15 O'12

Penny didn't cross Daring, he realized. His eyes drifted up, brows knit, jaw drooping to slack. He paused for a moment that way and then huffed out an irritated breath. A puzzle then. *Penny doesn't cross Daring*, he thought obstinately, but then a pensive, speculative part of his brain started to engage. *Ten*nyon did cross Pen*daring*. He rolled the thought around in his head ... close enough.

15 O'12 was three in the afternoon. It was a ways off—*five or six hours*, he thought. He decided he better go check in on his guest when he was interrupted again.

"Spare some coin?" a crippled man implored, laying inconveniently across the warped boards of the sidewalk. Holland hadn't realized he'd still been walking while sorting out the problem in his mind. He stepped over the man, Dain Burrough's industry of beggars having dulled his sensitivities to little more than the faint echo of tree branches clattering in a windstorm.

"Alms!" the man said emphatically, catching the hem of his pant leg and then pointing at the crumpled hat on the ground beside him.

Holland looked at him, dumbfounded. This was aggressive even by Dustbin standards. The man looked pointedly at the device still in Holland's right hand and then darted his eyes in the direction of the hat again.

Holland finally got it. Shaking his head in acquiescence, he tossed the device toward the open hat. The beggar was fast and caught it before it hit the ground, which Holland realized now could have damaged the item considerably. The crippled man looked at him indignantly while grabbing his hat, then got up and hobbled, bow-legged, off in the other direction.

He watched him go and then hurried back along his path, fearing he'd already drawn too much attention to the exchange. Whether sanctioned or otherwise, thugs paid a keen interest in the goings-on within city limits and were paid for their efforts. Holland's exploits a few evenings prior had left his coffers bare, so payment would be in flesh, and he didn't have much to spare in that department.

Holland returned to find the front door to his shop was already unlocked, though the closed sign hadn't been flipped. He didn't pause, but walked right in. "We're not meeting at three, then?" he asked the air as no one was visible within the cramped, L-shaped configuration of the sitting room, workshop, and kitchen.

"Nah. Ruse within a ruse. Never be too careful..." a mature but vibrant female voice replied.

"You still believe all that conspiracy then...?"

"Believe it? You'd do likewise if you had more than a pair of gray cells to rub together in that fossil head of yours."

Sensing something amiss, Holland scanned the space and felt a surge of panic when he saw the empty spot on the mat near the wood stove.

"She gone?!?"

"No," the voice replied. "She's upstairs in *your* bed. You've turned into a poor sort of host, Holland Finnery. Used to be a pretty girl could barely cross the threshold without ending up there..."

"Yeah, well, a lot's changed... You haven't."

"The more things change, ya know," the woman replied and stepped out from behind a stack of boxes on the far side of the shop. She was short, pixie-ish with black hair in a boy's cut peeking out from a tanker's cap. It was similar to Holland's but with the earflaps tied up and a bronze leaf stitched into the front.

"You're still a majore, then?"

"Of a sort. Hear you found trouble. Seen with my own eyes, it's true," she said, glancing up at the ceiling where Holland's bed would be, along with its current occupant.

"Of a sort, anyway." His own eyes settled on the mat on the floor and then took in the stack of dailies near the wood stove. "I need something ciphered."

"Figured as much. Let me see what I can do," she said, walking toward him with her hand outstretched. He realized she'd likely searched the woman and discovered the empty memplant. He hesitated.

"Good to see you, Nelv. Saw Malph. He looks the same."

"Yeah, well, he chose his destruction. I chose mine."

Holland assumed she meant his drinking and her involvement with the terrorists calling themselves the ToobRaiders. A name reminiscent of those that'd fought off invaders that—not wanting to brave the supposedly haunted bogs like the failed Bolsko-Cherjk incursion—had attempted to burrow *under* Dain Burrough to take it from the inside. It was a silly name and had proved to be a vain ambition. Malph and Nelv had split sometime after Holland sobered up, following the loss of his wife, Meri. The two women had been close. The four of them, inseparable. For a time...

"None of your ... *associates* can see this," Holland said, holding up the small crystalline kernel that was no larger than a stud earring. It was Nelv's turn to pause.

"Of course. I'm going to need another way out of here, though," she said, glancing to a place near the mat on the floor, "and a favor in return."

Holland frowned before giving a curt nod. She was one of the few who knew his secret, and he was surprised she hadn't come to him earlier. Still, he felt a bit like a fish that'd taken the bait and then wondered why such a juicy morsel was just floating around on the surface. He was waiting for the sudden jerk to set the hook.

Holland slid the mat aside with his foot and lifted a hatch that'd been cut into the wooden floor while considering this new turn of events. It felt like he was walking around with sticks of dynamite in his pocket: one for smuggling the odd orphan out of a life of addiction and slavery and into something better in the middle realm of Vellem. Another for owing a favor to the likes of the ToobRaiders, even if it was at the behest of a former friend. Last, was the beautiful Ekron agent sleeping in his bed upstairs, the Harbinger, Madrigal Timms. An agent who might be a serial killer, or at the least, the subject of a realm-spanning manhunt. And worst of all, she was someone who knew him from another life. Knew his secrets.

Holland realized he'd pieced this all together on his walk. The Madame Harbinger had asked him to help her find a killer, and she was who he'd shown the Elsewhere to as a child. Things didn't work out, and he hadn't seen her since. The fact that she was here now, this current and most tenuous dilemma, felt like the stick with its fuse dangling over a candle. But maybe not if he knew her secrets as well...

"Still not sure how you made a wayportal in your basement," she said, shaking her head in amazement. And then, "You look like hell, Holland," before she crushed him with a hug and rabbited down the stairs to the basement. Like many in Kirksfold, she could operate a wayportal if it already existed.

Holland was surprised to find himself blinking back moisture, while the corner of his mouth twitched involuntarily. Weariness dropped on him with a sudden weight. He felt as though he were holding back a horde of ghosts, threatening to overwhelm his defenses like a storm surge to a seawall.

Holland clenched down against the swell of emotion, swallowed, and dropped the hatch covering the stairwell. From below, a flash of bright blue light emanated from between the floorboards and was gone. He nodded to himself, rolled up the sleeping mat, and slid a rug that'd been hastily shoved aside, over the spot on the floor.

A comet was comfortable for ninety-nine percent of its life, hibernating in darkened silence. But that one percent...

Realm Brythe, Vantipolis,
Bureau Ekron on Dever's

"Yes, well, Bureau Ekron has its place in history, *not* because we manipulate the past, as you're so thinly implying, but because history wouldn't be what it is without us," a tall man replied into the telephone receiver, his head tilting in a small display of annoyance. He scrutinized manicured fingernails, secretly hoping to find some small imperfection to focus his attention on but found none. The conversation was boring and the man on the other side was dull, even if he was the Minister-at-Heads. This was a waste of Osmius's time.

He continued in his buttery smooth, perfectly enunciated tone, "No. I disagree most vehemently. Ekron certainly deserves the extraordinary budget it commands because, without it, history would no longer lean in favor of Brythe and the powers of stability and prosperity that she represents. We would be gone. In our exact place, our detractors would certainly be having this exact conversation if not something similar to it. We must ever be vigilant against this. And, to this end, Bureau Ekron is the tip, the haft, and the very hand that holds the spear. And before that, we are the idea of the spear whispered into the craftsman's mind."

He had changed the tense of that last sentence purposefully, though he doubted the Minister would catch it, or gather its meaning. Or realize the fact that Osmius had in essence agreed to the accusation that the minister had made, all while making it seem as though it was his idea—and the reason why the minister *should* agree to his terms—in the first place. The minister babbled on for nearly a minute more.

The tall man on the phone smiled and then affected a stern look. "Thank you, that'll be all. I'm sure you'll do what's best for Brythe and the Three Realms, your Honor. Now, I really must be going. Good day."

He gently placed the receiver on its cradle and looked thoughtfully toward the windows opening out on the bright gray of the Devers and the meandering park that followed its banks through the entirety of Vantipolis. Sunlight and pockets of bluebird sky peaked through cracks in the blanket of wispy overcast. It seemed the cloud cover might burn off after all.

Director Osmius Turnbull rose from his desk, rolling his shoulders before checking his timepiece and returning it to his pocket. He turned to the hardwood mantle and retrieved a long, fixed-blade knife from its display stand before slipping it into a custom-sewn pocket inside his jacket. He checked his teeth in a small mirror on the mantle, nodded, turned, and then strode casually across the generous open space of his office.

Darkly lit, appointed with polished mahogany, and sets of first edition books from floor to ceiling, the room echoed dully with his passing. He reached a place in the tall shelves that bulged outward, a vertical, cylindrical protrusion of shelving. It added a focal point and an understated architectural flourish to the otherwise uniform appearance of the wall.

He checked a timepiece, paused for precisely five seconds as the long hand swept to the top of the arc, and then a well-manicured hand caressed the underside of one of the shelves before him. The cylindrical shelf rotated on an unseen axis to reveal a man-sized chamber within, not unlike a phone booth in many respects. He entered, sat on a crimson, crushed velvet cushion, and retrieved an antiquated telephone handset from the facing wall. The bookshelf rotated back into place, with him still inside.

- / -

Almost as soon as it had closed, the shelf opened again and the man, who was now standing, emerged. He looked tired and energized at the same time and was perspiring visibly. He tracked wet footsteps across the floor to his desk, the room echoing with each squishy step. The man produced a cloth and cleaned the blade of the knife before placing it back on its display mount.

Osmius removed his shoes using the toe of the opposite foot and nudged them into a suitable location on the hearth before turning on the gas and watching distractedly as the fire flickered to life. It stirred up geometric patterns of orange upon the carbon-encrusted undersides of the logs. He tossed the bloodstained cloth into the flame.

Crossing the couple of feet to his desk, he pressed a button inset into the writing surface, after which a taut, but otherwise matronly voice issued from a wood-trimmed speaker beside it.

"Yes, Director Turnbull?" the voice asked.

"Miss Precept. Please send a message to the Kirksfold Propriety. I wish them to be on the lookout for one Madrigal Timms. She's been implicated in a series of rather heinous crimes and must be brought in immediately for questioning. Of course, notify them that certain measures must be taken due to her involvement with the Bureau Ekron. Do the same for Vellem and Brythe as well. All points. And let them know that this information absolutely must not be brought into the public arena until the proper time." He rolled his eyes and chuckled silently to himself, knowing what effect that would have on containment of the story.

"Of course, Director Turnbull," the receptionist replied, and then added, "Anything else?"

"No, that will be all," he answered. He knew she would be deeply satisfied to carry out this particular request. He didn't know why the woman manning the front desk to his office hated his star agent with such intensity, but the fact was evident and on display for all to see. And that, for as long as he could remember. But it would no longer be a source of awkwardness in the office or at holiday parties—the Harbinger was gone. And with her, any impediments to his plans.

He crossed from his desk to the wet bar in just his socks, humming softly to himself. Then he grabbed a tumbler, added ice, and poured a finger of shockingly old scotch, which he promptly knocked to the floor. The tall, trim, and well-dressed man stood there looking at it for an oddly long time. Then he looked at his timepiece, noting the sweep of the long hand as it crossed the top of the arc.

- / -

He crossed from his desk to the wet bar in just his socks, but he was suddenly too tired for humming. Then he grabbed a tumbler. A bead of sweat ran down his temple as he added ice, poured a sloppy finger of near-ancient scotch, and then splashed an equal part on top for good measure. His hands were shaking before picking it up, so he exercised great caution as he brought it to his lips and sampled it. He nodded to himself in satisfaction, whether for his actions, his plans, or for the scotch was unclear and perhaps, irrelevant.

He drained the tumbler and then, in the flickering of an eye, the Director of the Bureau Ekron, Osmius Turnbull, was in a darkly lit chamber in the catacombs below Nexus Ultimatum, the headquarters of the Guild of Ways, and home of the Operatrix herself. Only now, Turnbull, rather than bearing the resemblance of a tall, senior-looking man of trim build and stately appearance, stood likely on the sub side of five feet, as a woman who bore a decidedly bovine, and oddly sinister appearance.

Her large brown eyes searched the darkness. A penciled eyebrow arched at the sound of dripping water somewhere close by. And then again as a rustling of clothing and a body drew her attention. She inhaled sharply with excitement.

"My dear, you must be terrified. You haven't moved an inch," she observed, her sickly sweet voice echoing down unknown tunnels in the dim light. She breathed in deeply, relishing the bright scent of fear floating in the dank, subterranean air.

A faint sniffling whimper could be heard, but no response was forthcoming. The woman clodded across the floor in a sensible pair of pumps. Upon reaching a wall, the lighting in the space came up by degrees until the shape of a girl in dirty britches and an oversized and ratty button-up shirt could be seen huddled against a rock wall opposite the woman.

On the bare floor lay opened manacles attached to a heavy chain. Above her dangled a wrought-iron cage, roughly eight feet across and suspended above the floor enough for either of them to walk under without having to duck.

The older woman clucked in mock disappointment.

"Now you've gone and taken all the fun out of our little game."

The girl whimpered again, but didn't move. She curled tighter into a ball as if hoping somehow she might become so small as to be invisible. Soon, the woman with the large, fully dark, and wide-set eyes was standing over her. She shook her head with that same look of admonishment, but her face betrayed another expression; that of hunger. Suddenly, the girl's hand flashed out, slashing across the woman's cheek with a jagged rock, and she was gone, bare feet padding frantically down one of the darkened corridors.

The woman drew up in shock and anger, her hand clutching her cheek. But then, her eyes narrowed, as a dark kind of glee settled over her. She stared down at her hand and licked the fresh blood from her fingertips. She began to move in the direction of the quickly retreating steps when a chime broke the silence, and she drew up short. The woman brought her watch up to read the message scrolling across its face and then a slow, animal growl escaped her throat.

"Always, when I'm working!" she spat out. But then turned, walked a few feet, and disappeared into a blinding burst of light, which stretched her shape into something taller and decidedly more masculine.

CHAPTER 3

BACK DUES

Memplant Transcription:

[Subject X, presumably Madame Harbinger/Ms. Timms denoted as *Madame Harbinger*, italicized. Symbol -/- denotes possible time slip.]—E.B.

[Transcrypt starts 51years Prior]

[Multiple people, Madame Harbinger and a young boy (Holland Finnery) and a Man (possibly Agent Wilmes?) speaking]

Boy/Holland: "So, your job is to travel through Time, fixing things?"

Madame Harbinger: *"I fix things. Sometimes I manipulate time to do it."*

Boy/Holland: "You must not be very good at it…"

THE HARBINGER BROKEN

Madame Harbinger: *(Chuckling)* "Indeed. Some things cannot be fixed. And the Universe has a way of putting things back. Things it deems important. Time, like any stream, is not linear but follows the path of least resistance."

Boy/Holland: "So, if you can travel through Time, why can't you travel between realms on your own? Aren't you powerful enough?"

Madame Harbinger: "Silly boy... no one's that powerful. They'd be a god or at least a demi-god. Besides, I believe the powers are separated so that the people of the Three Realms are forced to work together. Like you and I, right now."

Boy/Holland: "But, if you can't do it on your own, then why do you all live in palaces, but we live in places like Dustbin?"

Madame Harbinger: "You mean Dain Burrough? Dain Burrough's ... nice. It's quaint."

Boy/Holland: "It's a shit hole."

Madame Harbinger: "Watch your mouth! But, yes, I guess you're right. It is a bit of a shit hole."

Man/Agent Wilmes: "Madam Harbinger, the Keysmith is ready. Is your apprentice friend ready to go?"

Madame Harbinger: "What do you think, Master Holland? Are you ready to take us to the special place you go to?"

Boy/Holland: "Mmhmm. But I don't think the people will like it."

Madame Harbinger: *"What people, Holland?"*

Boy/Holland: "The people that live there sometimes."

Madame Harbinger: *"The Ephemera? That's just a myth. No such thing."*

Boy/Holland: "They're real. I seen 'em. Kinda."

Madame Harbinger: *"'I have seen them.' And we'll agree to disagree. Now, are you ready?"*

Man/Agent Wilmes: "Madam Harbinger? We really must be going."

Boy/Holland: "Miss Timms ... why are you after him?"

Madame Harbinger: *"We're not after a man, we're after a group. They're moving through Time and Place. That's how we know there's more than one person and that's why we have so many with us."*

Man/Agent Wilmes: "Madam?"

Madame Harbinger: *"Yes, yes Agent Wilmes... Holland?"*

Boy/Holland: "Is he dangerous?"

Madame Harbinger: *"Them, Holland... Yes. Let's go. Off-time, out-of-place... they'll never see us coming."*

...

The Harbinger Broken

Madame Harbinger: "Is this it? Is this Elsewhere?"

Boy/Holland: "Yes."

Madame Harbinger: "Okay then, we wait until the minor window, which is in... just forty-five seconds. Okay, ready everyone?"

"And you're sure that you can get us back to the place where we were earlier?"

Boy/Holland: "The warehouse? Yes. I remember it."

Madame Harbinger: "Okay. We go on my mark."

Boy/Holland: "How do you travel off the timelines?"

Madame Harbinger: "Probably the same way you travel outside the ways. Quickly now. We must get this right. Stand next to me, Holland. Five... four... three... two..."

...

(Bustling of bodies, words of surprise, confusion)

Madame Harbinger: "No, no. This is all wrong. We're back where we started. Holland! Where've you taken us?"

Boy/Holland: "I... I don't know... I knew where I was going."

Man/Agent Wilmes: "Told you we shouldn't have gone outside of protocol and trusted an amateur."

Back Dues

Madame Harbinger: *"We had to go outside of protocol. The killers have been one step ahead the whole time. No. We can fix this. We'll just do it again. Holland? Holland?!?"*

Realm Kirksfold, Dain Burrough (Dustbin)

Present Time

"Yer burnin' up, lass..." Holland whispered as he leaned over his bed to feel the woman's forehead with the back of his hand. Her eyes were moving frantically beneath her lids. His eyes moved to the bandage on the right side of her stomach, soaked through with blood.

"No, no, no. Not good. You can do better 'an that," he chided. It was in a soothing voice he hadn't had to use for years. He cast his attention aside. "Nelv, look what you've done moving 'er to *better* accommodations..." he groused to no one, shaking his head with frustration. He searched the air for inspiration but settled back on the same conclusion he'd rejected several times already; he'd have to seek outside help.

"Doc, I hope you're in the mood fer surprises," he muttered before returning his attention to his unintended guest. "I'm sorry. You're not goin' to like this."

He reached down and scooped the woman up into his arms. She stiffened and moaned feebly. Holland glanced about the room to confirm the window shades were fully drawn. He nodded to himself right before the walls were splashed with brilliant blue light and then engulfed in darkness.

THE HARBINGER BROKEN

Realm Vellem, Antipole Sur, 1112 Warbleshom

Roald Smythe looked down at the lustrous black hair of his receptionist. She wasn't an attractive woman but, from this angle, the doctor had to imagine little to stay aroused. He fumbled with his zipper and belt. A tinkling of chimes rang out, and the woman bumped her head on the underside of the desk drawer and cursed. This was accompanied by hushed curses under the doctor's breath as well.

"Stay here. This will only take a moment," he told her, but began to think better of it when down her blouse he caught sight of her ribs and sternum, where he'd prefer to have seen mounds of ample bosom. His sneer of contempt must have been evident for the woman's eyes flashed down in embarrassment. *I'll have to fix that later*, he thought to himself. Good receptionists were hard to find, even more so, mediocre ones who were willing to shelve their inhibitions in order to keep a paycheck.

The chimes rang again. Roald zipped up some uncomfortable bits and bit back a flurry of curses. He paused to cautiously finish his task before making his way to the door that led down to the *other* surgical room—the one that was as profitable as it was questionable from a legal standing.

"Oh, by Jonnes, no," he exhaled as he took in the sight of Holland Finnery with a bundled-up woman lying on his operating table. "I don't do Pro Bono work anymore," he hissed. "You know that."

"Doc," Holland implored.

"The answer is no."

"Doc..."

"No means no," he said and then instantly regretted it as Holland leveled a gaze at him, all amusement drained from his face. "She told me she was of age," he pleaded. "How long do I have to pay for these crimes?!?"

"Crimes? Plural? What other *crimes* are we talking here, Doc?"

"I won't do it," Smythe stated defiantly, crossing his arms.

"You will do it because you know deep down inside, you're a sorry piece of work and that this is the only hope of makin' up for at least some of your sins before death. Which, by the look of you, is trundling down Warbleshom as we speak," Holland retorted, with no little venom.

"Roald?" a woman's voice queried from upstairs.

The doctor's eyes flicked to Holland, whose head tilted in a way that said without words, "Really?"

"Close up for the day, hon," he yelled up to the woman. *That'll buy me a little goodwill*, he thought. *Maybe make up for my prior indiscretions.* He returned his gaze to the woman on the table.

"Not another orphan. What's wrong with her?"

"Stab wound. T' the stomach." It was the doctor's turn to stare questioningly at Holland, which he ignored. "Found her. Think she's mixed up with sumpthin'."

"You think? Came up with that on your own?" Smythe asked incredulously.

"No questions, Doc. Remember?"

The man scrunched up his nose in distaste. He was about to wade through the pile of blankets to get a look at the wound when he caught a glimpse of her ashen face and stopped cold.

"Holland, you damned fool! What are you doing messing around with such things?!? She's Ekron. It's in the papers. She'll come back here after she's all better and bust us both up. In fact, she could be here now..."

THE HARBINGER BROKEN

The doctor cast a feral gaze about the room to make sure she wasn't already. His mind swimming with possibilities, he imagined phantoms of movement in every shadow, as if the different timelines were even now converging on the nexus of the moment.

Holland grabbed him by the shoulder of his smock and shook him.

"Do what's right, and you won't have to *worry* about consequences!"

Smythe stared at him, looking as if he was going to bolt, but caught sight of her face again.

"Oh look, she's dead after all. Nothing to worry about!" he said cheerily.

"If she dies, the two o' you will be standing at Jonnes's Fork together. But you'll be taking the low road, I imagine..."

Smythe looked at Holland. He could tell the doctor hadn't considered the threat might be real. Something in Holland's look made him change his mind. He got to work.

"I'll be back in an hour or so. Mind who you're dealing with..." Holland said.

"I know... she's Ekron," Smythe replied with a dismissive wave of the hand.

"She's not who I'm talking about," Holland retorted, maintaining eye contact so there was no misunderstanding.

"Yes. I understand. You should mind yourself, too, Holland. That implant you have looks old. One misstep and the Operatrix will space you. Banish you to Elsewhere, forever. She doesn't get on with freelancers bopping about wherever they may."

"Yeh. Well, one thing at a time."

Back Dues

Realm Kirksfold, Dain Burrough
(The Dustbin), 5 Wheadon

Holland returned home to find Prentiss waiting inside, despite his instructions.

"What're you doing here? I said go home."

"My folks didn't believe me. Said they understood why I didn't want to work for a crotchety ol' bugger like yourself, but that I had to go." And then the boy added sheepishly, "Told me not to tell you that part, too, I guess…" He scratched his head and grimaced, seeming to realize his mistake.

Holland chuckled, and then realized that might be concerning to the boy, since he'd rarely ever even seen him smile. If that were the case, the boy recovered quickly as his attention turned to the woman—her well-being and whereabouts.

"Is she well then?"

"I took her to a healer."

"Which one? Mrelda? No, she doesn't do the gory stuff. Ol' man Nat?" he asked, cocking his head.

"Neither. And don't you mind. Why don't you work on that piece I have on the bench? Just file gently where you see the markings. Push. Don't pull. An' use the magnifier. I want you to get small. Think small. If you can see tooling through the magnifier, it won't shine when you're done. Got it?"

The boy stared at him in a stupor, as if he had started to speak in bleats like a goat.

"Do ya got it?" Holland asked more slowly, realizing he hadn't let the boy so much as *look* at a tool in the entire year he'd been apprenticed to him. The boy was probably in shock.

Prentiss nodded twice, blinked, and then walked over to the bench, turning to look over his shoulder, perhaps worried this was some sort of cruel joke.

Holland smiled and waved him on. *What is coming over me? Where'd all this niceness come from, anyway?* He should be mortified, ruining his business in order to not ruin his life with the likes of Ekron agents and terrorists and shady Vellem doctors. *Next thing you know, I'll be running from Clan Karnal thugs*, he mused darkly.

Then he realized that he was actually enjoying himself. He remembered a different man, a hero rather than the cranky old ex-drunk. He was thinking this when large shadows crossed his storefront windows. At first, he was wondering why so much light was coming through in the first place, but then he realized what he should have initially, that men were coming to see him. Not patrons who tended to come individually and by appointment.

His eyes darted to the boy at the workbench, but the lad was born and raised in the Dustbin, he was already headed for the back of the shop.

"No, no," Holland whispered, and motioned for him to meet him at a spot near the woodstove. Holland was already positioning the rug so it was centered on the hatch and would lay back down properly when closed from below. The boy saw what he was up to and scurried over. But there was no neighborly knock at the door. The front door burst open and hands were grabbing them before either of them could make their escape.

"Now, where'd you be going at this time o' day, sir Finnery?" the one man asked, his eye patch decorated with black, red, and silver sequins in a pattern meant to resemble a demonic eye.

The other man, who resembled something closer to a tree with patches of curly black fur, chuckled grimly. His eye patch looked small on his stump face.

Holland stuttered something about going to fetch turnips from the root cellar, but the first man responded with a flash of a backhand that shot stars through his head and buzzing in his ears. It squelched any attempt to formulate a plausible fabrication.

He looked at Holland with raised eyebrows.

"Mmm, you were sayin'?" the man asked, almost pleasantly, while massaging the blood back into his knuckles.

"Turnips." Holland smiled back, maintaining eye contact while the tree-sized thug brought a sledgehammer of a blow into his gut, dropping him flat on his ass a few feet away. He gulped air, but his stare didn't waver.

"Hmm." The man's attention turned to Holland's apprentice. "Why don't we take the rat off yer hands until you develop a memory? Word on the street is you've been up to things and Karnal'd like to know the nature of said activity. Thinks maybe you might have forgot to procure the proper permits. Hmm?" He finished with a smile that looked more like a case of indigestion.

"Come to us with yer fees plus, you know, back dues, but be sure you're not tardy. Rat here, well, let's just say we got more 'an our fair share of rats." He did the grimacing smile thing again.

Upon hearing this, Prentiss's eyes bulged, but to his credit, he didn't whimper or say anything. He knew it'd only make matters worse.

With that, the two thugs walked out with the boy sandwiched between them.

Holland toppled over, gasping for breath. He smacked the floor with his fist and then pushed himself up. Stumbling to the door, he looked down the street to see the back of the behemoth walking away. He couldn't see the other man or the boy in front of him for the man's girth.

There was no way Holland could do anything now. No way he could talk or pay his way out of this, either. He'd have to fix this later. Tonight. The boy should be fine until then, he assured himself. But doubts still milled about in the back of his mind, refusing to be silenced.

Now he needed the information from the memplant more than ever. He hoped against hope that wasn't the activity the thugs were referring to. He no longer had the luxury of waiting for Nelv to get back to him. He tried to close the front door, but it swung away, the lockset having left a jagged chunk missing from the doorframe from when it had been smashed in.

Holland shook his head and slid a bookshelf in front of it to keep it in place, then headed back to the floor hatch. There was only one thing he could think to do, and it wasn't going to make things easier. He maneuvered down the hole to the cellar below, making involuntary noises with the strain of it. The hatch let down flush to the floor and within a second or two, a blue flash illuminated the seams between the floorboards.

CHAPTER 4

SIEGEWORKS

Memplant Transcription:

[39 years prior]

(Many voices, a man (Holland) and subject woman (Madame Harbinger) speaking over the noise, restaurant/party/bar?)

Holland: "You look very lonely over here."

Madame Harbinger: *"Shouldn't you be celebrating with your friends?"* (Subject italicized)

Holland: "Let me check... No. They're celebrating just fine without me."

"(Unintelligible)"

Holland: "I'm sorry, what was that? I just came from a big war, and I can't hear very well..." (yelling as if deaf)

The Harbinger Broken

Madame Harbinger: *"I SAID, move along soldier-boy, I'm not your type."*

Holland: "You *look* like my type. You look like *anyone's* type."

Madame Harbinger: *"You're drunk. Now, scurry along…"*

Holland: "What're you doing here, anyway? You're not from around here."

Madame Harbinger: *"And I bet you'd know…"*

Holland: "What do you mean by that?"

Madame Harbinger: *"I mean you look like you do very well with the ladies."*

Holland: "What was that, was that a compliment?!? Well, now we're getting somewhere…"

Madame Harbinger: *"Don't read into it."*

Holland: "Don't read into what? You find me attractive and you're just not comfortable in situations you can't control."

Madame Harbinger: *"That is untrue!"*

Holland: "Really? Then why are you sitting with your back to the wall and a view of both exits while everyone else is in a drunken stupor, reveling in today's victories?"

Madame Harbinger: *"I am not."*

Holland: "Good cover, Madam Agent. 'You're a spy!' (mock gruff voice) 'I am not!' (feminine voice, full of false outrage)"

Madame Harbinger: *"Well, you're certainly not what I was expecting…"*

Holland: "You're right. Walk with me?"

Madame Harbinger: *"Hardly. Do I look easy?"*

Holland: "No. You look very difficult."

(Seconds of silence. Then sounds of gathering coat and purse, barstool scraping on floor)

Madame Harbinger: *"You have no idea…"*

…

Holland: *"*Nice place. Is this your flat?"

Madame Harbinger: *"Don't act cheeky. We both know what we're doing here…"*

Realm Kirksfold, Dainsmire - Front Lines

39 years and two weeks prior

The blinding white phosphorous of a flare hung suspended in the fog a ways ahead.
"Right. Easy."

No response. The lightly armored personnel carrier's window slit lurched left.

"Right! Your *other* right, Dunsy," hissed Holland. He was navigating from the tank commander's seat that was a little higher up and about an arm's length away from Dunsy's position. Holland's tone wasn't all hard edges, though. It was something closer to the chastising encouragement one might receive from an older brother. He knew from experience how nerve-wracking this part was.

The view ahead was still an illuminated but indistinguishable wall of fog. It shifted right as the rhythmic clacking of the machine's tracks stuttered under input from the driver. It was impossible from the small vantage of that tiny gap in armor to see any difference in overall direction, but the light source seemed slightly more centered in the wide, thin, rectangular viewing area.

"Coming up on a trench now. Should be third-line. Aim between the jacks, right?" he instructed loudly over the groan of the engines.

"Unghh," was all Dunsy replied, too focused on keeping the perimeter-track crawler (a transport resembling a flat toolbox sandwiched between two large chainsaw blades), from stalling in the mud or tipping into the fifteen-foot-deep ditch he was attempting to traverse.

The light from the flare was visibly lower on the horizon now and another shot up from somewhere in the distance to take its place. For a minute, the fog was a brighter sort of opaque until the first flare dipped below some dark structure in the foreground.

The clacking clatter of chugging crawlers rumbled, echoing through the flats, but none were visible out either the port or starboard view slits. They too were crawling over friendly trenches, heading toward enemy siegeworks stuck in the mud farther on. A line of siegeworks that had nearly penetrated Dain Burrough's natural defenses—the perpetually mist-shrouded and miles-wide bog known as Dainsmire. It had been a bay once. Then one day, like a deadbeat father, the tide went out, presumably for cigarettes, and just never came back.

The siegeworks crawled at an interminably slow pace, but every night, they inched closer. They needed only to get within a few hundred yards of the city's fortified beachhead to reach the upper fort with their mortars, and erratic and unpredictable, unguided rockets. What they lacked in precision, they made up for in quantity.

In a similar vein, the Dainlanz Defenciary crawlers stood no chance against the mobile towers individually, but en masse, they could get close enough to deploy troops and sappers that could sabotage the structures. The plan was to render them immobile, at least, and bring them down, if at all possible. But that, too, was near to impossible.

A horrid screech of metal erupted as engines roared to redline, modulating and sputtering with the strain. Cries of the men within the trenches or within the tanks echoed. Someone had miscalculated a crossing and tumbled in. The roar of engines escalated and so did the desperate hollering,

"Get out, get out, get out!" someone cried over the chaos. Concern over the crawlers' occupant's not being able to get out in the case of an explosion—an occurrence that was horrifyingly frequent—colored the man's voice.

More yelling. The engines whined and chugged ferociously and then the fog flickered brightly right before the sound of a double explosion shook the lines of concertina wire, wooden ladders, and gangways. Yelling continued, but now it was not of the warning variety. Rather, screams of anguish from the injured and cries for assistance from those with enough courage to try to help.

Engines always preceded armory though. A bigger explosion was yet to come. The seconds ticked by and the inevitable, even larger explosion lit up the fog accompanied by a concussive boom rolling over the flats and echoing through the night.

Farther down the line to the port side this time, a similar episode unfolded. Holland's own tank teetered on the far side of the third-line trench. He darted a wide-eyed glance at his driver while his stomach lurched sideways and then climbed into his throat. The tank stuttered, one of its tracks spinning uselessly, flinging chunks of mud and spraying sludge high into the air.

In spite of the roar of his own engines, he heard the terrain scraping along the bottom of the vehicle. They were high-centering and slipping to one side, but then mercifully the starboard track caught. The steel beast lunged terrifyingly upward before lurching down and forward again. Holland peered over his shoulder. Nothing but tight-lipped grimaces and silent prayers as the soldiers lining both walls rocked and swayed with the machine's wild gyrations.

More yelling came from outside, but this time it was voices of celebration from the third-line trench. Soldiers, who before had been expecting to break for cover as things went wrong, now cheered them on.

Another marker flare shot up into the sky and for the briefest moment, Holland thought he saw the shadow of the behemoth in the dim distance. His heart skipped. He pressed his face into the magnifiers and strained through the fog to see it again, but with no luck.

Too close, he thought. *There's no way that the Bee-Cees are that close...*

The Bee-Cees were the Bolsko-Cherjk, two city-states from the other side of the once-bay who hated each other less than they hated the Dainzlanders. Hated and felt that the Hall of Ways and the Nexus Ultimatum, the home of the Operatrix, should be located on the right side of the Dainsmire where most of the population of Kirksfold lived.

Far to his right, a staccato of light and sound signified a firefight. Perhaps one of the crawlers had broken ahead and made it over the trenches faster than the rest of the line? Maybe the ground was firmer north of his own track? Of course, it could just be a poorly timed probing attack from the enemy. The nature of the bog made for poor visibility, which encouraged such incursions.

The nose of the crawler dipped again, and he realized they were entering Second-Line. Dunsy goosed the throttle and the twin engines burped and chugged louder even than before, rattling the insides of the machine and its occupants. This trench had sloughed off more in the constant dampness, making it wider but also less vertical. The front edges of the chainsaw-like treads just touched the far side as they drew close to what Holland knew would be beyond the tipping point.

Dunsy crammed the throttle all the way forward this time and smoke belched into the air, mixing with the mist all around the tank. The smell of it was thick already in the cabin, so much so Holland thought he might only ever be able to taste diesel and gunpowder for the rest of his life. Which, he conceded, may not be all that long.

He cast a glance over his shoulder again. Eight bodies all strapped in, lining the sides of their glorified pillbox. He and the driver were the only two out of the lineup, his driver in the low seat, he in the high one. All strapped in until it was time to man the guns, and all hell would break loose.

THE HARBINGER BROKEN

The machine climbed, nose-high, and as it crested the trench, came crashing back down again. One track smashed the metal "jacks" used as guideposts and gates for the crawlers. The concertina wire normally stretched between them had been laid flat only minutes before in preparation of the assault. The transport rumbled on, half-on, half-off of the jack before it crashed fully to the ground and could run unimpeded.

It lurched forward again under full power and with better traction. Holland felt the butterflies in his stomach as the tank accelerated and was about to say something when a loud bang clattered inside the cab and red mist coated his metal-rimmed goggles.

Panic choked him. He rubbed his face on his shoulder and upper arm to wipe the lenses clear. Through smeary streaks, he watched as Dunsy's headless body, still strapped into his seat, flapped his arms loosely at his sides. The tank roared forward, the engines rising toward the redline as it bucked and jumped at speeds ill-advised for the terrain.

The crawler slammed into the First-Line trench like a rampaging beast, plowing over the jacks with a screeching squeal as it canted drunkenly before dropping back to two tracks and rocketing forward again.

Holland looked back to find wide, terrified eyes fixed on him as sappers and infantry gripped their safety straps with both hands, swaying and bouncing off one another violently. All except one, who was clutching the right side of his neck, eyes scrunched tight in desperation as he mouthed a prayer over and over again. Holland realized he must have caught an errant piece of shrapnel from the round that took out Dunsy.

The closest soldier to the front, Malphius Coggins, struggled against his straps and got the buckles disengaged, only to fly across the open bottom of the cab as the crawler lurched again. He smashed into the corporal who'd been sitting across from him—a short spark plug of a girl named Nelv. She pushed him off as she, too, disengaged her harness. Only she managed to avoid becoming loose baggage in the process, riding the bucking floor with the prowess of a circus monkey.

Malphius, from his half-reclined position, backed into the bench, twisted his hand around a loose restraint, and held her upright by her jacket as she worked her way close enough to the pilot's seat to remove Dunsy's body and get herself strapped in.

In the back, one of the soldiers had unstrapped to apply pressure to the injured man's neck as the soldier's own hands flopped limply by his sides and his head lolled unconsciously. They were now tearing across No-Man's-land at breakneck speed and Holland saw now what he'd only guessed at before—exactly how close the siegeworks had come.

Gunfire erupted from the enemy line in sporadic bursts, even as large blooms of light issued from high up on the mobile tower. A few showers of dirt denoted mortar rounds that landed wide, but then quickly those passed away and it was a constant ringing of rounds bouncing off the crawler's armor. They were inside the tower's range of fire now, but were going to be right in the middle of the lines if they didn't die from impact with the siegeworks.

"Ready automatic rifles!" Holland managed, yelling at the next closest soldiers on the benches. "You three," meaning the sappers, "brace and ready to deploy!" The men repositioned heavy packs between their boots and sat back flat against the wall and held on tight.

The soldier holding his lifeless companion's head upright caught Holland's eye. Holland shook his head in the negative. The man, Petruval, he thought, ceased grudgingly and then struggled to reconnect his harness buckles with blood-slicked hands.

Holland turned back to Corporal Nelv, now strapped into the driver's seat and vainly struggling to pull back the throttle slick with blood and flopping lamely with the tank's gyrations.

Something is wrong, he realized. He could see the throttle—two vertical bars with a cylinder handle between them—was wobbling loosely in its travel. *Disconnected linkage*, he thought, with the distant clarity of one who knew he was already dead. Holland looked up in time to see corrugated metal and steel supports burst from the fog to fill the view slit before the tank upended with a bone-hammering jolt.

Holland didn't recall losing consciousness, but darkness, the smell of fire, and a conspicuous lack of engine noise were testimony enough to the fact that something terrible had happened. Cobbling the pieces together, unfortunately, was beyond his current ability. He felt the impetus to hurry up about it, though he was uncertain as to why.

He shifted and pain jolted through his body from ... everywhere. His eyes flew wide even as his hands searched for restraints that were nowhere to be found. In the absence of engine noise, he noticed a lot of yelling and some strange popping noises accompanied by flashing lights, which he couldn't place exactly until the sounds and lights grew louder and brighter.

A black cylinder, which was more holes than metal, pushed through the view slit of what he realized was his crawler. He recognized it as the muzzle of a submachine gun. His brain latched onto that image even as he began to remember the crash and his squad of sappers and infantry. Holland fumbled frantically to grab who he could, which turned out to be the cool-headed Corporal Nelv Kiml and the valiant Mr. Malphius Coggins. And then, when there should have been a flash of gunfire, there was just the brief sensation of nothingness.

Malph woke. The engines screamed, stuttering against the threshold of their ability to cycle, and then a deafening boom jolted through the rear of the crawler. The all-consuming buzzing in his ears felt as if his head was wedged inside a hornet's nest. As it faded slowly, vague but imperative voices came through, yelling in a language that was harsh and guttural.

The pop and peel of gunfire echoed. *Yards away*, he thought, though it sounded far off. He heard pinging as bullets rippled across the metal belly of the crawler. If they were farther away, he'd have heard the impacts first and been able to sort the distance, at least roughly, based on the time delay.

Malph looked over to see the commander slumped against his restraints. Just beyond him, the headless body of his childhood schoolmate, Hallard Dunsworth, lay in a grotesque imitation of a discarded mannequin.

He bit back the wave of nausea washing through him. As he did, he saw Corporal Kiml, was still strapped into the driver's seat, but her arms were straight up overhead as if she were being placed under arrest. That's when Malph realized he was viewing the whole convoluted scene from the roof of the crawler and that the vehicle was, in fact, upside down.

Worse things could happen. The machine could operate for a moment while upside down, but then he remembered the explosion. That's what that was, the engines. The smell of diesel and smoke was overpowering. Now it made sense. Something was pressing on his conscious mind, but he couldn't complete the thought.

Then, gunfire peeled again, much louder than it had been. *They're close.* Enemy soldiers started hammering at the port-side hatch. Malph realized he needed to move if he wanted to live. He went to reach for the corporal and his body erupted in blinding shards of pain. He looked down to find a large, dark stain below his right knee.

He'd broken it. Compound, judging by the protrusion from underneath. He looked away in an effort to settle his suddenly delicate stomach. He'd be put down if he were a racehorse, which he most certainly was not. But he needed to move in a hurry, anyway.

Grimacing, he inched forward. Popcorn bursts and the resultant pings prodded him on. If it weren't for the adrenalin, he wouldn't be able to move. He willed himself to stand, supporting himself on his good leg as he undid the corporal's straps. He caught her easily due to her petite frame, setting her down against the wall carefully before reaching for the commander.

He needed to know if he was alive and if not, find his cyanide pill. Malph was under no delusions as to what would happen when he was interrogated. He'd break and his friends and family would die as a result. He wasn't a coward, just a realist. Everyone broke, eventually.

The commander's restraints came undone, but Malph was unable to soften the landing as he was taller and thickly built. The two crashed to the floor, nearly on top of the corporal. Mal's teeth ground together as he neared to blacking out. The ringing in his ears returned. His body felt warm and then like he was going to throw up. He choked down unbidden tears as he wondered if he was the only one alive. And if so, why?

More gunfire and then a muzzle poked through the view slit. He realized he wouldn't need that pill after all. Malph closed his eyes and waited for the cold embrace of death. Then he felt an odd twisting motion, as if the world had just done an about-face beneath him and they were no longer in the crawler.

Malph knew he wasn't totally clear-headed, but nothing could make sense of this situation except waysmithing. Only, no one could transit between spaces without an established portal. He knew plenty of waysmiths. Not one of them could do what had just been done. If they could, the war would already be over.

Malph surveyed his new surroundings. He was sitting on a worn, unfinished wooden floor in a large room resembling a fort-like command center but with armaments lining the walls. The low drone of machinery rumbled beneath him. He squinted to see clearly because the room was lit with a muted red light.

He cataloged the equipment—launchers with rockets strapped down in triangular stacks, mortars with closed hatches on the walls, and a sloped roof. In the middle of the room, were large plan tables and radio equipment. There were roughly a dozen soldiers, but they weren't wearing Dainlanz Defenciary Forces uniforms. These were light gray, and the soldiers wore light blue berets.

Malph's eyes grew round. Sweat peppered his hairline and the back of his neck as he realized they were surrounded by Bolsko-Cherjk soldiers—though none seemed to be aware of their presence.

He saw Staff Sergeant Finnery stand to his feet, stride over to the closest soldier who was using a compass gauge on a map, and twist his neck viciously. Malph had always assumed it was a myth that you could snap a man's neck like that. But Finnery was a big man, and he had the element of surprise. The dead soldier slid to the floor.

The sergeant then strode softly over to another, also intensely engaged in his own task, only this time he snaked his arms around the man's head and neck and dropped down to the ground. It only took a few seconds before the man lost consciousness.

Kneeling beside his victim, he fumbled with the man's clothing. Procuring a pistol, he made eye contact with Malphius and tossed it to him. Malph checked it, disengaged the safety, and ensured a round was in the chamber before bringing it up to aim at the next closest soldier opposite the sergeant. Movement from the corner of his eye caused Malphius to turn. Corporal Kiml, was rising to her feet, her jaw set, mouth forming a thin slit.

The expression was unmistakable. A stiletto blade flicked out from her right hand as she slunk forward in a crouch, closing in on the man Malph had been aiming at. He quickly shifted the sights to frame the next man in line. There were about ten soldiers left by his count, the sergeant having taken one more in the intervening time. All were still focused on the task of taking the Dainlanz front lines.

Malph heard footsteps coming up the sloping ramp that entered through a rectangular hole only feet away from where he sat against the wooden wall at the back of the room. Holland heard it too. He scanned the armaments quickly and scooted over to a wooden box stacked on top of a pallet of others. It had straw poking out the top and so was obviously opened already.

Holland reached in and drew out two round steel balls. He tossed one to Malphius, who caught it easily with his off-hand. Heavier than a stitch ball, but roughly the same size. Though it was an unfamiliar design, he knew it for a grenade.

He looked back at the sergeant. The man pantomimed pulling the pin on top and then flashed a hand with outspread fingers. Was that an explosion or a five-count? Malph assumed Finnery knew that *he* knew grenades exploded. So, he concluded it was the time delay. With things like this, you just wanted to be certain. He nodded his head in acknowledgment.

Finnery held up the grenade as if toasting to their early demise and then reached to the pin with his free hand. Malph hurriedly copied his actions, and they both pulled the pins. Kiml crouched behind the distracted soldier and covered her ears. The sergeant rolled his grenade toward the front of the room and slid behind the wooden supports of a rocket launcher. Malph tossed his grenade underhand down the opening and heard it hit the ramp, bounce twice, and then start rolling toward the voices below.

A clamor of urgent shouts from below caused everyone in the room to turn just as tandem explosions shook the upper rooms of the command-and-control siegeworks tower.

On the heels of the explosions, Malph's head felt stuffed with sand that was still being pounded by heavy surf. Soldiers were scurrying, screaming, or shouting orders that went largely unanswered. Kiml was letting a soldier slip to the ground, grasping his throat while she charged toward another, just crawling out from beneath a table. Malph watched as another soldier spotted her and was headed her way. He placed a hole in the man's beret that did little to contain the skull exploding beneath it.

Malph watched as Sergeant Finnery strode over to a soldier attempting to stand from all fours and planted a square, bootlace punt across his face. He carried that momentum into another man, bloodied from head to waist from the grenade blast. He drove the man to the far wall and right out the open window, then turned to survey the action.

Malph steadied his aim on the last man standing, a soldier who was somehow taller and broader than even the sergeant was. He began to squeeze the trigger but eased off at the last second when Corporal Kiml flew in like a cat from a barn fire. She wrapped herself around the enemy soldier's torso and slit his throat before he had time to react. She rode the man down as he toppled over, stepping off like a messenger from a steed, and wiped off her blade before retracting it back into its handle.

Malph gulped. He couldn't remember a moment when his feelings about something were more convoluted. Was he shocked or terrified? Or something else? The woman's grit was certainly ... admirable?

He was yanked back into reality when the mobile tower bucked under a blast from somewhere farther below. Then he remembered the tank. *The armaments have finally blown*, he deduced. It had only been a couple of minutes since they were inside the crawler. Someone had definitely performed an impossible feat of waysmithing to carry them from there to here—two distinct locations within a battlefield—without the use of portals.

Urgent voices from a couple of levels down clamored. *How many troops man these towers, anyway?*

Finnery was already moving toward a rocket battery. He flung open the hatches, revealing another siegework farther to the south, barely visible except for the glowing nebula of a flare illuminating the mists. Holland slashed the straps on the rockets and loaded a rack of five, twisting the fuses together and then lighting them with an igniter dangling from a chain on the side of the apparatus.

Then he ran to a mortar station and flung open those doors as well. Comprehension dawned on Malph as he watched in awed silence, still planted on his butt near the ramp. The sergeant adjusted the mortar, ranging it for the next tower, while Nelv catching on, mimicked his actions on the opposite side.

Soon voices and the thudding of boots from levels somewhere below became evident. Malph scooted closer to the entrance, wincing and sweating through the pain of his broken shin. He hollered at the sergeant for more grenades, and the man grabbed the box and ran it over to him. He looked down at Malph's leg.

"You good? You should be in shock."

"Yeah, I think. I can do this, though," Malph replied, pointing at the box of explosives.

"Holland. I know we met but..." the sergeant began but was cut off.

"Yeah, I know. I'm Malphius. I was friends with Dunsy."

The sergeant shook his head, looking angry and ashamed.

Malph started in again, "Wasn't your fault. Now, go over there and give 'em hell. At least until this thing burns down or falls over."

"No. I've got other plans. We'll do a helluva lot of damage. Break the line and light this place up like a supernova. But we're not dying today," Holland said, which caused Malph to raise an eyebrow through a pained grimace. His teeth ground down to their roots as every jostle of the tower sent shards of white-hot pain through his whole body.

"If we make it outta this, you're buying while you tell me just what the hell happened down there," he said looking pointedly in the direction of where he thought the crawler had been, "to end us up here," he finished, pointing at the floor of the command control room.

The sergeant stared at Malph and nodded. For the briefest moment, the sergeant's pale blue eyes held twelve kinds of danger. But then Holland nodded once more, as if concluding a conversation only he could hear, and strode purposefully back to the lineup of armaments. Just then, the first rocket flew, followed quickly by the other four all at once. They shot out into the night, spiraling, streaking yellow-white sparklers behind them and then exploding everywhere but on the opposing tower.

Sergeant Finnery dropped a mortar into the tube and ran back to the rockets just as Corporal Kiml's rockets began to light off one by one. The first mortar struck the tower mid-way up. Holland lit off the next set of rockets, ran back over to the mortar, and adjusted for elevation, while another thump came from the corporal's side.

Malph couldn't see where hers hit, but he faintly heard the explosion and noted she didn't make any adjustments before dropping another mortar down the tube and then another before heading back to reload the rocketeering station.

There were no voices from below, but Malph heard the scuffing of boots and he remembered his own job here. He pulled the pin on two grenades and lobbed them down even as a blue beret popped up through the opening. Mal fished for the pistol. The man's face only had time to register shock before he fell back down with a crimson dot on his forehead. The crack of the pistol barely registered before two booms in quick succession followed and then a much larger boom from below signaled the other towers were fighting back.

Holland yanked off handfuls of fuse wire from a reel on the wall and began quickly knotting together the ends of the rest of the rocket fuses in the stack, not bothering to place them in the launch tubes.

Realizing what he was up to, Malph pulled himself up onto his good leg. The pain stole his breath and shrunk his peripheral vision down to just the battery of rockets. He hopped forward twice, a third time, and then the whole siegework lurched beneath him, sending him to the floor. He cried out, tears welling in his eyes as he dragged himself the remaining few feet. Malph forced his hands into motion, focusing on tying each fuse together rather than on the mind-numbing pain.

Fire and smoke exploded from the front of the room, tearing off part of the roof and exposing the front of the siegeworks to the night air beyond. Malphius realized he was lying on the floor several feet away from the stack of rockets. To his shock, he saw some of the fuses were now lit. In fact, much of the room was on fire and smoke was quickly filling the space.

Then Malphius realized the corporal was nowhere to be seen. He struggled to pull himself back, the pain nearly causing him to gag. He searched the floor for her body but was blind in the growing blanket of smoke. And then a muffled cry came from nearby.

Shocked, he realized she had been blown out the window and was hanging on by her fingertips. For the second time that day, Malphius pulled her from peril and into his arms. In his mind, he decided to never let go.

The hulk of Holland's body came sliding into the two as another explosion racked the tower, only this time the tower lurched and slunk sickeningly beneath them before shifting faster and faster the other way.

Malph felt that perplexing movement again. Suddenly, they were no longer in the toppling structure of the siegeworks, but planted firmly against a muddy wall. They were sitting on wet boardwalks and looking up into an obscuring fog illuminated by white phosphorous flares and the orange glare of explosions. But they were well away for now.

Present Day

"What do you want, Gurlish?" The man with the eye patch asked tiredly, looking up from objects laid out before him on an antique desk. The desk had been placed prominently at the back of a large warehouse filled with row upon row of highly stacked crates. Tarnished light fell through skylights and high, opaque windows scattered around the perimeter, most of which were invisible for the racks of inventory. It seemed part warehouse, part lair.

"I want your people to show up when they're paid to do so. I want port authorities to look the other way when *they're* paid to do so. I want my shipment back!" Gurlish cried accusingly.

"Yeah, well, we all want something, right? You'll get your money back," said the first man, waving offhandedly and then motioning to yet another man standing a dozen or so paces away. This man had short, slick, black hair and was thin with a tailored-looking suit. Not common in Kirksfold. He looked very much the mob lieutenant. Most called him Straightz.

"I don't want *money*. You don't understand. I'll lose my *life!* Shipped into the ways and left to die. I *need* my shipment back!" wailed Gurlish as he wrung his bony hands and adjusted his driver's cap, looking as if he'd wanted to pace nervously but was stuck to the floor as if nailed there.

"Well, we both know that's not going to happen. That ship has sailed."

"Karnal, I won't put up with this and you know when *she* hears about it, it's going to be you that gets lost—"

"Gurlish," Karnal interrupted calmly from behind his desk. "Don't pretend to threaten me. You're as replaceable as your inventory." Then he looked over at his lieutenant, who was standing off to the side wearing an eyepatch with a sequined symbol in the shape of a demonic red eye. "Straightz. Fetch Bigg Baby and have him find something for Gurlish here before he says something that gets himself stapled to one of these crates."

"Ummm. We got a kid," he suggested, shrugging.

"Yeah? Give it to him."

"Well," the man known as Straightz interjected, stepping forward and grimacing painfully, "we was holding him for collateral 'til we could figure out what kinda funny business the old man's been up to."

"You mean Finnery? Is he coming here?" Karnal asked, returning his attention to the objects on his desk.

"Yeah."

"Well, then, what do we need collateral for?" Karnal asked, looking up at Straightz meaningfully. "That used-up old man has outlived most of his generation and used up all the goodwill I have to offer."

"I see your point. I'll fetch the rat." Straightz turned and strolled casually toward one of the rows of crates, presumably leading to rooms elsewhere within the facility.

"One kid? I lost half a dozen in that debacle! Not to mention my cages..."

Karnal lifted his gaze to the man, but said nothing.

"Errm... right. I'll take the kid. Plead upon her good graces." He laughed nervously. "Maybe she'll be in a charitable mood?" he ventured, shrugging, and then stood there awkwardly now that the negotiations were concluded. They'd ended as they always did, with Karnal giving only what he was willing to give and nothing more.

"Smarter than you look, Gurlish. Now, stand over there somewhere and don't touch anything," he finished with a distasteful curl of his lip and a dead, shark-like gaze from his visible eye, and then returned to examining his goods.

"C'mere rat," came Bigg Baby's resonant baritone.

"It's Prentiss," the boy replied in a small voice.

"Mantis? Like a bug? Ok, bug. You're coming with me," the huge man instructed. Prentiss went with the man, but didn't like the situation at all. The thugs would double-cross the old man given the chance. He just didn't know what he could do about it. He needed to figure out an angle. A way to keep himself out of the fray or to avoid it entirely.

He had thought if he made himself real small and quiet, they'd forget about him, and then Holland would come and sort things out. He knew the old man would come. He was grumpy, but he was right-hearted.

That's how he knew he'd help the woman when he'd found her that night. That's why he hung around for months on end, even when the old man wouldn't let him glance at one of the silver crafting tools, let alone teach him how to use one.

Prentiss had lied to him, of course, about his parents. He'd been sleeping on the streets for as long as he could remember. Correction: As long as he *cared* to remember. He didn't think about the days before that particular bit of nastiness. He just remembered seeing Holland talking to a merchant one day. Paying full price for a clearly rotten cabbage from the woman, Toolie. He knew then that the man was different than he looked. Different, too, than the way he talked.

Prentiss figured out the old man was Holland Finnery. The Holland Finnery from the stories of the war even though he didn't look the part. He had decided that apprenticing under the man might be worth his time.

Learning a trade was a pipe dream for most street rats. They'd end up dead, missing, or addicted and then dead by the time they hit their teens. Prentiss had stalked him like any good mark. Learned his habits and schedules and then showed up at his shop, claiming to be so-and-so's nephew from company such-and-such, and wasn't it a coincidence they'd bumped into one another at the market...

Prentiss was pretty sure the old man knew he was lying. But he'd accepted him as interim apprentice, anyway. Prentiss had good instincts.

Right now, his instincts were telling him to run. But there was nowhere to go. The house they called a man, known as Bigg Baby, had a hold of his arm. Bigg Baby's fist engulfed Prentiss's entire upper arm. As it was, he was hopping as much as walking beside the behemoth.

"Scrawny, isn't he?" Gurlish observed when the two had returned with Karnal's lieutenant, the unreasonably well-dressed Straightz.

"Yeah, but he's crafty, this one. Doesn't look like much, but those little wheels are always turning," said Straightz making a circular motion near his head, probably meant to imply gears working rather than that he was mentally unstable.

Bigg Baby looked down at Prentiss. A hint of a flicker of sympathy passed across his face, but was just as quickly replaced with that implacable wall of granite.

"I'll keep that in mind," replied Gurlish sourly, adjusting his green vest and then his driver's cap, looking very much put out.

Great, Prentiss thought. *I've been outed.*

Gurlish grabbed Prentiss by the scruff of the neck, but not before he'd managed to place a sharp kick square into Bigg Baby's shin. An action that hurt Prentiss far more than the mountain of a man, he was sure, but he'd seen what he wanted to see. Baby, instead of reacting in anger as he should have, ignored him and looked the other way.

Good, Prentiss thought, *serves you right*.

And then he walked along with the not-quite-right man known as Gurlish. True to his name, he had an oddly effeminate way about him that contrasted with his dock worker mannerisms. But beyond that, there was a repressed hostility beneath it all. *A contempt for weakness, for himself*, thought Prentiss. This man *was* evil.

The boy's stomach sank lower somehow, but his eyes were constantly on the move, drinking in information from any and every source. Information that would save his life if he had the wits to act on it. Street kids could see things, but right now, Prentiss didn't like what he was seeing at all.

Holland could follow the ways. That's what nobody knew. They also didn't know he could travel without them. Only Malph and Nelv knew that. And Agent Madrigal Timms, of course, the Harbinger. That'd been over fifty years ago, though. Holland had always hoped she'd forgotten.

Holland performed his special trick now, following Nelv's path of travel from earlier. He was surprised at how easy it was, though it'd been a lifetime ago since he'd tried it. Before that day, when he'd taken the Ekron agent to the in-between place people called Elsewhere. Before that fateful moment that changed everything and caused him to give it up and run away.

Holland found himself in a root cellar, of course. No one did this sort of thing out in the open. The fact that Nelv could go "off-roading" which meant to use an established way portal to start a journey but to finish where there wasn't one, was shocking enough. The fact she continued to operate without discretion, however, was even more shocking. Her being able to elude capture meant either the Operatrix wasn't as all-powerful as most believed, or she just couldn't be bothered with the likes of the resistance.

Trouble in Kirksfold wasn't trouble as long as the ways remained in operation. And to the present, the resistance—the so-called ToobRaiders—hadn't devised a way to interrupt that precious life's blood.

Stepping from a stone-lined room into a narrow corridor, he tripped on a wire, triggering chimes that could be heard way down the hall. He threw his hands up.

"I'm unarmed!" he yelled for the benefit of whoever was sure to be crashing on his position, weapons ready.

"I'm unarmed," he said again loudly, not moving for fear of tripping something more deadly. A body emerged from the end of the hall and a shot rang out, shattering the one working light. A bright blue flash followed, and Holland was now standing behind his attacker. He bounced the unfortunate man's head off the stone wall.

"Sorry for that, friend."

"No worry. Brighton's an idiot. Stupid should hurt," said Nelv, the source of the slight pressure he felt in his ribs being her pistol.

"That you Holland?"

"Well, of course it is. Y'know anyone else who can do that?"

"Don't know. There's been some strange talk of late. A demon that can do time and space."

"Pshaw! Nonsense... no one can do that. They'd be a god." The words came out, but Holland couldn't recall where they were from exactly. Just something he knew, but didn't know why.

"Yeah. Well... just the same. Come on. I'm sure you're here for the transcripts." She slipped her sidearm into a hip holster.

"Transcripts? Not the audio?"

"No, the machine just spits it out."

"Bloody inconvenient."

"Tell me about it. Now, come along. And about that favor..."

"It'll have to wait, Nelv. Clan Karnal come and stole my apprentice. Gotta fetch 'im first."

"I don't think you understand the nature of our deal."

"No, Nelv. You don't understand."

"Hard-ass, huh? Since when?"

"Since I needed t'be. That kid's got no one. I let 'im sleep where he wants to sleep but other 'an that... he's as good as my own."

"Yeah, well, I'm sure he'd be surprised to hear that."

Holland looked wounded, but then, after a moment, nodded in agreement. "Yeah. Prob'ly so."

Nelv darted a look in his direction. "Holland, you'll... Well, let's just say that some of what you're about to read will be a bit surprising. After that, though... Well, let's get that kid back. Then we can talk about the other stuff."

Holland reached over and pulled her in close as they walked, her head coming up to his ribs. She rested her head on his side for a couple of paces and then pulled away as they approached a green metal door on the left side of the stone-lined hallway.

"Here it is. Forget you ever saw this place."

CHAPTER 5

NO GOING BACK

Memplant Transcription:

[38 years prior]

[Many voices, a man (Holland) and a woman (Madame Harbinger) speaking over the noise, restaurant/party/bar?]

Holland: "You look very lonely over here."

Madame Harbinger: *"Shouldn't you be celebrating with your friends?"*

Holland: "Let me check... No. They're celebrating just fine without me."

(unintelligible)

"Pretty smooth operator there," Nelv observed, much to Holland's discomfort.

He was completely lost. "I mean, it sounds like me. Kind of..."

"Oh, it's you."

They continued reading down through the stacks of paper.

...

Holland: "Don't read into what? You find me attractive and you're just not comfortable in situations you can't control."

(No response)

Holland: "No response to that? Well, I... I guess I'm sorry for wasting your time."

Madame Harbinger: *"I'm not."*

Holland: "What do you mean?"

Madame Harbinger: *"I mean, are we getting out of here or what?"*

Holland: "Oh, yeah. I mean... Yeah, 'course."

(Sounds of gathering coat and purse, barstool scraping on floor.)

...

Holland: *"Nice place. Is this your flat?"*

Madame Harbinger: *"Don't act cheeky. We both know what we're doing here..."*

Nelv looked at Holland, scanning down farther. "See, it's just the same thing, over and over again. It repeats, year after year."

"For how long?" he asked, somewhat baffled.

"Years."

"How many years?"

"I don't know, maybe ten? Eleven?"

"The same thing...?" he asked incredulously. "For eleven years?"

She nodded. "Almost identical. Well, until here," she said, pointing to an earmarked spot well into the stack. "It's different here."

[27years prior]

(Many voices, a man (Holland) and a woman (Madame Harbinger) speaking over the noise, restaurant/party/bar?)

Madame Harbinger: *"Is this seat taken?"*

Holland: "Hmm? Oh, no."

Madame Harbinger: *"Are you waiting for someone?"*

Holland: "No. Not really. Just in my head, I think. We won the war today, I'm sure you've heard. It's as good as won, anyway. "

Madame Harbinger: *"Yeah, that's what they're saying."*

Holland: "Are you a journo? You don't look like you're here to celebrate."

Madame Harbinger: *"No. No, I guess I'm not. I guess, I just ... wanted someone to talk to."*

Holland: "Oh. Oh…"

Madame Harbinger: *"Would you like to? Talk?"*

Holland: "Umm... yeah. I mean, yes. Of course."

(Sounds of gathering coat and purse, barstool scraping on floor.)

Holland blinked in surprise. "Sounds like the tables have turned a bit. She sounds ... desperate," he said, wondering at the shift in roles.

"Uh-huh. You're a slut, by the way. Five sentences and you're going home with a stranger? Certifiable man-whore."

Heat rose in Holland's cheeks.

Nelv smiled. Having received the desired response, she continued, "And then, there's this one." She pointed to the next section of prose farther on.

[25 years prior]

(Many voices, a woman (Madame Harbinger) by herself, restaurant/party/bar?)

Madame Harbinger: *"Holland, you magnificent bastard. You don't even see me anymore...*

"Goodbye, Holland. I loved you."

(Sounds of gathering coat and purse, barstool scraping on floor. Walking away.)

Silence. Holland's eyes searched the ceiling above, but they were actually searching his memories for any hint of something like what he'd just heard described over and over again. The transcripts of what was supposedly their shared experience.

"I have no recollection of any of this. Not a single thing."

"Of course, you don't. She *undid* it. Right then, when she didn't speak to you after you stopped noticing her." Nelv shook her head in disbelief. "The power this woman wields... I'm surprised she didn't smite you with a lightning bolt," she said, picking a piece of lint off her wool jacket sleeve and then rubbing her fingers together until it drifted away.

Holland didn't respond at first. He continued trying to sort the information, hunting for clues to memories that had never been there. Some meaning to their absence.

"Twelve years..." he mused.

"Right. It's all a bit weird. But, each instance, for you, that's the year you met Meri. So, she kind of did you a favor. I mean a beautiful Ekron agent? Who could compete with that?"

"My Meri could," Holland said, his jaw set.

"Well, that's nice that you say that Holland, but back then?"

"Why didn't she stay? If she loved me like she said. Why'd she just toy with me like that?"

"Who's to say? But you can ask her yourself. Get some answers, if it helps," Nelv provided, attempting to organize the dog-eared stack of papers into neat piles on the worktable.

"I need answers alright, but to this other stuff first. This trouble she's in. It's big. I mean, maybe as big as the war itself."

A wall clock ticked loudly in the silence, reminding him of its significance. With each passing second, a killer drew closer to finding her. And if not him, then the law. With each passing second, his apprentice was in even greater danger at the hands of lawless thugs.

He glanced back at the mess of papers. "What else is there?"

Nelv turned from Holland to the transcripts. She worked her way to the end of the mess and drew her index finger down to a spot that had scribbled text and underlines around it.

"The last bit. It looks like, well, it looks like she meets with the head of Ekron, Osmius Turnbull. And he goes on about a stray dog in the park. Very weird, very cryptic. A little creepy considering what happens to her right after that exchange."

"Hmm. Yeah, for sure," Holland replied, contemplative, tapping his temple with a long, thick finger.

"And then there's this bit about wanting to meet with the Operatrix," the resistance leader, his old friend and closest friend of his years-dead wife, said, looking up at him.

"But when the Operatrix isn't there, that seems to lock in some idea in the woman's mind." She returned her attention to the page and continued, "And then, after that, she goes to meet the killer. I wish we could hear the actual voices, but this machine doesn't do that. It's just scraping the meaning off of the audio. We'd need a real NeuroVox to get it. I'd say what we have is ninety-five, to maybe ninety-eight percent accurate though. We've tested it."

"Have you?" Holland asked, eyebrows raised, questioning the morality of their experiments more than their efficacy. It would have to have been tested on someone with a memory implant and those were hard to find in the Dustbin.

"Yes. But I think we'll leave the details vague for now. You wouldn't want to be found complicit with the resistance, now would you?"

"No. Prob'ly best you don't tell me."

"So, she meets her boss. Then she tries to meet with the head of the Guild of Ways and then she meets a nasty end. Almost... and it sounds like she was surprised. Like, her would-be killer did something unorthodox. Or maybe, considering your girl's abilities, something ... inhuman." Nelv looked at him knowingly. "Seems like she's been tracking this guy for some time."

Holland thought again about their first meeting, when he was a young man. She'd been searching for him even then, fifty-plus years ago, though for her it was considerably less. As few as twelve based on the transcripts record, though he imagined it was more.

"Yeah. Yes, she has. He seems to be playing a very long game." Holland stared off someplace beyond the beige office wall. "I need to get back to her. And then I need to save that boy. Tonight. They won't expect me to do that, but if I don't show for the boy soon ... they'll expect something's up."

"Start with the woman, Holland. Maybe she can help you undo the whole thing with Karnal. It'd be best if it never happened at all."

"You saw her, Nelv. She's in no shape to be sorting time."

"Still, if what you're worried about is true. Our *reality* is at stake," she said, motioning to everything around them. "Nothing's off-limits. You could be unborn as easy as this conversation could cease to be..." she said this last, looking around, hoping to catch the out-of-phase images that sometimes preceded a time-slip. What people sometimes confused with ghostly apparitions.

"Yeah." Holland shifted a couple of thin copper coins between his fingers over and over again. "Best if I can get 'er stitched up and back to health. The fact Director Turnbull thinks her dead, I need to use that if I can. An' I should avoid drawing the attention of the Operatrix as well. Tho', gonna have to slip out to Vellem and back... The doc. He said my chip's old. Is that true?"

Nelv scrunched up her nose and nodded. "Yeah, most likely. You should upgrade. You still in touch with Prator?" she asked. Then, seeing him nod affirmative, added, "Yeah? Be best if you could get him to boost you up. God knows you can afford it. Don't know why you ever stuck around here..."

"Yeah, well... lot 'o that's gone. Silversmithing in the Dustbin, ya know. Still, I ain't never left, cuz ... well, this was all I known. I dunno. I guess I just couldn't. Meri's still here..." he said, trailing off.

"Holland. You know she'd want what's best. She'd want to see you happy, not rotting away in that dingy little shop." Nelv placed a sympathetic hand on his shoulder, though it was a reach and she had to draw close to do it.

"Dingy?" he said half-heartedly, looking down at his boots. The top leather was dry and scarred, the soles still wet from his walk back from Ciller's Still. "Yeah. 'Course..."

"So, I can't have you go offroading from this location, Holland."

"Sure. Makes sense. Oww!" He reached back for his neck where he'd just been jabbed with a needle. "Dammit Nelv, what'd ya—"

Her years-old friend crumpled to the floor.

The young guard from earlier stepped into the room.

"Brighton, you think you can handle him this time?"

"Yes, ma'am," he said with a bit of an evil gleam in his eye.

"Alright. Don't take him back to his place, though. Take him to Prator. Have him upgrade his chip. The old man's good for it. If Prator has any trouble with that, tell him we'll cover his costs."

The young man's eyebrows came up at that.

"Don't start. Holland owes me now, and I need him to make good."

With that, Brighton slung Holland over his shoulder, struggling under the weight, and then flopped him into a wheelbarrow that'd been prepared for the purpose, before rolling him out the door.

Holland woke. His head must have had a chasm running through it wide enough for a crawler to navigate. In fact, it felt as though a crawler had done exactly that. A stabbing pain shot through his neck and into his right ear. The dead weight of his legs dangled uselessly beyond dully throbbing butt muscles. The pain in his buttocks, though, took second place to the sharp knot in his back. But then, when he thought about that, it just made him more aware of how badly his head hurt.

This inventory of suffering looped endlessly like a raucous band seated on one side of a slowly rotating carousel until he realized most of this could be attributed to the fact he'd been sleeping in a wheelbarrow. That broke the feedback loop, and he was able to take in his surroundings with fresh eyes.

At first, he couldn't place where he was, but then he heard a distant foghorn. Some of the trees looked familiar. Then he saw a stone cross atop an outcropping of rock, and his stomach dropped. He was in the cemetery at the top of the hill.

Dew dripped onto Holland's face from mist-blackened branches above him. Someone had left him there. No way they'd come up from the harborside, though it'd been close to a century since there was an actual harbor there. Still, that way was too steep. He must have been brought here from the upper city, though he couldn't imagine by whom.

Then he remembered his encounter with Nelv. Remembered the conversation about Prator in particular, and his stomach dropped another level. Given free rein, what might the demented scientist have done?

Prator was tight with money but infinitely curious. The possibilities of what he *might* have done were endless. Experimental plugs? One-off gear? Holland didn't want to find out. He wanted to go back to sleep and forget the whole thing. But the bitter cynic inside him couldn't be contained long.

"Always thought I'd be laid to rest here, just not quite like this..." he said out loud to any ghosts who might be fooled by the mist-squelched sun into thinking it was still night. "Wouldn't ya know... couldn't even get dying right," he continued as he placed knobby hands on the sides of the wheelbarrow and pushed.

He got to his feet and instantly regretted it. Bile filled his mouth, and he was certain he wasn't going to keep down whatever it was he'd eaten last.

Holland crumpled to the ground, head pressed into the cold muck as he breathed through the feeling of vertigo. Lights danced behind his eyes, the smell of ozone was in his nostrils. The ground was below him, his face was pressed into it for Gadd's sake, but it still felt like it was spinning around him. He wanted to throw up just to make it stop.

"This isn't right. This isn't right…" After what felt like an hour but was only a matter of minutes, the spinning slowed and started to fade.

After another minute, he lifted his head, did a quick physical inventory, and was pleased to find no new stitches in his abdomen. That was good. At least he still had all his organs, though now he wondered how he'd paid for whatever services had been rendered. Or to whom he was now indebted and quickly his mind flashed back to his meeting with Nelv, again. His headache surged back into the fore.

"Great. I've been pressed into service… This complicates things."

Holland tripped over a root and only then realized he'd been walking while sorting out his thoughts. He found himself standing face to face with a familiar headstone. It was one he hadn't seen in nearly a decade. One he'd commissioned himself. His mouth went dry, and he worked his jaw as if to say something by way of apology for an inconvenience, but realized there was no point.

Meri had always seen right through him. Even now, he was certain she could do the same. There was no point in apologizing for her benefit, but he couldn't help himself. He babbled, sank to his knees in the wet grass, and kept on babbling. Apologizing for not coming more often, and for not coming at all, and for not being able to save her, for not knowing he needed to keep her home that night, for not sensing it somehow when it had happened. He should have known, shouldn't he? How could he not know she needed him? He pounded fists into the grass, dead leaves, and black mud.

Holland wrung himself out. He was unable to tell how long he lay there in the chill damp. He wore no watch and there was no sun to gauge the day by, just a dully luminous blob that had moved from one place in the sky to another. He assumed it was west and judging by the wan light, it must be getting on near to dusk. That jogged his memory about some of the other more pressing matters. The living he needed to tend to.

"Forgive me, Mer. Forgive me," he pleaded, swallowing thickly. He crossed himself and departed down the steep steps to the harborside. Holland exited through the arched trellis at the wrought-iron gate he'd been unable to enter even up to and beyond the day prior. He turned left toward his shop. But he wasn't going to his shop. He needed to get back to the doc and to his patient. *And* he needed to get the kid.

Drawing close to dusk, he figured Prentiss was in more pressing danger. The Harbinger had chosen her path. The kid, well, he'd been sucked into circumstances that weren't of his choosing. Holland had known there'd be hell to pay for saving souls. He figured it was nigh time to make good on that debt.

"Save the kid, Holland," he told himself as he walked to the place where he'd been accosted by the homeless not-quite-cripple just a day before. He turned up a narrow cobblestone street heading away from the harbor and toward the warehouse district where Clan Karnal's "secret" headquarters was known by all to be located.

The front of the place was a rectangular wall made up of corrugated metal, windowpanes, and a large double door made chalky pink by years of exposure. Behind it was a large Quonset-type structure stretching back another twenty feet before it intercepted the monolithic face of the larger warehouse. There were four street heavies standing, leaning, or sitting about the steps outside.

Holland walked by, averting his eyes, keeping one or two people between himself and the men at all times. One of the men stood, stretched, and then walked inside, giving Holland a decent view into the interior.

It looks doable, the old soldier inside him thought. He continued walking past and turned a hasty right into an alley. A pop of blue light followed his entry into the narrow space.

Instantly, Holland was inside the front doors of the warehouse, watching that same guard from moments ago, walking away. His footsteps echoed in the silence inside the building. Holland padded to the right and down the first break in the rows. He walked smoothly on the sides of his feet from heel to toe to avoid thudding steps.

Paralleling the henchman's path, he made it seventy or eighty feet before the man cut in front of him down a broader walkway. Luckily, he didn't look down the corridor. Holland, too, turned down the wider path and saw it ended in a stairway going down to a lower level. He assumed this was where they were keeping the boy.

Holland had to deal with Karnal before, and this seemed like his way of doing things. He'd known Karnal's uncle in the war. That was probably the only reason Holland had been given any grace at all. He'd been brought in and essentially extorted into paying some sort of insurance, but in the end, they'd let him walk on a one-time get-out-of-jail-free kind of deal.

He knew then there would be a comeuppance. Apparently, that time was now. And there was the thing the shorter thug had mentioned about the activities he'd been up to, which he assumed was the bit about smuggling orphans out of Kirksfold and into the middle realm of Vellem.

They wouldn't understand this was a charity service, rather than the child trafficking it resembled. They'd want their money, assuming there were profits to be gained.

Holland frowned, and then followed the stairs down. So focused he was on keeping his steps quiet, he was surprised to find the thug at the bottom, waiting for him with a five-inch blade flipping in his hand. The blade caught the light like a fish lure. A wicked smile played across his face but turned to shock when Holland disappeared in a blaze of blue light and was suddenly behind him and wrenching his arm up high behind his back.

Holland drove the man forward, ramming his head down onto a tabletop just beside the stairs. But it was Holland's turn to be surprised when the man's head came up with the knife sticking out of his fake eyepatch. That didn't quite work out as he'd expected. He had intended to at least question him first. Killing had been a last resort.

"Jonnes great briny bollocks," Holland cursed under his breath as he dragged the body toward a maintenance closet just across the hallway. He pushed the body into place, but each time he went to close the door, a foot or a hand or a head would block it. Finally, he pushed the body back and slammed the door against it until it clicked. He lowered his head in exhaustion and noticed the trail of blood stretching across the walkway. Then he heard footsteps behind him.

Holland woke for the second time that day with his head splitting. For a moment, he wondered if he was reliving that same moment from earlier in the cemetery when he heard an unmistakable voice.

"What the scud, old man?" a booming baritone asked.

Holland looked up and struggled to consolidate the many Karnals seated before him. They began to coalesce, just as the man rose to his feet, walked around his desk, and leaned against it, arms folded. From this position, it was easy to see how he'd risen through the ranks of the local thuggery to achieve his current status. The man was a knot of muscle. He had no neck to speak of, just slanting slabs of tattoo-riddled flesh from his ears to his shoulders.

"I say again, what ... the ... scud?"

"Uhh... um," was all he could manage.

"Umm? That's all you've got to say for yourself. I have a dead associate and I find you in my warehouse? Straightz." Karnal gestured in Holland's direction.

A loud smack assaulted Holland's ears as stars exploded in his vision. He tasted metal but knew it was just blood from being punched in the side of the face. He blinked away distorted vision and looked down to see blood and drool streaming down into his lap. That's when he belatedly realized he was tied to a wooden chair that'd been placed directly in front of Karnal's desk. He struggled to regroup, but another smack to the side of the head scrambled any attempt.

"I said..."

Holland heard the shuffle of suit cloth as Straightz reared back for another blow, but then there was a flash of light, and Holland found himself standing behind his assailant. The man dropped to the floor, his head and neck flopping sickeningly before coming to rest in a very unnatural way. In his punch-drunk stupor, Holland had transited and broken the man's neck all in one lethally efficient movement.

He looked up from the gruesome scene he'd just created. Karnal was staring at him bug-eyed, but regained his composure quickly. The man known as Bigg Baby was standing on the other side of the chair Holland had been occupying only seconds ago. Bigg Baby's jaw was moving, but no words were coming out, making him look much like a landed bass.

Locking eyes with Karnal, he could see equal parts surprise, awe, and calculation. A man like Karnal would always find a purpose for other people's possessions. Or in this case, abilities.

Holland transited again. This time, back to the cross hallways in the lower level. He shuffled hurriedly down the hall, still blinking away the beating he'd just received.

He headed back to the location of the first encounter, certain the man who had caught him unawares must have been coming from somewhere important. He hoped it was from checking on prisoners. He wiped blood from his mouth and checked for loose teeth as he ran. Swelling around his right eye was beginning to crowd his vision, but he barely noticed. It was the agonizing ache in his head that felt like a sizzling branding iron had been jammed dead center into it.

He stumbled over careless feet but kept moving. Instinct and desperation somehow managed to keep him upright. A gray-painted door slid past, and he came to an abrupt halt. The brass lock and hasp on it appeared well-used. He peered through the thick metal mesh of the window set in the door. Inside was what appeared to be a stable that'd been converted to individual pens.

He blipped through to the other side to get a better look. There were six pens and there were beds in each of them. But none held the boy.

Holland's stomach was slowly rising into his throat, cramping into a ball of molten lead. The nausea returned. He searched again, hoping he'd missed something, but there was still no one there. The pens looked recently used, though.

The knot in his stomach drew tighter as he realized that as hard as he was working to save the children of

Kirksfold, there were forces more powerful and equally bent on oppressing them. The room burned away in a bright blue light.

For the second time that day, Holland found that he'd shifted without intending to.

"Where's the boy?" he demanded, standing again before the desk of the self-proclaimed king of thugs.

"Well. You *are* surprising, old man. All this time, I'd dismissed you as a washout. Just another spineless has-been."

"Maybe you were right. But now you've gone and done what you shouldn't. Even you know better'n this, Clephus," he menaced, using Karnal's given name. "Where's the boy?"

"Gone," he replied, his face growing a shade darker, his one eye flint-like.

"But your man said—"

"Yeah. Well, those are the breaks. We had a pressing need. Business…" he said, shrugging, as if trading the commodity of human life was no less consequential than that of bulk flour or recycled tires. Which, to him, it apparently was. A statement about Dain Burrough as much as anything else.

"Where'd he go?"

"What's it worth to you?"

"Karnal. If any harm comes to that—"

"You'll do *what,* old man?!? You think you can take me when I know you're coming? Try it. That trick you pulled on Straightz, that's a one-time gig."

"Yah, well, we'll see."

"We will. Now, when you're all good and cooled down. You come and see me. We'll see about this boy and a job I have for you."

"Not likely."

"Yeah, well, can't say I envy the life that kid's gonna live. At least it'll be a short one, from what I hear…"

Light flashed and Holland appeared next to Karnal, his face right next to his ear, Straightz's namesake, a bone-handled straight-edge knife gleamed as it pressed the flesh on the side of Karnal's face.

"Whatever happens to that kid ... happens to you," he whispered as the strap to the thug's eye patch severed and fell away to reveal a scarred mass of twisted skin... And then Holland flashed away again.

There was silence for a moment. Then Karnal spoke up, dabbing at the thin line of blood on his cheek, but not bothering to cover the tortured mess of an eye.

"Baby. Give Straightz a proper burial."

"The pigs?"

"Yeah. And Ratchit, too. Then find that kid."

"What about Gurlish? He works for the lady. He's right. She won't be happy."

"Baby. Did you *see* that? I don't care what the lady is. She's never seen anything like it. Soon as we get the old man on our side, we're taking this pathetic little circus interdimensional." He made a quick circling motion with his index finger, seeming to imply the entire operation. "The Klan will be in Vellem, in Brythe, maybe other places we ain't never heard of. Explains a lot about how our hero managed to sneak into one of those siegeworks back in the day."

Bigg Baby nodded in appreciation. "How're you going to get him to help us? He doesn't seem very ... pliable."

"All the waysmiths have that hardware in their head. It's authentication for when they travel between realms. You don't got it? The Operatrix comes and finds you. She's like an air traffic controller for the way portals. But a guy like

Finnery? Someone that can go anywhere he wants. Well, he'd need something special to stay under the radar. Only guy I know that can do that sorta work is Prator."

Karnal steepled his fingers and stretched a kink out of his neck. "The thing about Prator, he backdoors everything. You want the old guy to blip you into some powder wig wearin' parliamentarian's pad in the middle realm? Well, Prator can get it done," he said, locking eyes with Bigg. "Besides, I already know the old guy's been smuggling kids into Vellem. Paying for civvie packs. The whole deal."

He leaned back and kicked his feet up onto the desk. "Man must be fighting off some serious inner demons to fork out that kinda cash on some filth-eatin' street rats. Figured him for some kinda creeper, but turns out he's legit."

He pulled a switchblade from his pocket and examined it as he spoke. "We can appeal to his tender side. And if that doesn't work? Well," Karnal flicked the blade out and jabbed at the air, "we'll shove a white-hot poker up his ass, courtesy of that neural jack he's wearing." A broad smile crept across his face. He knew that with the eye patch missing, it looked horrific, which was as intended.

"I see," Bigg Baby said, unironically.

"Be sure that you do, Bigg. Now that Straightz is gone ... I need someone with a cool head."

"You got it, boss. Head like an ice block."

Karnal looked at him sidelong, but kept his thoughts to himself.

Bigg Baby, on the other hand, looked down at the blue-faced corpse of his former partner. He reached down and hoisted him up onto his shoulder. "Ahh, scudding Straightz. Figure that guy to die with a boner."

"It's called a priapism."

Bigg Baby looked at him in disbelief. "No shit?!? Why would you *know* that?"

Karnal shrugged. "I'm the boss. Gotta know a lotta shit."

Baby paused and then nodded grudging agreement before sauntering off in the direction of the second corpse.

"Hope Ratchit doesn't have a priapism... that'd be just too weird, carrying around a couple of stiffs. Ha!" The big man laughed at his own joke as he sauntered down the aisle carrying the cadaver. "Stiffs... too scudding good."

Prentiss felt the box jostle as it was moved from the back of a van, presumably to a loading dock. He wanted to kick the box or call out, but he'd been bound thoroughly and gagged just as well. It was possible he'd been drugged, too. He wasn't sure how, but his head felt squishy. That was the best description he had for it. Squishy and warm. It felt oddly comforting, but then made him even more concerned, and he felt panic begin to rise up.

There were three holes near the top of the box on opposing sides. He focused on those holes. Through them, he made out the harsh yellow light of high-bay lamps. That's how he knew he was on a loading dock.

Probably at the Hall of Ways, he thought sadly. Just like a few days prior, but on the wrong side of a thin wooden box.

No way they'd go through all this trouble just to move him locally. Plus, there'd be no need. Street kids were a dime a dozen. If that. He was definitely going to one of the other realms, but he doubted it was going to be pleasant. Even if anywhere was supposed to be better than Dain Burrough.

He settled back and listened, committing every detail to memory. And then the box was moving again, down a long hallway before being set down once more. A flash of dim blue light burst through the holes in his box. And then he was scooted a few feet farther. Another flash of blue, a little brighter this time. And then he was moved forward a few feet more.

"Where's this one 'eaded?" asked a man, most likely a dock worker or maybe even one of the waysmiths.

"Looks like, ooh, *private* residence. Only one o' them." A swift rap came from the top of the box. "Tough breaks kid," the worker called to him through the wooden sides of the box and then patted the top of the box twice more. "Tough breaks..." he said, this last trailing off as he shuffled away.

At that moment, Prentiss decided it might be a good time to try out religion. Prentiss's gag was going to be a problem for praying. *I could pray in my head*, he thought. But what if Maker couldn't hear him? He didn't want to get x'd out on a technicality. He maneuvered his head this way and that, managed to get his thumbs under one edge of the kerchief, and wiggled some more until it slipped down over his chin. Small victories.

"Umm, Maker?" he asked in a small voice, but speaking as loudly as he dared. "I know you're busy and probably couldn't give two shits about us down here in the Dustbin, but..." and then he had a disturbing thought, "Do you shit? I mean, I wouldn't think so, but then I look at people like Karnal and Gurlish... In any case. If you could smite them up something terrible.

"Maybe start with their balls. Ya know, make 'em swell up to the size of pumpkins and then maybe explode into a pile of blood-sucking worms that feast on their bodies and are horribly painful. I'd appreciate that a lot. Thank you. Over." And then he remembered one more thing. "Oh, and

... can you get me out of this box? Okay. Over, over. For reals this time."

And then the box was moving forward again.

A young girl crouched in the dark, a hunk of granite clutched against her chest. Her dress, dirty, ragged. Her hair, similar. She huddled in the darkness, careful not to breathe too loudly, though her heart was thumping in her chest so fiercely she was sure the woman could hear it.

"Where are you, precious?" a syrupy sweet voice called from the dark somewhere down the tunnel to her right.

"Hmmm? Dear, is that you?"

And then the girl heard a sniffing sound as if the woman could actually smell her down here in the cold, damp of the subterranean caverns.

"Yessss. There you are."

Shuffling footsteps from down the corridor grew a little bit louder, closer, and then paused. This was followed by more sniffing and then a few more hesitant footsteps.

The girl's heart pounded harder; she heard it in her ears. As the footsteps drew within a couple of feet, it was all she could do to not cry out.

"Oh, that's right. You should be afraid," came the sickly sweet voice of the woman, half-whispered in the darkness.

A long inhalation came, as if the woman were exulting in the smell of the child's fear.

And then there was the faint sound of chimes. Then silence. Then the chimes came again. "Ugghhh. I swear, Malvor, if this is another false alarm, I will *wear* your *skin*!"

A purple flash lit up the cavern and for a brief instant, the woman and the child's eyes locked and then she was gone.

The Harbinger Broken

Marceline broke into a run. Into the darkness she sprinted, going off of memory, her night vision ruined by the bright light. A dip in the floor caused her to stumble and reopened wounds still unhealed from fumbling around for days prior.

She scrambled back to her feet. She was at an intersection of tunnels and as she turned, trying to reestablish her bearings, something in the darkness caught her eye. Something she'd never seen before. But when she looked again, it was gone. The young girl stopped and forced herself to step backward, terrified she would bump into the woman stalking her in the dark. And then she saw it once more.

Something high up. She barely made out the faintest light. It was indirect, but it definitely was light casting off stone somewhere and the air tasted … different.

She felt for the wall and pressed up close against it. Taking one small step at a time, her feet found the tiniest footholds along the wall, each a little higher than the last, and eventually leading up to a ledge she was able to crawl onto.

The dim light was brighter up here and as she rounded an outcropping of rock, she saw a hole in the wall ahead, with portcullis bars, but beyond them was blue sky and wheeling gulls in the distance.

The rock slipped from her hand as she ran to the opening, pressing her face to the bars and breathing in the moist sea air. From this vantage, she couldn't see much, just sky and the horizon, but she could hear crashing waves far below. Her heart sank as she realized even if she could break her way out, she was looking through a hole high up in the cliff wall.

Her only solace, it seemed, was if she could break through, she could at least end her life on her own terms. And deny that wicked woman any satisfaction whatsoever. So that's what Marceline determined to do. She walked back, found her rock, and started working at the joints where the bars met the mountain. Her stomach cramped and grumbled for lack of food or water since she'd hit the woman in the face with that very rock two whole days before. Marceline worked through the discomfort, energized by thoughts of freedom—if only fleeting.

CHAPTER 6

Going Back

Thin light ventured through a high basement window. The window wasn't high above the floor, but it was pressed as high as it could go against the ground-level floor above. Roald Smythe fiddled with a hangnail, wincing and muttering under his breath when the skin began to pull the wrong way.

He reached above the patient's table and flicked on an overhead light, revealing the woman lying there and casting her in stark white light. She looked pale; her lips ashen but starting to regain some of their natural color. She'd been very close to death. Very close indeed. Roald, as it turned out, was as capable a doctor as he could be loathsome a human being. Which was to say, quite.

He checked the woman's temperature and then studied her features consideringly. She was middle-aged, like himself, and not unattractive, in fact, much to the contrary. Her features were regal, almost haughty, but softened in a way that just made her look serious. He generally liked his women a bit more curvy, but then he had highly elastic standards.

He brought the thermometer up close enough to read the tiny print. Her temperature was below one hundred for the first time since she'd shown up on his table with that damnable do-gooder, Holland Finnery.

His half-hooded eyes drifted back to the subject on his table, and he felt that familiar longing warming his loins. He thought maybe she needed a more thorough going-over. He was a doctor after all... Replacing the thermometer in his breast pocket, his hand started to drift toward her crotch even as his other hand drifted toward his own.

"I'd say you've done enough, doc, don't ya think?"

"Godammit Holland! Don't you know how to knock?!? And besides, I was just—"

"Yeah, I can see what you were just... Is she good? Stable?"

"Oh, looks like you've had some work done as well," the fat man observed, looking intently at the side of Holland's face, much pleased to change the subject away from the woman on the table.

"My face or the implant? Damn. I'm gonna have to grow eyes in the back of my head to keep the streeties offa me now... Patrol-Civil too, for that matter."

"Yes. Prator does good work. It's Prator isn't it? The implant sits well on the skull behind your ear there and the skin's not all puckered and fester-y. Plus, I don't know what model it is, but it's very sleek. Maybe his own? Why he stays in that hellhole, I'll never know. Uhh... no offense."

"None taken," Holland replied, smiling wanly. "She's doin' better though?"

"Yes. She seems stable. I was just..." Then the doctor's cheeks reddened. "Well, she's fine. She could come to in the next couple of hours, I imagine. Meanwhile, I should take a look at that eye of yours," the doctor said, crossing the distance to get a closer look at Holland's swollen face.

"Still got all your teeth?" he asked cheerfully.

Holland hated using Roald for situations like this, but he'd had no choice. He was glad he'd come back when he did.

There was movement from under the blankets, and then he heard the wounded woman's voice. "I'm awake." It took him back decades, to when he was a kid.

He looked at Roald and then back at the woman he'd known only briefly as Agent Timms, but whom he'd known much more intimately as Maddie, just in a time stream he was unconnected to. For all intents and purposes, it was as if it had never happened. At least for him.

"Who are you two, and what am I doing here? Where's... uh... oh, never mind. I should just be going," she said, straining to get up and then thinking better of it, laying back down.

"Ms. Timms. You really shouldn't be going anywhere," said Roald.

"I'll be the judge of that—" she tried to respond but was cut off.

"No. You won't," Holland interrupted, stepping into the light from the overhead. "You're in no shape, and 'sides, Ekron's after you. And certainly, the local Propriety have all been notified."

"They're what?!? Why...? What's the meaning of this?" she demanded.

"Maddie," Holland started, resting his hand on her arm still covered by the blanket.

She jerked away at first and then, blinking away confusion, looked at him as though for the first time. Comprehension washed visibly across her face. He could tell she recognized him through the added years and his unkempt appearance. And even his swollen face. For her, it'd only been a handful of years, though he'd aged considerably more than that.

She let out a long breath. "It's you, isn't it? Of course, it is…" she sighed. "Well, I didn't expect our next meeting to be like this." Maddie sighed wistfully and tried to sit up again, but stopped abruptly. She pressed her head back into the pillow. "Oh, bloody hell, that's a good one, isn't it?" she asked through gritted teeth.

"No, no. Relax," the doctor interjected. "The stitches are good, all three sets of them. But you've got plenty of mending to do still. You were really lucky, actually."

"If I was lucky, I wouldn't be here," she retorted.

"Roald, will you excuse us?" Holland asked.

The man looked up. "Yes. Yes, of course." And then made his way toward the stairs, nibbling at his hangnail as he went.

"Maddie. Is there anywhere you can go? We can't stay here. I'd take you to my place but…it's not safe neither."

"Holland. Just so you know…" Her hazel eyes searched his. "Well, how much *do* you know?" She gulped, paling even more. *"Everything?"*

"Mmhmm. I think. Maybe not everything. Though, what I know's enough," he said, nodding, a finger poking at the spot behind his ear where his—and her—implants were located. He did this while looking anywhere but at her.

"Holland, you have to know, I…" She reached toward him but paused partway.

"Now's not the time. Later… perhaps," he said, his mind a convoluted mess of emotion that probably showed as clearly on his face.

"Right." She stared at him again, as if searching for any memory of what they'd shared together. Holland was sure she didn't expect there to be any. She'd made sure of that. His only memory of her was as a child, scolded for screwing things up on an Ekron bust and then running away, ashamed and confused.

"Later then," she agreed. "There's a place. You wouldn't know it, of course…"

He nodded. "Of course… Kirksfold then?"

She looked around the room, probably making sure that they were indeed alone, and then said quietly, "The Inn at Badbriars. North of the harbor side, near the Dainsmire."

"I know it. Mad, that's … a bit of an area."

"Isn't all of Kirksfold? I think I remember distinctly, you calling it a shit hole? Of course, that's been ages for you…" She looked away, her cheeks acquiring a little bit of color. She composed herself and then continued, "It's in order. I assure you."

"At least no one will be looking for either of us there," he muttered under his breath and leaned down and scooped her gently up. She winced but said nothing and then rested her head on his shoulder. Her eyes were moist, he thought.

In a blue flash, the room was empty but for a blood-soaked blanket lying on a patient's table.

Holland and Maddie appeared in the space between buildings. Gulls could be heard keening in the distance and beyond that, the ever-present grind of a foghorn. He stepped out from the alley to see a three-story gabled building in need of much repair. Its shingled siding had been painted yellow once. That was a very long time ago. Much of what remained was covered by pale green lichen or, beyond that, just patches of unidentifiable filth.

"Honey, we're home," Holland said, attempting levity, but cringed when he realized the comment was much closer to home for her than it was for himself.

"Around back. There's a walkway that leads to the second floor of the main building," she told him. "I can walk, though. We'll just have to take it very slow."

"Nonsense. You're in no shape."

She didn't argue, which he was thankful for. She shouldn't have been moved if they could help it. But they couldn't. She was a fugitive, and he had just threatened a mob boss.

He saw now that there were secondary buildings. Single-story affairs with multiple apartments, two rows deep and flanking the motel on either side. They were crowded with an overflow of articles, more possessed of long-term residents than the vacationing kind. He hurried along so as not to draw suspicion, carrying around a woman in a bad neighborhood like a bride across a threshold...

A narrow street, cobbled in the old style, cut into the hill and wrapped behind the building at such a steep angle that it seemed unlikely to carry motorized traffic. This was old. The motel itself had been the harbor master's manor from back when the city was founded. He thought he remembered something to that effect, anyway.

As Holland mounted the steep drive, he was greeted by dripping tendrils of foliage that hung from the hillside. Vine runners stretched across the stone pavement nearly to the other side. Clearly, this road didn't get much traffic. It continued up and around behind the motel where a suspended walkway extended to a second-and-a-half story. Something added, probably during one of the building's many renovations over the decades.

The entrance to the suspended bridge was a gate with a leaning trellis. If it was any indicator of what lay beyond, he wanted nothing to do with it, as it projected boldly out into the naked space between the hillside and the inn.

It was only about forty-five feet from the road to the doorway, but every inch of it looked just as likely to fall through as the next.

"You say everything's in order?" he asked hesitantly, concerned that they were about to break themselves upon the overgrown statues and planter boxes moldering in the cramped gardens below.

She nodded. The side of her face was warm against his chest. He tried not to notice. Too, the faint traces of perfume which still managed to cling to her hair in spite of the trials of the last few days. A dull ache blossomed in Holland's chest as he unlatched the low gate. Ignoring it, he stepped forward and was greeted by an ominous creak. He took another step, and the walkway groaned under their combined weight.

"Holland, you fool, just trust me."

His cheeks flushed, but he bit his tongue and strode quickly to the far end.

"It should be open."

He glanced down at her as if she'd spoken in some long-dead language. "In this neighborhood?" He shook his head but reached forward, regardless. It was just as she said.

They stepped through, and it was a completely different affair on the other side. The room smelled clean, lightly fragrant with the same floral profile as her perfume. *Gardenias*, he speculated. It was a vast improvement over the molding leaves, rotting wood, and perpetual low-tide stench from outside. He closed the door with his foot while she nodded toward a light switch near the tarnished, filigreed handle. He flicked it on and a solitary lamp in the ceiling rose to a glow.

Across from a humble kitchen was a day bed whose sheets, quilted comforter, and pillows appeared to have been recently turned and fluffed. Indeed, the smell of fresh linens wafted gently as he laid her down. He propped up pillows and helped her into a semi-seated position before pulling up the blanket that had been folded at the foot of the bed and gently tucking her in. She watched in silence.

"Tea? Coffee?" he asked.

She nodded. "Tea would be great."

Maddie winced as she tried to adjust her position in order to direct his efforts, but stopped short. It was clearly not a battle she was ready to commit to.

"Just sit back and rest, Mad. I'll get it; just tell me where."

"Why do you call me Mad?"

"I don't know. Should I call you something else? Madrigal seems a lot of work, but then I guess no more than Holland..." he said, shrugging.

"No, Mad or Maddie is fine. It's just... that's what you called me. Just, I thought you'd be different now. But you're not."

"No, I've changed," he said, shoulders slumping. "I think you've got me wrong."

"No, I think you've got yourself wrong. Now, to the right of the breadbox, there's a jar. Kettle's on the stove. The tap works."

Holland gave her another one of those dubious looks, but turned the knob and a coughing sputter preceded a clear flow that chimed as it splattered on the bottom of the ceramic sink.

"Huh. Better'n mine..."

"As I said, everything's in order," she said pertly.

"Well, you're not. You sure you're safe here?" he asked, looking around at the space.

"Yes. Safe as anywhere."

"Ekron doesn't know about this place? Seems you've got some enemies within the bureau..."

Holland placed the kettle on the stovetop, turned the knob halfway, and pressed the igniter, which evoked a loud clicking noise just as a spark ignited the gas into a soft blue crown of light. The gas whirred quietly in the intervening silence. He turned it up to an emphatic whir and stepped away to let it do its work.

Holland felt like a giant in the modest space. Grabbing a chair from the small dinette set, he spun it around so that he could sit with his forearms stacked across its back and rested his gray-stubbled chin there.

"You need something to eat. I've got some things to attend to. I'll pour your tea, fetch you a meal and then return as quick as I can."

"Holland." She tried to sit up again, but growled and slumped back. He was there in an instant to help her up. She grasped his forearm, and they locked eyes. "I'm so, so sorry. I didn't mean for it to happen this way. In the beginning, it was... I just felt ashamed. Coming back to see you again and again. My own private affair...

"And then later, I just couldn't do it. I couldn't commit. The killer was still out there. But then, when I realized that I could lose ... what we, well... For you, it was this celebratory fling and by then, for me it was, like, I don't know. But it was too late. I couldn't let you remember me that way. So desperate..." Her eyes stared off into an empty space. "I tried to come back, later, when we were a little closer in age again maybe, but..."

"Meri," Holland provided, feeling deeply conflicted about invoking her name in the present situation. It felt like a cheat.

"Yes." Maddie nodded, her jaw firm but her eyes still soft. "You looked so happy when you were with her."

Holland pulled away and was relieved to hear the faint whistle of the kettle beginning to boil. Crossing the small space felt like wading through molasses. It felt like the air was thick and his ears were warm and buzzing.

It was just too much, too weird. The memories of Meri and then all the things he couldn't remember because they were taken from him ... by *her*, the notorious Madame Harbinger—experienced by another self, in another stream of reality that was lost to him.

"You've got a lot of nerve," he wanted to say, but instead it came out as, "Cups? Oh, ne'er mind." Two ornate teacups sat overturned on a kitchen towel as if they'd just been cleaned and set out to dry that afternoon. That, too, made him mad, but he wasn't quite sure why.

Holland took one, filled it with the steaming, pale, amber liquid, and walked it over.

"You don't strike me as the cream and sugar sort."

She nodded, her gaze pinned to the painted bars that made up the foot of the daybed. Her lips were pursed as if holding back a gush of words she yearned to tell him. Holland found himself wondering what kind of time they'd spent together, here, in this very room.

He felt a rush of heat as his mind went to exactly the kind of time he knew they'd kept. He pushed through that trap to something he could hold on to.

"Mad, you're in a heap. I've got troubles of my own and I need to see t'them as well."

"What kind of trouble?" she asked, blowing away steam, seeming thankful for the change of subject.

Holland squinted, his ragged features hardening as he recalled the lives he'd taken and the man he'd threatened just hours before. And then he remembered the reason for it all: the boy, Prentiss. The boy who'd woken him in the middle of the night to come to the aid of the woman now resting before him. The boy who, in so many ways, had saved

Holland himself. He'd been in a pretty dark place when the kid had connived his way into an apprenticeship with him.

"There's some bad men after me. And there's a boy they've taken. I need to find him." His eyes came up to meet hers. "He's the reason you're alive. He found you. Woke me up in the middle of the night," he said, shaking his head and smiling just a little bit. "Good kid... if there's such a thing."

"Holland, you don't need to explain any of that. I know you, even if you don't know me in the same way."

He breathed a deep sigh and nodded. "Yeah. The tapes suggest as much."

She paled a bit. "Do you know where to look for him?" she asked, guiding the narrative back to something safer.

Holland didn't really want to get into it but gladly let the focus shift back to the drama at hand rather than this other one that seemed, somehow, even more dangerous.

"No."

"Who are these men? Can you ask around?"

"No. I've done enough askin'. Beef's with Karnal himself."

"Dammit. Really? Holland, what did you do?"

"It's kind of a long story. They took the kid. I went to get him. Maybe killed a couple?" he offered, squinting again. "Okay, *definitely* killed the sorry bastards," he said, staring at the floorboards. "Anyway, Karnal doesn't have the boy no more, but told me he'd find him if I helped him out. I can't see any other way."

"So Karnal knows what you can do? Holland, how could you be so careless?"

He looked up at her, but her face held no judgment, only concern.

"Was desperate. They're taking kids off the street. I don't know what they're doing with them. But it ain't good," he said, his jaw clenching involuntarily.

"I know that kids show up in Vellem from time to time," she offered.

"Yeah, well, I think that's largely my fault."

"Oh, Holland... Seriously? What *are* you doing? That's serious. The authorities will string you up and that's if the Operatrix doesn't get to you first!"

"Yeah, well, some of these kids just need a better chance than they've been given. But the kids I bring through, I can only afford to help so many. There's much more 'an that that Karnal's thugs are providing. I seen the pens, Mad... Pens. For children."

"Pens?" she asked in disgust. "Well, they still have to be going through the wayportals. I still have never heard of anyone with the abilities you have. And believe me, I've looked," she said and then cocked her head, as if a thought had just come to her. "Holland, a long time ago you told me you thought the killer was a 'him.' Why did you think that?"

He shook his head and looked down at his boots. "That was a long time ago, Mad..."

"What is it? What are you holding back?"

There was a long pause. He was at war within himself. He'd never shared any of this with anyone before. His eyes met hers briefly before his shoulders dropped as he shook his head. "Nowhere to hide with you, is there? You wouldn't believe—"

"Believe what Holland?"

"The *people*, Mad," he said, still shaking his head, massaging his temples now, barely believing he was going down this path. "The people told me, okay? They told me to watch out for the devil. Guess I just assumed that the devil was a *he*."

"The people. You mean the *Ephemera*?"

Holland rolled his eyes, seeing where this was headed. "You see, this is why I didn't want to tell you."

"No. I believe you," she said quietly, staring into her cooling teacup.

His eyebrows knit in disbelief.

"I believe you, Holland. I'm sorry I didn't at the time. You were just a kid, and I was so sure of myself that I had it all in order…" It was her turn to shake her head. "Having stood face to face with the Devil. It makes it easier to believe in the impossible." She was staring off into a memory but then pulled back to the present, looking at Holland intently. "The people, Holland… do they still … speak to you?"

He sighed. "Yeah. Sometimes… That night when the kid came. First time in a long time, they told me to get outta bed." He chuckled, musing at the irony of the Ephemera telling him to save the Great Madrigal Timms, when it'd been her, so many years ago, that boldly asserted they didn't exist.

Her eyebrows rose a little, but she just continued sipping her tea, contemplating.

Realm Brythe, Vantipolis,
Bureau Ekron on Devers

40 years Prior

"The markers have gone all wonky in a tertiary stream," Osmius Turnbull told Agent Madrigal Timms in the smooth, rolling tone that was somewhat of a trademark with the Bureau Ekron's director.

"Wonky, sir?"

"I mean, someone has been fiddling with some very large and important events and we are no longer riding the main wave. We're something closer to the fifth..." he said absently, looking up and to the left, seeming to calculate something in his head.

"You'll have to elaborate, sir. I don't think they covered this in Temporal Mechanics. It sounds like you're referring to Jainip's Fifth Law, but I've never heard anyone speak about it in waves, or even a ... tertiary stream, was it?" Maddie asked.

"Agent Harbinger, while I find your provincial understanding of the subject matter ... endearing, I'd appreciate it immensely if you'd clamp your lips and listen to the assignment, hmm?"

"Yes, sir." She pasted a smile on her face that she hoped didn't look too patronizing. "I believe you left off at 'wonky,' sir?"

Turnbull returned to pacing in front of the high windows looking out on the gray sky and the sprawling park that straddled the Devers as it bisected Vantipolis.

"Indeed. You will need to meet with Professor Wilkens-Bernst. Perry. Dumb as rocks, but he knows enough about temporal harmonics and standing waves to be dangerous. He should be able to help you suss this out."

"So, my assignment, sir, is to *timestamp* a *divergence* in a tertiary stream of reality that is causing *dissonance* and therefore is presumably the source of the 'wonky markers' in hopes of returning our reality to the main one, sir?"

"Aptly put," he replied to her, smiling, and then under his breath, "...surprisingly..."

"And upon successful completion, sir?"

"One step at a time, agent." He chuckled, smiling as if through severe gas cramps.

"Very good, sir... Thank you."

"Thank you? For what?"

"For the opportunity, sir. For trusting me."

"Oh, trust has nothing to do with it. You're simply the only agent of a suitable class available. I don't have any delusions that you'll actually succeed in the matter," he replied offhandedly, waving her away as he returned his attention to the stacks of paperwork on his desk.

Maddie stared after the man, teeth grinding. "Sir," she said by way of dismissal, smiling tightly, and then strode back to the double doors from which she'd come only minutes before.

Osmius Turnbull heard the door click shut. He smiled smugly as he tapped his index finger on pursed lips. Nodding to himself, he stepped away from his desk, smoothed the wrinkles from his gray trousers, straightened his tie, and disappeared in a flash of light that for the briefest instant revealed a much shorter, bespectacled man with white mutton chops and a tragically misused tweed jacket.

Not-yet-Special Agent, Madrigal Timms, strode down the wide, black and white checked hallway that was, for now, devoid of students and echoed loudly with her passing. An ornate, dual-faced clock protruded from the wall proclaiming the time (as it was being experienced at least) to be Thirteen and Thirty-Four O'Twelve. She'd timed her approach to avoid the indignity of fighting against the press of coeds bustling between classes.

Maddie thought it strange. Only a couple of years ago she'd been one of the many students here, studying time and its mechanics. Now her view of it was entirely different. It was personal. Intimate.

She'd been on the agent course at that time but even her professors had no idea what she was truly capable of. To be fair, she hadn't either until one day, it had changed forever.

The matrices of time that bound all realities together were so structured, but on that day, the framework just seemed to melt away. She didn't know if it was a coming of age or some other environmental factor, but suddenly the pathways and appointed moments were no longer immutable laws, but mere suggestions.

On that day, she'd watched a woman step in front of a bus. It was precisely Nine and Eleven in the morning. The sidewalk erupted into chaos, the bus's tires screeched, causing birds to light from the wires overhead.

Maddie had dropped her travel mug, full to the top with a robust brew of Grindinger's. She watched it tumble and then shatter on the sidewalk. The bus screeched past and shuddered to a stop, but there was no body left in its path, just a red streak punctuated by one black, patent leather pump.

And then, impossibly, it was Nine-Eleven again. The matrices dictated that time slips could *only* occur on wholes and fifths, Nine-Ten or Nine-Fifteen, but never Nine and Eleven.

She remembered being short of breath, panting even, and then it happened again. The body, the bus, the birds, her tea. And then it happened again. She felt beaten. She was gasping for air. Her arm could barely be bothered to reveal her wristwatch. And then it happened again. Nine-Eleven, but at that point, she didn't see or hear anything. She was unconscious on the ground.

Her classmates had thought she'd fainted. But she remembered what happened. And kept it to herself. Years later, it might come in handy.

Maddie found herself standing before a wooden door framing a large, opaque pane of glass. The name Prof. Rhees Wilkens-Bernst, Ph.D., was stenciled in black and gold. She knocked and waited. Knocked again, louder this time, and after a minute was greeted by a man with large, round, gold-rimmed glasses. He had similarly round cheeks that showed a couple of days' growth of soft white hairs that had been trimmed into a mustachioed mutton chop arrangement.

"Didn't you hear me?" he asked, a patronizing smile on his face.

"I'm afraid not. Professor Wilkens-Bernst? I'm Madrigal Timms, Agent of Ekron," she said, clipping the words and smiling her best, most professional smile as she extended her hand.

"Hmmph. What sort of trouble have you gotten yourselves into now?" he asked, turning and retreating back into his office, which Maddie took as an invitation to follow.

"Director Turnbull said you might be able to help me sort out some issues with markers that are ... out of sorts? He says that there is a dissonance, well actually, that was my word. He believes we've, possibly, shifted streams?" she said, looking at the professor tentatively to see if he was buying any of this or about to have her thrown out on her ear. He didn't move toward his phone, so she forged ahead, "He thinks the Fifth, if that makes any sense…"

"Yes, third, fifth, seventh… harmonics, you see?" He smiled in that patronizing way again, assuming she didn't. Without waiting for a response, he turned and walked to the windowed wall, grabbed a pole, and used it to pull open a hinged window several feet higher up. It let in a warm, humid breeze that smelled of some waxy-leafed shrubbery or other.

"That's better," he smiled again, which Maddie was beginning to believe was a nervous tick. It was her belief that all professors, at their core and in direct proportion to the size of their ego, were deeply insecure.

"Tell me more," he said, hands moving wide, looking not unlike a priest offering a benediction.

"Well, that's it really. The director believes…"

"Enough about the boring *Mr.* Turnbull, tell me what *you* believe." The professor looked at her now, the smile gone. Something sinister crossed his face, but fleetingly. She wasn't sure she saw it right, but it seemed almost predatory, like a hungry wolf eyeing a stray shearling.

Saliva worked in the back of her mouth. She swallowed it down before continuing.

"Well, I believe that *Director* Turnbull has some very enthusiastic ideas about the nature of our own reality. However, the idea that we could detect discrepancies between our current one and another that has been altered, would mean that we'd have to navigate between those streams. Very progressive, but rubbish, I think."

"Indeed…" The professor looked up at the ceiling, tapping his upper lip as he did so. "Of course, the harmonic thing is just a theory I've been playing with, but I've conceived of a device to do, well, not that, but to discern the places in our existence which are most likely to … overlap, with others."

"You're saying that you believe him?"

"No, I would never go so far, but … I am saying that his theories and mine, in this one precise instance, are not in complete disagreement," he replied, with a toothy, altogether wolf-like grin.

"That's great," she pressed forward, "but that still doesn't help me discern where this snarl of timelines has originated," she complained, hands on her hips as if to affect a posture of aggravation when in actuality it was just a way to place her dominant hand closer to the telescoping baton hidden within her belt at the small of her back.

"My dear, if that's what you were looking for, you should have just asked," he replied, closing the distance between them but then retreating a step to lean with his backside against his desk.

"What do you mean?"

"Well, only an event of some magnitude could cause such a mess. Obviously, if your boss thinks it's kicked us off the, what did you call it, the *main wave* and into some far removed, subordinate time stream, well, that would have to be something, wouldn't it?"

"Yes, I suppose, but what? And more importantly, when?" she asked, almost disbelieving that she might actually be onto a thread that could make this dreadful encounter worthwhile.

"What's something big that everyone knew would end up one way, but didn't?"

"You mean like an election? That happens every time. Depending on who you ask."

"Something bigger. And mind you, it doesn't have to be just here in Brythe. And it can't have been long ago for the impact to be so large, Wilkens-Bernst's Law of the Orders of Magnitude as it Pertains to Temporal Sequences..."

"Never heard of it."

"That's because I just made it up. Sounds good though," he mused boyishly.

"Well, there was the Battle at Dainsmire. But that was a foregone conclusion..."

"Not to those that were there..." he replied, all mirthfulness suddenly absent, as if remembering the event in person.

"You were there?"

"Oh, Gadd's no," he said wistfully, grabbing the sides of his considerable belly, an odd twinkle in his eye. "This body was built for pleasure, not pain."

"Uh-huh. Well, this has been very ... informative, Professor. Thank you for your time," she replied, making the most discrete and professional beeline for the door that she could manage, which was to say, not very.

"Sure sweetheart. Come back anytime," he called, but was cut off by the door slamming behind her.

CHAPTER 7

Bramble Pigs

Realm Kirksfold, Dain Burrough,
New Fort Pendletharp

29 years Prior

The dull, thudding booms of far-off explosions rattled the rafters though they were a long way off.

"What's going on down there?"

"Mmm?" An elderly fellow in a green military uniform with a considerable scramble of gold leaf embroidery on his shoulders responded distractedly before his attention was pulled away.

"Nooo... not there, you idiot!" he said, pointing to a place on a long and broad table containing maps of a battlefield. "Are you sure you're not related to anyone in the Convening of Magistrates? Regiment Ell-Gee is clearly spread across trench lines one, two, *and* three... quadrant twelve, you see? For Gadd's sake, man!"

"Sir? The explosions?" asked Maddie, or Agent Harbinger, as she was known due to her constant proximity to horrific events.

"Ahh, yes! That would be the crawlers. An eighty-three percent rate of effectiveness crossing trench lines on those. Not bad 'til you have to cross *three* sets of them. What is that?" he asked, searching the air and then leaning toward one of his marshal staff.

"Fifty-seven percent, sir," Maddie interjected.

"Yes! Right. Are you sure it's not more than that, Agent?"

"No, she's right, sir," offered one of the officers from a desk crowded to the side of the Command Strategy and Control Center. The C-Sack was located in a tall building overlooking the New Fort Pendletharp at the top of Dain Burrough proper.

Maddie was standing near a wall of glass, looking out at a thin blanket of fog whose tendrils stretched from the miles-deep mire and probed the city's streets and alleyways tentatively, alien in the way an octopus might probe some morsel before pulling it into its eager maw.

"Only fifty-seven? Oh..." he replied, breathing in through a grimace and looking at the map anew. He blew out through puffed-up cheeks that made his face, with its cotton and cork-colored beard, resemble something like a ground squirrel. It was not very warlike, and it did *not* exude confidence.

"So, you're saying only about *half* of our forces will even make it to the enemy siegeworks?" Maddie asked, staring through the large windows out into the foggy night, illuminated vaguely by what scarce light was allowed past curfew in the city below.

"Yes... something like that," replied General Crum.

The Harbinger Broken

"What happens if they don't bring down the towers?" she asked.

"Well, they don't have to bring down *all* of the towers. Just enough."

"And how many is enough?" she pressed.

"Gran Major Chardrim, how many is enough?"

"Sir, our estimates say about fifty percent," the gran major responded in a clipped, and not entirely domestic accent.

Maddie cast a skeptical eye in his direction and then continued, "We have to take out at least *half* of *all* of their siegeworks?!? With only half of our troops?" she asked, looking a little ill.

"Oh no. Not *half* of our troops. Half of our *transport crawlers*. There's only a handful of men in each and not enough crawlers to go around."

"And women, sir," offered the gran major, clearly proud of how progressive the Dainlanz Defenciary Forces had become of late.

"Right. And women," General Crum offered cheerfully, as if the conversation were taking place at a press conference rather than preceding the most consequential battle in all of the war. One that, in at least one stream of reality, they lose.

"So, we have to take out a majority of their siegeworks, with a fraction of our troops, and only half of which will even make the journey. What are the odds of success if they *do*? Make it across No-man's-land, that is," Maddie asked, mortified by what the answer might be.

"Mmm. Very slim, I think," the general said, shaking his head and tsk-ing remorsefully.

Maddie's brows shot up. "Then *why* are we fighting instead of negotiating or planning something else?!?"

"Never thought they'd make it this far, to be honest. Diligent sons-a-bitches… if nothing else."

"Indeed, sir," chimed in Chardrim, similarly unhelpful.

"Okay," Maddie said, massaging her temples, searching for some glimmer of hope in this quagmire of apathy. "What would it take to win? Walk me through *that* scenario."

Maddie was beginning to question whether she'd chosen the wrong event. There was no way, in light of the vast incompetence standing before her, that they had won this battle under *any* circumstances.

"Well, take this field glass," the general said, walking to the wall of windows facing out over the city proper and the Dainsmire beyond. "See the phosphors? They illuminate each of the mobile towers," he said this while helping her aim the glasses and getting an eyeful of his own, she was sure.

"Do you see them?"

She did. Far in the distance, dimly, she could make out the fifty- or sixty-foot-tall towers that looked much like lookouts but heavily fortified at their base and on up their scaffold-like structure. The one in particular she was looking at was dead center of the line and was half again the size of the others, from what she could tell.

The enemy line looked like a miles-wide castle wall set out on some isolated, misty peninsula.

"What is this one? It's bigger than the others?"

"Mmm. Indeed. That's the command center. Bugger of a thing. Bigger. Better defenses. More armaments. Admiral Zonovovich's own design. Clever bastard."

"Clever. And diligent, sir," Chardrim added.

"Yes. Right."

"Admiral *Sonofabitch*?" Maddie asked incredulously.

"Mmm. We don't know his real name. Intelligence came up with that. Not bad, really. Sometimes the ol' boys come through."

"Aye, sir."

Maddie arched an unamused eyebrow and returned to the field glass, watching in dismay bordering on disgust as fire after fire lit up along the closest lines of trenches. *Fifty-three percent*, she thought bitterly. She refocused on the behemoth of a command center.

"So, what if we were to take out the command center?"

"Impossible," the general scoffed.

"So, what if we were to ... *theoretically*?"

"Mmm." He nodded soberly. "*Theoretically*, that would cut off all coordination. Wouldn't be quite as effective *now* since all the siegeworks are in place, backed up by Sonofabitch's main force, but it'd cause a *hell* of a stir. Boost morale. Could even turn the tide when it comes down to hand-to-hand, which it inevitably will.

"I don't envy those poor bastards, trading lead, clashing steel to steel while knee-deep in the putrid muck. Bombs going off, enemy chain guns mowing down squads at a time..." It was the general's turn to look pekid.

He changed the subject, "Now, while we're on the far-out and bat-shit crazy side of speculation. If we were to seize that tower and turn it on the adjacent ones. Well, that could break the line! But as I said... Bee-Ess-Cee."

"Ha! BSC, sir," echoed Chardrim while stuffing a pipe with tobacco leaf.

"I'm sorry?"

"Bat Shit Crazy. Keep up, Agent. One-in-a-million chance of that happening, though. But it would be something..." the man said, stealing a less than discreet glance at her chest before turning his attention back to the board that had not changed in the intervening time since he'd checked it last.

As the top brass were chuckling about the idea, Maddie watched a lone crawler careen across the lines to near impale itself on the very tower they had been discussing. No one, however, escaped before troops descended upon it and it exploded in a brief, pathetic blip of light. Maddie decided she needed a closer look at the action to make an appropriate assessment of her odds. *If this was the event that had been altered*, she reminded herself. She had her doubts.

While she was still working the problem in her mind, absently staring through the glasses, she saw a flash of light from *within* the command center. *That was odd*, she thought. Not like the explosions of the crawlers or the brilliant pinpoint phosphors, it was blue, like the arc of a welder. The flash, she realized, was clearly created by a powerful waysmith.

"General Crum. Are the enemy forces using waysmithing?"

"Rubbish. There are no *wayportals* in the mire. Can you imagine?!?" General Crum scoffed.

"No, sir. Waysmithing in the field of battle!?! Beyond just being poor form, that'd be an outright slaughter," Chardrim offered. "We'd already be drinking warm ales and snuffing powdered poppies from the backs of our hands if that were the case!"

They both laughed loudly, the general wiping the corners of his eyes and shaking his head.

You won't be doing that with your heads on spikes, Maddie thought morbidly, thinking of what would *actually* happen if they lost the war to the invading Bolsko-Cherjk forces. Her memory of the event was already growing a bit murky.

She'd always assumed it should be black and white. This happened and then this happened, but once something got un-happened, it was much more nebulous than that and, as it turned out, heavily weighted by perception. The more the new fact was perceived, the more real it became. And then sometimes, the universe rejected the change entirely. All your work, poof! Gone. Back to the way things were.

Maddie pulled her wandering thoughts back to the present. This present.

"I don't know what they're teaching in the Ekron academies *these* days, but it's clearly not warfare, Madam Agent." The general smiled, seeming deeply saddened by her misfortune, yet still suffering from residual bouts of chuckling which caused his guts to buck like an out-of-balance washing machine. He wiped his eyes again when the fits stopped.

Maddie breathed a deep sigh, sensing she should be offended but honestly, drawing a blank on what the conversation had been about. *Oh yes, waysmithing in battle. Crazy.* Yet, she'd seen what she'd seen.

"Very true, sir," she conceded graciously. "I'll leave the heavy lifting to those suited to it then, sir. Thank you for your..." she looked at her watch as the minute hand swept toward Nineteen and Five O' Twelve, "...time."

And then, to the general and the gran major and the rest of the marshal staff of C-Sack, it was as if Agent Harbinger had never visited at all.

- / -

"Not there, you idiot. Are you sure you're not related to anyone in the Convening of Magistrates? Regiment Ell-Gee is clearly spread across trench lines one, two, *and* three... quadrant twelve, for Gadd's sake!"

"Thank you, Waysmith Gaines. Give my regards to the Operatrix," Maddie said, looking again at the delicate timepiece resting on her similarly delicate wrist. *Let's try this again, shall we?*

"Should I wait for you here, Ma'am?" asked Gaines.

"No, I think not. This may take a bit."

Of course, she could always just get things done and then blip back in time to this moment, just after she transported through the ways, but there was a strong chance she would waste an immense amount of energy completing the mission at hand. And it wasn't Ekron policy to slip unnecessarily.

In fact, the opposite was true. Slip the least amount possible and only redo a moment if absolutely necessary so as to maintain the integrity of the temporal stream. The things the director had been speaking about—tertiary streams, harmonics, standing waves—all that was quite theoretical and, by Maddie's understanding, highly speculative.

She was quite surprised the Director of Bureau Ekron itself would engage in such discussions. *An odd one was Mr. Osmius Turnbull.* Not at all like his staunch and steady predecessor.

Maddie puzzled somewhat over the fact she couldn't immediately recall his name. She made a mental note. This was a flag, and these things needed to be inventoried. Out of instinct alone, she activated her memplant. Ordinarily, an agent would only use a memplant to chronicle something they were going back in time to repeat. She just felt that... well, she didn't know what she thought, she just didn't want to miss it.

Maddie stepped out of the portal entry, past thinly populated queues, and into the broad, echoing hallways that were the Kirksfold end of the Ways. Not well-appointed, tending more toward utility than luxury like the hubs at Vellem and especially Brythe. The floors here were wood and worn to a warm but dull polish.

Others walked amongst the halls, either coming from or going to meet up with their respective waysmith and some, possibly a keysmith if they were going somewhere with higher security, such as the Bureau Ekron assigned portal.

At the far, far end, crates could be seen moving to and from larger portals under high ceilings and sparsely populated lights. This was another distinct difference between Kirksfold and the other two halls. Realm Brythe's back-of-house business was conducted at the far end and around the corner of the truly massive, almost-palatial, L-shaped building. A very different affair indeed.

At this end of the Dain Burrough upon Kirksfold Hall of Ways, thin-threaded and crumpled business suits were the commodity. Maddie stood apart, wearing well-fitted, if well-worn, fatigues in typical army field print. Being that Dain Burrough was under martial law, it wouldn't do to be sporting about in her usual black business suit and polished patent leather heels.

She dressed the part, but her olive complexion betrayed her as someone not from the perpetual fog and sogginess that was Realm Kirksfold and the ironically named Dustbin itself. She would have chuckled at the oddity of it if she wasn't so preoccupied with the purpose of her visit. She was always preoccupied that way.

Maddie, or rather, Agent Harbinger, strode purposefully through the meandering crowds and then out into the moist filth of downtown. Five checkpoints later found her in a loud, boxy, knobby-tired transport, buzzing her way to the third and closest line of trenches that was nearly all that was left of the battlefront.

The frontline had been pushed all the way to the backline. All that stood between Dain Burrough and the enemy was a demarcation zone about half of a mile wide, known as No-man's-land and this meager handful of trenches. At least the supply lines were short, she thought to herself as they bumped along and then skidded to a sloppy halt.

"Thank you, Corporal ... Eystes, was it?"

The man blushed deeply and nodded. She'd not needed to show any papers, her stately appearance and authoritative demeanor did most of the convincing. The blacked-out Ekron opposing chevrons on her collar—which intentionally looked like an hourglass—helped a bit, too.

"Now, just down this ramp and right and I should find the field HQ?"

He nodded again, apparently unable to speak or make eye contact with the agent.

"Very good," she said and then stepped out into the mud which engulfed the better part of her boots, making her glad she'd tied the cuff and tucked them into her boots per DDF guidelines.

She unstuck her foot and trudged down the ramp of sullied straw and laid flat chain-link fencing that afforded the barest amount of traction. The bottom of the trench was sopping and had gangway planks laid down, which she was thankful for, and which made the going much easier. She continued through the labyrinth of intersecting trenches, following signs that had been hastily scribbled and then scratched out.

It appeared the HQ had moved frequently and with no apparent regard for order or common sense. She found it several rampways farther down (the general would be absolutely mortified to find out). She laughed inwardly, feeling a little bit sorry for and then considerably appalled at the general lack of order and leadership she'd witnessed thus far.

She found an open door with a soldier standing outside, which she correctly figured for the headquarters. The signs had in no way influenced this assumption. After a cursory introduction, the man led her inside.

"Ekron Agent Harbinger!" the soldier announced, standing at attention, eyes focused on empty air in the middle of the room. A forty-ish man with dark hair, short on the sides and slicked back on top, turned casually from the map board he'd been consulting and stood up. He turned to the far wall where a radio officer sat with headphones on, leaning over a microphone while speaking in hushed tones. The crackle of static interjected between sentences.

"Tell Ell-Gee to push up ahead of those crawlers. The enemy is giving us a gap and I'm going to make sure they damn well pay for it," he said in an easy but commanding tone.

The man turned back to Maddie, lifted his chin, and looked at her expectantly. "And how may the Dainlanz Defenciary Forces assist you today, Agent...?"

"Harbinger, sir."

"Agent ... Harbinger." The word seemed to taste bitter in his mouth. "Well, that is ominous, isn't it?" he chuckled, looking her up and down before turning back to his maps. A soldier rushed up from another set of radio equipment with a piece of paper.

"Hmmm. What *are* you up to Zonovovich?" he asked in a musing whisper, and then returned his attention to Maddie. "Well? Is this 'Show' or 'Tell'? I never know with you people."

Maddie stepped forward. "Colonel Culbreck? I need to get to the front lines. Well, that's not true. I need to get to the enemy command center."

The colonel's eyes lit up in amusement. "Well, darling, while I think you might get the good general's attention, I don't think you'll be able to talk him out of the beat-down he's about to unleash upon the loyal Dee-Dee-Eff, here," he said sweeping his hand broadly to encompass the length of the wide but egregiously shallow set of trenches displayed on the board.

"It's of critical importance. It will most assuredly make or break this defense, sir. Otherwise, I wouldn't waste your time."

"Too late for that, Miss ... Harbinger? Now, if you'll excuse me, I've got a war to win," he said over loudly and then looked up. "Radio! Cancel that thing about Ell-Gee. Zonovovich's already compensating. Send up Ell-Aitch."

"Sir," Maddie persisted.

"That'll be all, Madam Agent," he said without looking up.

Maddie pursed her lips, biting back vitriol. She contemplated replaying this moment. It would cost her a considerable amount of energy to slip so short. It hardly seemed worth it. There had to be another way.

"Okay, ready the crawlers. Mark. Tee minus twenty," the major called to the first radio operator who echoed it into the mic, adjusted a dial, and then echoed it again, adjusted the dial once more, and continued on down the line.

Maddie stepped forward, none too certain about what she was going to say next. "Sir," she whispered so that none of the other officers could hear, "I've seen this battle play out..."

He stood upright, his eyes searching hers, jaw clenched. His look was hardened steel, but then something seemed to snap. It was clear he also knew how this was going to play out. His hands drifted behind his back in a loose parade rest. Lips pursed, chin out, he drew in a deep breath, then sagged. With one eyebrow raised, he asked, "What do you need?"

"I need to get across No-man's-land. One of your crawlers will make it to the lead siegeworks but then get caught up, somehow. I think they make it up into the command nest, but I believe there are other agents at work. *Not* Ekron. I need to counter their counter, sir."

"Well, there's no way to do it, but if anyone *can* do the impossible, it's Halleck," he offered and then spun. "Radio!"

"Yes, sir."

"Message Bramble Pig Squad. Tell them I've got someone who needs an escort. Authorization Hambone Cartwheel Feline Nine One Gander Osprey."

"Yes... sir???" the radio operator asked, turning in his chair to look at the colonel directly.

"Do it." And then to Maddie, "He'll meet you at the main tunnel in five minutes. Better hurry."

"Sir?"

"Specialist Stanleigh can get you there."

A tall, thin soldier, in his early twenties, came up beside Maddie, paused, and then headed for the door, ducking so as not to bump his head on the low lintel.

Maddie, seeing him leave, nodded and mouthed a thank you to the colonel and followed him quickly out.

"Tunnels," she asked the tall soldier. "What tunnels?"

He turned, a gleam in his eye, smiled mischievously, and shuffled on ahead, clearing ground at a surprising speed for his lanky frame.

It took them every second of that five minutes to rush up and out of the third line, navigate the maze of trenches that was line two, and then rush up the ladders and over to the first line, dodging the couple of potshots that zipped by with activity above the trenches. The tall soldier, Stanleigh, she remembered, led her to a door facing away from the enemy lines.

Once inside, she found the room cramped full of bodies, each gawking at her with the feral look of rabbits huddled in a warren—if those rabbits could also look savage and bloodthirsty. They were all smeared with shoe polish and the smell from the room was oppressive, almost violating. This is what war actually looked like. She'd seen it through the centuries due to the privilege of her position and giftedness with the craft.

One man stepped forward. Stanleigh acknowledged him and left without a word.

"Sgt. Halleck?"

"Mhmm. Welcome to Bramble Pigs," he said, chewing a large wad of gum. "So, you wanna see the other side, do ya?" he asked nonchalantly, as if they were discussing investment strategies rather than a likely suicide mission into the heart of the enemy's line.

"Yes. And time is of the essence. I need to get across before the crawlers do," she looked at her watch. Eighteen and Thirty-Seven O' Twelve. "The charge will start in thirteen minutes. My crawler gets across very fast. I need to be there before him and sneak into the command siegeworks."

Nervous laughter rattled through the space but was extinguished by her solemn expression.

"Pardon my Brythienne, but no shit?" Sergeant Halleck looked around at the dark, glistening faces crowded around him and turned back with a broad, hillbilly, toothless smile. "Well then, mish," he said and then swiped the carnival dentures back out of his mouth and tucked them into his shirt pocket, "we'd better get to it!" The round of sniggering from the men gathered in the tiny room didn't give Maddie a warm fuzzy.

Heedless to her unamused expression, he smiled and winked and then stepped back to make space about a grating on the floor. One of the soldiers lifted it, revealing a ladder that ended in a puddle looking like mercury on asphalt as it reflected the light from above. It was twenty or so feet down.

"After you…" the sergeant said. But when Maddie made for the entrance, he retracted. "No, no, just wanted to make sure you were up for it. Cartwright. Mitchell. Velkers. Gitty the scuuud up!"

With that, the men collected their weapons and started filing down the ladder in fluid motion. It was clear they were very familiar with the routine.

"Alright, Miss, your turn. Mansignol, Copper, and Poe will bring up the rear."

The tunnels were not much different than the trenches—wet and sloppy with gangways scattered over the worst of it. Lanterns were scattered sporadically so most of the navigation was done by touch and sound, sandwiched between bodies fore and aft.

They were making good time. Maddie realized she was huffing and puffing. A thin sheen of sweat covered her from head to toe in the cold, heavy air of the subterranean complex. The group shimmied around a boulder protruding into the tunnel and came to a halt in a small, low-ceilinged room.

Poe stepped up from the rear and a small furry head poked out near the collar of his shirt. The shiny black fur of the creature rippled as it slipped out of his collar and into his ready hands. Maddie was surprised to recognize it as a ferret, or maybe a weasel. She realized then she didn't know the difference. Poe gave the creature a light peck on the top of the head and, crossing to a circular opening on the far end of the room, let it go. It bee-lined ahead and out of sight.

"Elbows and assholes from here," the sergeant told her. "Mansi, you're on rearguard."

"Ahh, that's bullshit..." the large, ruddy-complected man with brown, almost black eyes complained but peeled out from the crowd and crouched in the corner of the room, submachine gun resting across his trunk-like thighs.

The sergeant spun on him. "Any more of that and I'll give you a permanent set of these!" he said pointing at the prosthetics in his pocket and gave him a meaningful look, shifting his eyes in Maddie's direction as if to imply that he was trying to impress the brass.

"Aye, aye, Cap'n," the huge man responded unenthusiastically with a half-wave for a salute.

"What's with the ferret?" Maddie asked.

"Chumley? Oh, he's kind of a mascot. Regardless, he lets us know if there are enemy soldiers ahead without us finding out the hard way." He made a pointing motion toward one temple and then an exploding motion out the other side and smiled gruesomely. "Now, let's bite this bugger on the backside, shall we?"

Maddie smiled gamely but her heart was pounding, and it felt like a stampede of butterflies was caught in the space between her stomach and her chest. She knew she could re-rack a moment gone badly, but that was only if she *survived* it. The odds of success on this little encounter, by her estimation, were plummeting.

She looked at her watch. It'd been twenty-one minutes since she had convinced Colonel Culbreck in the command bunker to get her across the demark zone. The crawlers would be underway. She hadn't heard any of the explosions she'd witnessed earlier in her first meeting with General Crum at the New Fort Pendletharp Command HQ, or C-Sack as they'd called it, but she knew they'd be coming soon enough. A dull thump from back down the corridor seemed to agree with her timeline, pressing her to jump up into the cramped, egg-shaped tunnel.

Once inside, she discovered there was no way to crawl on hands and knees. One had to belly crawl their way forward. Maddie had never been claustrophobic, but suddenly, all she could think of was hundreds of tons of oozing muck filling the space and her choking on mud right before being crushed to death. She focused on the shuffling of bodies ahead of her as the light from the vestibule disappeared behind.

Doggedly the team pressed forward into the dark. The *whoosh-whoosh* of dirty fatigues on sandstone, mantra-like. When she finally emerged from the tunnel, she sensed and then could smell cool air and gunpowder. Her hand went to her pistol, and she reassured herself the safety was off. She reminded herself that she'd already loaded and cocked it in the tunnels along the way. To do so now would be unnecessary and the noise could give away her position.

The sergeant crouched low and started forward, with her following close behind. They passed four or five bodies of enemy soldiers, all with black pools of blood around their neck or chest. The trenches here were little different from those on the side closest to Dain Burrough—deep, muddy conglomerations of dirt, corrugated metal, and wood.

As she came around a corner, her heart jumped into her throat. A hulking structure that had been hidden by the trench walls and battlements loomed overhead, a halo of barbed wire in row after row about its lower sections.

Suddenly the world erupted into high-contrast black and white as a new phosphor burst into the air before the monstrous siegeworks. Now she heard shooting and saw mortars and larger guns firing from high up above. Dull booms in the distance began to grow louder. Too, the whining chug of big engines echoing through the fog. One, in particular, whined louder and her pulse jumped again.

"We have to go, now!" she whispered emphatically. "That crawler goes crazy and shoots across the demark before it blows up. Right here," she said, pointing at the ground they were standing on. "We have to get up into the siegeworks before that happens. That's where I believe the problem starts."

It was right then they bumped into the others, huddled near an entrance to a gangway going up the structure of the siegeworks itself. Several more bodies were sprawled about the open space.

"They'll pick us off if we go any farther," one of the soldiers told Halleck in a sing-songy accent.

"Velkers is right. We need a distraction," the sergeant said, mostly for Maddie's benefit, she realized.

"There's one coming up right now." She glanced at her watch. "A minute from now, and that crawler will literally be on top of us. The Bee-Cee soldiers collapse on it and then it explodes, but we need to be up there *before* that explosion. Plus, if we stay here, we're dead anyway when they come."

Just then, the firing began to intensify as the noise from the crawler re-doubled.

"Now or never, Sergeant. They're focused on the crawler. We've got to go."

"Okay," he said. "Cut the lock. Bonnie-Cherry's be damned."

Mitchell pried the gate with a crowbar that appeared in his hands as if he were a magical mechanic. They started up the gangway, running around the interior perimeter of the structure and indeed, it did seem the enemy was too busy firing on the incoming crawler to notice them.

Once they'd turned the corner, they could see it bouncing across the terrain, making a direct path toward the siegeworks. Maddie was amazed at how small it looked in comparison. Explosions were going up all around it, but somehow none hit directly, and nothing seemed to phase it. *The driver is either crazy or dead*, she realized.

It kept charging. They too pressed forward, one section at a time, on up the tower. Even when the Bramble Pig soldiers on point had to take out the guards at another check station, the soldiers from below didn't seem to notice...

It was when they stacked up outside the access door to the command center's upper levels that the crawler struck the tower. Maddie hazarded a glance down and watched it roll over on its side. The engines already on fire, exploded and the crawler yawed farther onto its lid. She knew now was the time. Just as Halleck's squad of specially trained soldiers breached the command center door, she heard another noise, the tuk-tuk-tuk of a heavy machine gun from somewhere inside.

Bodies tumbled like bowling pins as golf ball-sized holes punched through the corrugated steel walls and door. Maddie watched in horror as the entire squad was wiped out in a handful of seconds and then a secondary explosion from below knocked her from the gangway where she'd been crouching, hiding from the wall of lead flying overhead.

As she tumbled through the air, time seemed to slow down to a crawl. The ground raced up to meet her. She concentrated on a moment, and just like that day in front of the bus, she slipped time, out of time.

- / -

"They'll pick us off if we go any farther," one of the soldiers told Halleck in a sing-songy accent.

Maddie caught herself. The transition from falling to her death and standing upright was more than a little disconcerting.

Sergeant Halleck looked at her quizzically but continued, "Velkers is right. We need a distraction."

Catching up to the moment, she chimed in, "There's one coming up right now."

She looked at her watch Eighteen and Fifty-Nine O' Twelve and continued, "A couple of minutes and that crawler will be on top of us. The soldiers collapse on it and then it explodes. We need to be up there *before* that happens. Otherwise, we're dead if we stay here."

Just then, the firing began to intensify as the noise from the crawler, too, grew in intensity.

"Now or never, Sergeant. They're focused on the crawler. We've got to go."

"Okay," he said. "Cut the lock. Let's go. Bonnie-Cherry's be damned."

She grabbed his arm. "One last thing. Do your guys have grenades?"

He nodded his head slowly in the affirmative, scrutinizing her now even more intensely. She could tell he was a little bit spooked. Probably suspecting some of what had happened.

"Use them. At the top of the gangways, when we get to the command center. Use all of them."

Halleck nodded, and turned to work his way to the front of the squad.

They mounted the ramps going up. Once again, she saw the crawler careening across the demark zone known as No-man's-land. Once again, the crawler collided with the structure, tipped over, exploded, tipped over some more, and the soldiers descended upon it. But this time, when the Bramble pigs breached the doors, they were low and flooded the room with grenades. Tuk-tuk-tuk-tuk, holes filled with light from inside punched through the behemoth's metal skin in chaotic swaths. With nowhere to take cover, Halleck's squad pressed down into the gangway as if they could become one with it.

Shots began to pop off from below, but they went wide and then the enemy soldiers below seemed to realize they might be shooting at their own troops and stopped. The seconds droned on, and Maddie felt the urge to abort, to just reset again, but in the wake of the excitement, she hadn't realized how much the first timeslip had taken out of her. She realized that now.

Then a quick succession of deafening booms issued from inside and the metal walls looked like a starry sky for all the pinpoints of light pressing from within. The squad flooded in but for Mitchell and Velkers. As they filed forward, Maddie's stomach clenched. The two men she'd crawled through tunnels and crept through trenches with, were shredded beyond recognition. She swallowed down bile and pressed forward.

Her lead hand stayed glued to the sergeant's back. Her trailing hand clutched her bureau-issued Brenner autopistol. Its familiar heft normally gave her comfort, but here, it suddenly felt small and insignificant.

Submachine guns bantered back and forth. She heard someone yell, "Grenade out!" and she hit the deck behind a low wall of supply shelves. Waiting for the inevitable explosion, she saw stairs that led up to the next level and prepared herself to charge for it, but then realized she still did not understand how this event had been turned. The room exploded in light and noise and her head, already buzzing from before, just went silent as though she were underwater. She stumbled toward the stairs when a strong arm pulled her down. Bullets peppered the wall above her, and she saw it was Halleck who had grabbed her.

He was leaning against the wall, machine gun in one hand, holding a growing pool of dark crimson at his abdomen. Then a metal object like a baseball smacked into the wall next to them. He pushed brutally away and rolled onto the object right before it exploded, lifting him off the floor and dropping him like a sack of rice. Maddie lay there, quite literally, stunned for seconds that stretched like minutes. She felt as much as heard the clomping of boots up the stairway and then heard more explosions, but dully.

It dawned on her that they needed to try again, that she needed to reset. The moment was lost but then commotion from upstairs battled to infringe upon her senses. There were loud, snake-like hisses which she recognized as rockets. Then she heard thumping noises and realized that they were mortars being launched. Explosions from some distance outside the tower followed.

Her mind raced. This was how she had imagined it happening, the theoretical win. The command center would turn on the other siegeworks.

But her team hadn't made it upstairs... Comprehension clunked heavily into place. They hadn't made it, but someone had. This was how the war had been won. A waysmith. An extraordinary waysmith...

"Dammit," she cursed. She knew if she wandered upstairs, she'd be shot before they knew she was on their side. Her only hope was to make it downstairs and back into the tunnels, where she'd likely be shot by Mansignol, who was waiting for a team that wouldn't be coming back. She got up and stumbled out the door and down the gangways. No one shot at her. The scene was utter chaos.

Explosions wracked the command center as well as the adjacent towers now. The fog was luminous, with pulsing explosions from all over, like the inside of a thunderstorm. She made her way to the trenches, but found she was completely at a loss about how to get back to the tunnels.

Maddie realized now she hadn't even thought about an exit plan. She'd been too focused on the task at hand and at least a small part of her assumed she'd have to reset and search for another moment in time. Or at least that she'd have *some* of the members of Bramble Pig to guide her back. However, in hindsight, the sheer number of heavily armed soldiers in the command center seemed unlikely.

That was the counter. They had assumed an attack from below and if Maddie hadn't come with Halleck's squad, they would have decimated the "insurgents" that had somehow made it up into the top of the tower. *The same way they had Halleck's squad*, she thought, her breath catching in her throat.

She wanted to go back and redo the whole thing, but with every attempt, she grew weaker and each one brought new opportunities for failure. Doing that would jeopardize the main goal of fixing history in this timeline at all. Maddie stared down at a muddy pool and caught her reflection in a flash of orange. She was haggard and exhausted, with smears of mud, ash, and carbon across her face. What struck her was the luck of resignation. She had to take what she'd been given... but it was bitter medicine. This was what it meant to be an agent of Ekron. Do the impossible. And then deal with even more impossible consequences.

Her eyes followed the trenches running away from where the wreckage of the crawler rested, still smoldering. Something moved. It was small. She expected it to be the hand of a wounded soldier, but it turned out to be a small, furry creature, nearly black with a white face and bandit mask. Its eyes sparkled in the firelight.

"Chumley?" she croaked. The creature looked at her, paused, and then scurried down the line of trenches. She saw no better alternative, so she followed. The ferret stopped at an intersection and continued when it saw her round the corner. She was struggling to stay upright, but she was determined to just put one boot in front of the other, to make it out alive. If for no other reason than to watch Director Turnbull have to eat his words about the impossibility of her succeeding.

In light of everything that had happened, that seemed a hollow victory. She resented herself for even thinking it.

Maddie's throat grew raw from breathing smoke, diesel fumes, and spent gunpowder. She stumbled on, turn after turn until she found Chumley standing on its hind legs, sniffing at the body of a soldier near the back wall of a vaguely familiar room. She rolled the soldier over and found the hatch they'd come through previously. Chumley darted into the hole, and she followed, not bothering to close the hatch behind her. She was unable to reach it now that she was in the confined space. How they'd managed it before, she wasn't sure.

The crawl back was interminable. Pitch black. Silent but for the swishing of fabric on sandstone and her own breathing. When she paused to give her elbows a break, resting her head on the cool stone, she could hear her own heartbeat and the gurgling of her stomach. It reinforced the reality that she was alone. The only survivor of a mission she had authored. It was a terrible feeling. She might have been sick, but for the fact there was nowhere to go if she did vomit. Somehow, she fought back the urge and pressed on. Most times, the return trip went faster than the way out. This time wasn't like that at all.

When she finally made it back to the vestibule, she found Mansignol there, holding Chumley, stroking its fur, its tiny body dwarfed by the huge man. She looked at him, her stomach threatening to jump out of her throat. Maddie tried to work up the courage to explain what'd happened to his friends, but he just turned and started down the tunnel. She realized that Mansignol, when the ferret had returned without Poe or another member of the squad, had known the others were KIA.

"I got a kid," he said, breaking the silence from a little way up the tunnel. "That's why Halleck made me stay. He's just a week old. Wife hasn't even named him yet. Just thought he'd be a junior, ya know? Not now. Gonna name him Thomas, after Sarge. No one in my family with that name, but…" The big soldier shrugged and let the thought drift off. Maddie did what came naturally in that moment, as a fellow soldier, and just sat with it.

The two trudged in silence for the rest of the way and when they reached the end, he looked at her, smiled a weak smile, and then walked away. Maddie heard the roar of soldiers yelling and boots stomping on walkways and ladders as men poured forth from the trenches out into the No-man's-land.

Errant bullets whistled overhead as she walked. Still, they poured forward like ants ahead of a forest on fire. More and more of them.

As it turned out, the general was right. Seeing the command center and adjacent siegeworks burning had boosted morale immensely. She continued on against the flow of bodies. The urge to get out of her fatigues, to get showered and wash everything away was visceral.

And then she remembered there was still a loose end, niggling at the back of her mind. What was it? Oh, yes… the waysmith. Transporting out of place, outside the Hall of Ways. Extraordinary. She'd only ever met one person who could do that. At the end of the war, he must have been, what… twenty-four? Twenty-five?

Maddie navigated her way to the closest inn. Something on the north side. Something out of the way…

In the distance, a lonely foghorn groaned. She smirked weakly at the sound, bone-tired and emotionally spent. *Who could it possibly be warning?* she wondered.

Maddie looked back over the trench lines, out into the fog, with blooms of light stretching into obscurity in either direction. She listened to the low din of yelling, exchanging lead, and clashing steel in the mists—the sounds of men making ghosts. She was reminded of what was at stake when she ventured back and forth in time, changing a little thing here, fixing something small there. Did Halleck and his men survive in that other stream of reality? Or did Tommie Mansignol grow up to make his mother and father proud in this one? She looked at her hands and sighed.

It wasn't for her to decide. She just did what she was told. She had to trust in the knowledge and judgment of her higher-ups—the odd Mr. Osmius Turnbull. He must know something she did not.

She reached the pavement and scraped the mud off her boots on the curb with conviction. Then she continued on, not caring that the street beyond was just as filthy. She ignored it and picked up her pace.

She wasn't about to let the infinite dullness of this place dampen her spirit. She'd stay here just long enough to find out what she needed to and not a second more. *Find the waysmith and move on*, she concluded. She started walking again, leaning forward to shield her face against a cold mist that couldn't decide if it was fog or drizzle. The foghorn grumbled again, and she found herself doing likewise. She needed a drink. She'd get cleaned up, fresh clothes, and go to that place; what was it? Ciller's Still?

CHAPTER 8

CATACOMBS

Unknown

Present

A blue light flashed and suddenly it was dark. Very little light came through the breathing holes in the wall of the wooden box, but on one side, it was noticeably brighter than the other. Suddenly, something struck the crate and the grating screech of nails pried from wood caused Prentiss to jump. The wall of the box fell away to reveal a solitary suspended ceiling light, a slick granite wall, and the knobby-kneed, not-right-in-the-head man called Gurlish. He reached in and hauled the boy out with surprising strength, dragging him scrabbling to the far side of the cavernous room, where he manacled him to large, rust-pitted chains bolted to the rough stone floor.

"Best you don't move. Lest you lose a leg or an arm… or worse," the man said offhandedly, as if imprisoning children was little different to him than filling out bills of lading at the loading docks. He stood up and walked back toward the light with the slightest limp, as if one leg were just a bit shorter than the other. Prentiss was too terrified to move. He looked up and saw something darkly metallic swinging slightly in the obscurity of darkness above.

The sound of metal grating on metal assaulted his ears and was followed by a fury of ratcheting noises. Then the object above drew closer and closer until it dropped finally to the floor with an echoing *thud*.

It was a cage. Prentiss jumped up and ran for what appeared to be a door, but was tripped up by his manacled leg. He crashed down on the cold, hard floor. Smarting from the impact and struggling to force breath back into his lungs, he crawled back, sliding his non-manacled leg beneath him.

From the far side of the room, he heard the man chuckling to himself from farther on, out of sight.

"Happens every time..."

And then a blue flash bloomed and faded, and Prentiss was alone except for a solitary dripping noise echoing faintly from the darkness.

"No wonder I never had much use for religion. Out of the box and into a cage," he said pitifully, rubbing the spot where the manacles had bit into his ankle.

"You been in some scrapes before, Ol' Prentiss, but this one's ... well, ya done it good this time."

Marceline heard the sound of one of the cages being dropped, way back in the caves somewhere. *Fresh meat*, she thought bitterly. She was tempted to leave it alone, but the hunger in her stomach felt like something gnawing at her from the inside out. Also, her hands were raw and bloodied and her arms were almost too sore to lift from trying to dig out around the bars of the opening. She wouldn't be getting much work done right now. And she was cold. Always so cold.

She slipped from her hiding place. Ventured in the dark, moving by feel and largely by memory at this point. She'd been down in these tunnels now forever, it seemed. There'd been others in the beginning, but each time a cage would lift, it was only a matter of hours before the hunt would start and then the screaming would come. And then the silence. And the waiting.

None of the others had fought back, but then, none of them had been so lucky with the wretched woman's responsibilities elsewhere. Twice the woman had been called away when it looked like it would be the end for her. Marceline knew there wouldn't be a third time.

She drew closer to the main room, stopped and listened, and then, when she was satisfied, crept closer. The overhead light was on, illuminating the side of the room opposite the holding area—the area with the lever that lifted and lowered the cages, Marceline had come to realize. Only one of the cages was down. In it, she saw a small boy, only a year or two younger than herself, maybe. She crept still closer, and the boy's head shot up as he heard her.

"Shhhhh," she whispered as she drew up to the bars of the cage. The boy looked at her with big, brown eyes, wet with tears. She was surprised that he seemed terrified of her, recoiling as she kneeled down, and then she heard it, the shifting of sand on the rock floor and she spun to see the woman's hideous face distort as her body swelled and her arms stretched like tentacles.

Marceline screamed as the woman's chest burst into a vertical slit of dagger-sharp fangs. For the first time ever, she was stuck, frozen in fear. The creature lunged, engulfing the upper half of her body. Fangs sank into her flesh, and she heard the sickening snap of bones as the monster's jaws crushed her chest. Then she woke with a start.

Bolting upright, the waif of a girl rested back on her hands, heart pumping, lungs aching, the sound of her own pulse pounding in her ears. Relief washed over her as she realized that it was just a terrible nightmare. A dream, not the actual nightmare she'd been living in for days innumerable.

And then she realized that she *had* heard something. The ratcheting of the lever. The clanking thud of the hanging cages. Her stomach dropped. *What was she going to do?* She was safe here in her hiding place, with a view of the real world outside. She looked down at her shredded hands, dried blood black under her fingernails, and then she felt that gnawing hunger, just like in the dream. She would starve to death before she made it out. Or die of thirst. She tried to swallow; her tongue was a thick wad of sandpaper.

It only took her a second to make up her mind. Not everyone was like that, she knew. She'd always been quick to act. Sometimes that was a bad thing...

Marceline decided she would see who was down here, how many there were. Get some food and come right back. She didn't think she could listen to any more of the screaming. But she meant to survive. *First things first,* she told herself, and walked slowly back to the edge of the shelf on which her little cubby was perched.

She stretched out one bare foot, sliding it against the stone column there, stretching to find the first step down to the cavern below. Her toe slipped over the rounded edges of it and she had to press hard into the rock to keep her balance. Her heart thumped hard in her chest, and she tried again.

There will be a point when I am too weak to do this, she realized. Too cold, too hungry, too bruised and sore. The woman was her enemy, but the clock was no ally either. She had to investigate this new activity. She needed food. Even if it meant putting a face to the next set of screams to echo through these damnable caverns, as hard as that would be to stomach. Marceline steeled herself. She'd feel no pity. She would survive. As far as she knew, this was the longest anyone had.

Her thoughts carried her to the very edge of the light, and she was shocked to find herself so close to the holding chamber already. She stopped cold. Before her, just as she'd dreamed, one of the cages *had* been let down and within it, a small, miserable little boy lay sniffling quietly into folded arms.

He seemed somewhat well looked after, though he was clearly poor. Not from Vellem certainly. She'd seen the people that lived there. No, it seemed that all the children that came here were from the Dustbin or one of the other cities of Realm Kirksfold. She wasn't as familiar with those as Dain Burrough was often at war with them. It seemed everyone was mad at everyone else almost all the time. Indeed, she had hate in her heart, she had to admit. She'd been taught that that was wrong, but she'd met so few that were deserving of anything else.

"I can hear you," the sniffling boy said in a diminutive voice, but it was directed out and not directly at Marceline.

She studied him. Gawky, small, mouse-like features, oily, sand-colored hair poking out in tufts from beneath an oversized driver's cap. He wouldn't even make a morsel for the evil lady. Marceline had seen firsthand. She hadn't meant to, but her and Neldrid Kinnebruk had run faster than the others. Neldrid, because she was older, making her taller and longer-legged. Marceline because she had always been fast.

The evil lady had appeared in front of them and eaten her in two bites—snake-like the way that her jaw unhinged, and her mouth seemed to be as big and wide as her whole body. Neldrid had kicked and screamed. So much so that Marceline thought she might just flail and flop her way out, but then… that sickening crunch.

Marceline squeezed her eyes shut, trying to erase the memory. This poor boy. At least he wouldn't have to go through all that. The evil lady would take him in one big gulping bite. And then look around for more…

It was then that Marceline realized she was still standing there at the edge of the light. Hands balled into fists, trembling, breathing ragged breaths. The boy was looking directly at her now.

"I said, I can hear you. I know you're there."

Marceline slunk back into the dark of the tunnel. Her stomach twisted into knots and not just from hunger, she realized.

After a minute, a bloom of purple light from the direction of the holding room told her that the woman had been there all along. A shudder ran down Marceline's spine and she collapsed to the ground, hugging herself for warmth and comfort. She leaned into the rock wall the way she used to lean into her older sister Marza in their tiny, two-person shelter when it was raining too hard to go out to panhandle or steal. Marza always wore the same threadbare, knitted sweater and she could smell it now. It smelled a bit of wet sheep, but then always the tiniest hint of roses. Marceline knew that that was impossible, but she held on to the memory of it, and it was her turn to cry softly into her folded arms as she huddled in the dark with only the dripping of water in the distance to break the silence.

THE HARBINGER BROKEN

Holland was exhausted. He scratched at the gray stubble on the side of his face and then rubbed his face vigorously with his hands to wake up. This was more walking in a day than he'd done in ages. And all of the transiting was taking its toll. He realized that Maddie must be starving, too. He'd taken her cabbage soup and a bread roll earlier in the day, but that'd been hours ago. He'd not even had butter for the roll. Thoughtless.

So much of his life was in a state of neglect at the moment. He'd thrown every waking moment into scheming how to get some of the kids off the streets. It just seemed so wrong, their situation. With Mer gone, he just felt like he needed to do something to justify his existence. To give meaning, but maybe Smythe was right. If he had the means, he should have just dragged up and moved on to Vellem. Leave all this in the rearview.

It didn't seem like anyone would miss him much. Except for Nelv, but she had her own agendas. Malph in his way, but that... that was a lost cause. Holland didn't know if he could watch that slow-motion train wreck play itself out. The man was killing himself with alcohol and seemed content to do it. Plus, he was sure he was connected one way or another to the corruption that wound through Dain Burrough like veins of cancer. Holland wondered if that wasn't the true reason behind the man's suicidal habit.

Prentiss was the only thing worth sticking around for and certainly, Holland could take him with. He *should* take him away from this place. *Maybe that's what I'll do? Settle my affairs and make for greener pastures.*

Holland needed to find Prentiss, but he was just running in circles now. None of the packages that'd left that day had led anywhere. And he'd checked them all. Well, everything on the manifest anyway. Cost him more than he had to get a copy too. But that, he realized, was his mistake. Whatever was going on was most likely off-book.

He needed a new tack. He'd go back and check on Maddie, get cleaned up, then he'd have to go back to the warehouse. It was the only way. He found himself scratching at his beard again. *Yes, get cleaned up*, he thought to himself. Then the warehouse. There'd be more kids.

Karnal wouldn't halt the operation just because of some pesky old man sniffing around. Holland would see where they were taking the kids. How they were getting through customs. He could break the whole thing wide open while finding Prentiss.

And then he'd deal with Karnal. Holland felt his blood beginning to boil and had to calm himself when a blinding slice of white light felt as if it'd split his skull in half. He stumbled and caught himself on the wall in a far corner of the Hall of Ways.

His knees shook with the pain. It was like someone had taken a red-hot knife to his skull and was trying to pry it open. He collapsed farther onto his elbow, pressing his head against the wood paneling, hoping in vain that *that* pain might crowd out the other.

The pain doubled. The pressure felt like a vice screwed down on his temples, like a hand was reaching through the back of his spinal column into his brain, searching for a lost set of keys. It was maddening, all-consuming. His mouth went dry. His stomach threatened to empty itself. And then, all of a sudden, it was gone.

Holland was left panting, leaning against the wall and wondering what the hell had just happened. He reached up and his hand found its way to the implant behind his ear.

Prator... What the hell was going on? Was it his implant? Was his body rejecting it, or was there something wrong with the hardware? He'd need to sort that out.

He looked around and saw people staring at him. Later. Hopefully, it wouldn't happen again. Or get worse.

Holland took a couple of wobbly steps and was going to transit back to Maddie's flat, but thought better of it. If there was trouble with his implant, he may not have some of the protections from being seen by the Operatrix that he had come to rely on. Transiting from the Hall of Ways itself was asking to get caught. He started walking back toward Maddie's, albeit on legs that were none too steady.

It was a long, wet walk. Not rainy, just damp. The mist was blowing hard from the south so was colder than usual and by the time he got to the Inn at Badbriars he was soaked through and freezing. A bad day to be on the streets...

So much so that he almost didn't think about the precarious walkway as it swayed and creaked with his passing, feeling somehow even more wobbly than earlier that morning. He knocked at the door, the prearranged sequence, and heard the snick of a handgun de-cocking. Apparently, she'd heard him coming. He thought again about the creaky walkway and how it may be more purposeful than he'd first realized. Then the sounds of her shuffling to the door greeted him. It made him mad, and he couldn't understand where the misplaced anger was coming from.

She shouldn't be getting up; it'd only been a few days since she'd been stabbed and left for dead. She had been truly lucky that the blade hadn't lacerated an organ, but he'd been through war and seen many things that defied logic. That bit with Dunsy being one of them... that turned out decidedly much worse. The door opened and, much to his surprise, he was still looking down the barrel of a black Brenner semi-auto pistol. Apparently, the decocking was a ploy as well. This woman was full of surprises.

He lifted the brown paper bag he'd been keeping dry in his jacket during the walk. "They're still warm, I think. Sandwiches. Hedva took care of me even though I didn't have cash on hand. That's rare these days. Even among friends."

Maddie smiled weakly and turned back toward the bed. Holland could see the pain on her face and rushed up to help her, first to the bedside and then getting situated on it. There was fresh blood on her bandage, too.

"Have you been up and around?"

She shook her head no, and then sighed and nodded yes.

"Let me get that taken care of."

"No, you get cleaned up and into something dry. I have a set of clothes for you there," she said, pointing to the shelves across from the bathroom in a short, narrow hallway visible from the kitchen.

He looked at her with a wry expression.

"They're yours. If you're wondering," she said, not rising to the bait. "They look like they still ought to fit. Maybe a little out of date, but doesn't seem like things change here all that much."

Holland nodded acquiescence, but didn't comment. He moved on instead. "Can I bring you something to eat or drink?"

"No, I'll wait 'til you're done," Maddie told him.

"You sure?"

She patted his hand and nodded.

"Okay, suit yourself," he said with a pursed-lip shrug.

He walked over and started a pot of tea, and then disappeared into the small bathroom just beyond.

When he came out, he felt refreshed and clean. He'd shaved, combed his hair, and dressed in a thick knit cardigan and denims. Even his boots were newer and polished to a shiny black.

A low whistle preceded a weak laugh. "Look at you. You clean up really well. And with the gray hair, you look quite dashing," Maddie said, looking him over and then self-consciously down at her own crumpled, bedridden self.

Holland pretended not to notice that last bit. Women were always so worried about how they looked. And Maddie was a beautiful woman, no matter if she was without make-up or a proper shower. Some women just had a presence. And she was definitely one of those women. His cheeks flushed again. He grasped for a change of subject,

"I'd forgotten about these boots. I loved these boots," he said, crossing to the teapot that was just beginning to whistle. "I wore them through the soles, twice. But here they are... Good as new," he mused.

He turned off the gas and poured two cups of Grindinger's. He brought them and the bag with the sandwiches over to Maddie's bedside and swung a chair over from the dinette. "First food and then your bandage. It doesn't seem to be seeping so, should hold for a bit."

She nodded, still looking at him. "It's amazing. You look ... the same. I'm used to this, to the moving back and forth around a time or an event, but seeing you then and now... it's, I guess it's kind of eerie. Like looking at a ghost." She shook her head, her eyes a little misty. "You've been a ghost to me ... for years now."

"Eat up, Mad. You need your strength."

"I will. I just... Holland, I want to clear the air. What I did was *wrong*. Selfish." She looked down, tracing her fingernail along the hem of the comforter, turning it over and over again absently. "I hid behind my position and my power." She looked up to meet his eyes. "Coming to visit you, it was reckless. And dangerous. And, well, morally gray if not a little bit creepy if I'm being totally honest. But it was all the best moments of my life. I couldn't let them go and then before I knew it, it wasn't my choice to make anymore. I had power over time, but not over you. You made your choice, and you didn't even know you were doing it."

"But there is what I did and what I didn't do. What I did was to rob you of your memory, of us. That was selfish. And what I didn't do was to tell you how I felt... *feel* ... about you. That makes me a coward."

Holland swallowed dryly, trying not to look as uncomfortable as he felt. He looked at the beautiful Ekron agent before him. A woman who had her fingers in every defining moment of his life since childhood. He struggled to take that in. His mind swirled in an anarchist's cocktail of thoughts and emotions. Disdain at how cavalier she was about manipulating people's lives, *his* life. Intrigue at her beauty and what obviously transpired between them.

He was flattered that she was still taken with him, especially in his advancing years, when not a morning passed, that he didn't wonder why he was still here. Butterflies in his stomach made his cheeks flush once more. Was he a teenager that he couldn't control his emotions? Knowing what they'd had together. Here, in this very room...

If he was being honest with himself, truly honest, he yearned for that. Wished he could remember those intimate moments that, for him, never even existed. He was jealous, he realized, of some other version of himself in another swirling eddy of existence. Lucky bastard. He scolded himself for letting his mind wander. Nagging at the back of his consciousness, there was something bigger and more important than anything. This one glaring thing—the boy. Every second he was here, he wasn't out there looking for him.

"You're not going to say anything?" Maddie asked, her eyes betraying woundedness. "Serves me right, I guess." They welled up, and she lifted her chin, choosing to own her shame in the face of the man she loved and betrayed in equal parts.

"Mad, look, I... well, that was another me. I... I don't have the memories you have. I'm sure you realize that."

"Come. Here." She gestured with a curled finger that turned over to point down next to her. The look in her eyes was still plaintive, conciliatory, but there was something else. A knowing. Even if her confessions were earnest, this was still the woman from the tapes. The one that'd seduced him, year after year.

Holland turned the chair around and scooted closer, committed to letting her down easy.

"Don't make me work for this," she said, her eyes searching his. "I'm broken," she said, and he knew that she meant it in more ways than one. He leaned closer, meaning to stop part way, to tell her all the reasons why this was a bad idea. Why it wouldn't work. Why he had too much baggage to deal with. He was too old, too...

All those reasons fell away as his eyes met hers. Gravity or some equally undeniable force urged him forward.

They kissed. Her lips were soft and warm. Felt like they went on forever. The fluttering in his stomach intensified, his body grew warm, tingled all over. He couldn't remember the last time he felt this way.

Her kiss, tentative at first, turned into something more earnest. He met her there, their tongues touched with electric intensity and the feeling of desire turned into something desperate. He kissed her deeply, longingly, the years of loneliness clawing back his façade of stoic placitude.

Feelings welled up. Fears and desires, more fears, and then just an overwhelming yearning. There was something more he couldn't describe. Something he didn't know was there.

Her hands drifted to his face, slid back and her fingers were in his hair, pulling him to her. It felt so good, the warm touch of a woman, this firebrand of a woman, who shined so brightly it seemed the universe itself shrank back from her brilliance.

Maybe it was as simple as being alone for all that time since Mer passed, but it felt deeper. There was something right. Some truth that wouldn't be denied. He helped her sit up against the headboard and her hands were touching his chest, sliding to his waist as she pulled him toward her. He wanted to follow, but then it was like the enchantment faded with a snap of fingers. The temptation to lay down beside her was still there, but the guilt of where Prentiss was right now and what he was going through re-emerged in his psyche. He pulled away. His breath difficult to draw when it wasn't entwined with hers.

"Mad, the kid's out there. And there may be more than just him," he said, breathlessly.

Maddie nodded and looked away.

He took at the lines of her profile, her hair like spun gold as it hung down and splayed across her chest. He felt ashamed for wanting her. For these feelings that seemed to come from nowhere. He struggled to sort them in light of his loyalties. There was Prentiss. But there was also Mer. Long lost Mer.

He'd only just visited her grave, so afraid was he of the devastation it might bring him. It had always been better to just keep running than to face the specter of that loss. And then, through no intention of his own, he was forced to face it. To look at her headstone, to feel the soil at the foot of it. Feel the finality of it. All its emptiness. The terrible wrongness of her being beneath the dirt and he above it.

She should have outlived him. Suddenly, and for the first time, he was glad of that burden. Glad to have spared her that anguish. He knew she forgave him for his shortcomings, his inability to visit her. And he knew she'd forgive him for this. She'd have wanted this. He was always so stubborn... her the pragmatist.

He looked again at Maddie, the smooth, perfect skin of her face, just a few little wrinkle lines at the corners of her eyes. What was she, in her forties? He was sixty, mere days ago. This was a nice release. A moment, but he didn't see how this worked out long-term. She still had her life ahead of her. That was, of course, if they could capture a killer. A killer who could manipulate time, and maybe more.

He hadn't put much thought into that until now. He'd been so preoccupied with his own dilemmas, but that was significant. The Director of Ekron and maybe the Operatrix, both in on a plot to take out Ekron agents. But for what purpose? And what did Maddie have to do with it all? Was it because she had figured it out, as the memory chip implied? If that was true, then the devil had truly come.

What the Ephemera had warned him about. He thought about that. What was so important that they would even care? They were beyond such things. They were trans-dimensional in the truest sense, living in the space between spaces. He hadn't given them much thought either, to be honest. It'd been so long since he'd seen or interacted with them, limited as it was. He had been a child at the time. And now again, just recently—in a dream.

Holland could not run away from this. Hide it like he had his abilities for all those years. Perhaps the Ephemera had thoughts about the transport of children through the ways for nefarious purposes. And that gave him pause, too. What were the children being used for? His mind went instantly to the lowest common denominator, was well acquainted with the depravity of man. One need only look to Roald Smythe for confirmation of how sick and twisted the manifestation of man's desires could be.

He focused back on Maddie and felt that flicker of shame. For his own small indiscretion? In whose mind did that transgression lie? Certainly not Maddie's... or Mer's. Just his own, he guessed.

Still... Suddenly he was aware that she was looking at him, her eyes at first doe-like, but then as she took in his posture and countenance, they seemed to harden a bit.

"What are you thinking about? Why are you looking at me like that?"

"Oh, sorry Mad. I was just lost in thought, is all. This situation with the Director and maybe the Operatrix."

"It's not maybe. They're one and the same. I don't know how, but—and don't lose me here—they're not human," she said, searching his face to gauge his reaction.

Holland drew in a slow breath, weighed those words.

"So, if he's not human, what is he then?"

"I don't know. What I do know is that he can bend time, out of time, like me, but that he can also transit. I imagine that he can do that out of place, off the lines, just like you can. The Operatrix can do that, so it stands to reason. To be frank, it's absolutely terrifying," she said, rubbing her face and then running her hand through her hair. She winced.

Holland rose to help her. She grabbed his arm and stared into his eyes. He tried to look away but found he couldn't. "I just wanted to be sure that you feel it, too."

He broke his gaze away. Tried to say something, but it just came out as stumbling gibberish and stopped. He gave a small, purse-lipped nod.

"I don't know what I feel but…" And he nodded again without looking at her, searching vainly for something else in the small apartment to focus on but could find nothing.

"Our time together Holland, after the Battle of Dainsmire, it was … amazing, consuming. I knew it couldn't just be, you know, some kind of fluke. Some fleeting moment. But you felt it. You felt it too." She grabbed his hand, interlacing her fingers.

She looked at him but didn't bother waiting for a reply and just nodded knowingly to herself, a small smile playing across her face. His eyes drifted over her, this younger woman, and he couldn't deny it.

Then that blinding light shattered his vision. Burned away his consciousness. He thought he might fall down, but then it was gone. He stood there shaken, ashen, breathing ragged.

"Holland. Holland, are you ok? What happened?" she demanded, sitting up farther in her bed.

"I… I don't know. I think maybe it's this new implant. Nelv had Prator get me updated, so I didn't trip any alarms with the Guild of Ways, the Operat… Operat—" he struggled to form the words, still feeling the aftershocks of the pain.

"Here, sit down for a minute. What's this about an implant? I didn't know anything about this."

Holland sat down on the edge of the daybed, rubbing his temple and then running his hand back to where the implant sat behind his ear. It was warm to the touch.

"Dammit, Prator," he said, squinting and shaking his head gingerly as if to clear the cobwebs, but without rattling it around too much. "I've never felt that before with an implant, though my exposure to it isn't all that much. Not much use for gear like that here in Kirksfold."

"Wait, let's get back to this situation with the implant. You got a new one?"

"Yeah, Nelv got me hooked up after she transcribed your chip."

"Nelv."

"Yeah, she's an old friend."

"And she just happens to have the kind of equipment it takes to transcribe memplants?"

"Err... yeah," he said, feeling suddenly like he was drifting closer to the falls without a paddle.

"And she's the one that got you a new implant that you're suddenly having trouble with."

"Yes, well, we traded. She decodes your chip so we can figure out what kind of trouble you're in, and by extension, I'm in since I saved you and you were staying in my shop. And I do her a favor at a later date," the words came out, and he instantly wished he could take them back.

"What kind of favor, Holland?"

"Umm, well, that's hard to say. She's one of the few people that know of my abilities."

"Except for Karnal, of course."

"Yeah, except him. And yourself."

"Who else knows?"

"Um, well, Malph, but he's kept his mouth shut all these years."

"Malph?"

"Malphius. He was with Nelv and I, in the command center, when we knocked it over."

Maddie's face clouded over, as if lost in troubled thoughts. He remembered that they had met right after that battle. Had she been involved, doing Ekron business? Of course she had. That's why she was there. The look on her face was pained. "You alright?"

"Um, yeah. So, I feel like there's so much for us to catch up on and talk about and we haven't really had a moment, but this thing with your implant… that could be serious. If it's going wrong, that's one thing. If it's intentional, that's something else."

"What do you mean?"

"Well, I've heard of certain … doctors, and I use the term loosely, embedding a backdoor in their implants. Kind of an insurance policy against unhappy customers. Your implant could be corrupted, or not taking properly, but it could be worse than that and it's actually being used against you."

"But who would do that?" he asked and then started shaking his head. "Oh, you're not thinking Nelv… There's no way. She just wouldn't. She's a lot of things and she has a hard side, I mean, we both have done stuff, but Nelv and Malph have been my closest friends, Mer and I, for years. Decades."

"And yet you had to strike a deal to elicit her help?"

"Well, we've been out of touch for a while. And it was kind of a big favor. But, no, there's no way it's Nelv. Though, other than Prator, I don't know who would want to do a thing like that. Or why he'd go along with it."

"What about Karnal? Does he know you've had recent work? This is a relatively new thing, gen three and later."

"No, I don't think so, but a man like Karnal knows a lot of things he shouldn't. Who's to say?"

Maddie looked solemn, contemplative.

"Well, nothing for it. You need something to eat, and I need to check on those pens. The only way to find Prentiss is maybe to see where they're taking 'em. You've no idea? Haven't seen anything in Vellem? Or Brythe?"

Maddie shook her head. "No. Nothing on the scale you're talking about. Plus, it sounds like most of what I was picking up was your doing," she said, shaking her head again and blinking with the outrageousness of that statement. "So, Holland, we really need to formulate a game plan. Obviously, I think you should try and find the boy, but there's Karnal to deal with and beyond that, the situation with the director. We don't know what we're dealing with there. This could be one lone, magnificently powerful psychopath, or this could be the ground forces for an invasion.

"We just don't know, and I, well, I'm afraid that what's been happening has been the systematic destruction of our understanding of things outside our own dimensional space and of time stream mechanics.

"I can't prove this but," she looked around as if uncertain herself of what she was about to say, "I think the director, and the Operatrix, and who knows how many other personas he's using, are covering something up. The murders are, sadly, just collateral damage. That's why there was no standard MO for the killer. No bragging about his accomplishments, taunting the authorities, things you'd see with other serial killers. Just prolific death, all aimed at a specific outcome. But what that is, heavens knows.

"The systematic rewriting of our history and maybe even our science? Can you believe that? I mean, can you just get your head around that?" She was shaking her head again, but it seemed to be too much for her, either the thought or the exertion. She laid back with her hand over her eyes.

He could see her hand tremble and stood up to smooth her hair back, but found her forehead was moist and warm.

"You've a fever again. Let me round up some meds and something to put on that wound to draw it out. I'll be back soon, and we can formulate this grand plan of yours," he said, still smoothing back her hair, and within minutes he could hear her breathing, low and long as she slept.

Holland crossed to the bathroom, closed the door and the small curtains. And then a bright blue light enveloped the room.

CHAPTER 9

Unlikely Allies

Maddie shuddered and then flopped down beside her lover, purring contentedly. They both wore a sheen of sweat, though it was cold and miserable outside. She ran her fingers through the slick, dark hair of his chest, tracing little patterns in it.

"Mmm... I could do this forever," she murmured, stretching and nuzzling his ear.

It'd been nearly a week, and they'd rarely ventured outside, though they'd no lack of exercise.

"Then stay," Holland replied, interlocking his fingers with hers and looking into her eyes. They were slightly crossed on account of how close their faces were to one another, an endearing look.

She pulled back to see him more clearly. "You know I want that, Holland."

He continued staring into her eyes but said nothing... gave away nothing of what he was thinking.

"I want to, but... as it is, I'm going to have to slip back a whole week. I don't know how I'm going to justify that to the director.

He'll bust me back to... I don't know, but something lower than a cockroach in bureau terms."

He traced a line from her clavicle down her sternum and then slowly, barely touching the skin, inched toward the curve of her breast, an amused eyebrow raised as he drew closer and closer.

She bit her lip. "Ooh, you have to stop that!" she cried and rolled on top of him again, burying her face in his chest.

"I'll think about it. Okay? Maybe," she said before sliding up to kiss him, playfully biting his lip and pulling back to let it slip from between her teeth with a light pop.

"Hey," he protested, grabbing her wrists and pulling her back down until he had her pinned beneath him.

She smiled devilishly.

Four hours later, she left for good. She left a note with a heart on it accompanied by one solitary white gardenia flower and that was it.

Maddie replayed the memory in her mind. It felt good to remember, but it ached, too. More bitter than sweet lately. She played the memory again, remembering each nearly identical instance of it as it had played out over a decade of her lifetime. Year after year after year. Her a little bit older, him the same. Each instance ending with a gardenia flower and a note with no words. What could she possibly say?

"What a wicked fool I've been," she said aloud into the lonely silence of her tiny Dain Burrough flat. "What a wicked, selfish fool."

Drawing the covers back, she grabbed a knee and rocked upward slowly so as to engage her damaged stomach muscles the least amount possible. She examined the wound in her abdomen. The bandage was clean and in good shape. She'd been so lucky.

A thousand times that scenario could have played out and 999 of them would have ended with her dead. But she had a chance now. If Director Turnbull thought she was dead, she had the tiniest sliver of an opportunity. However, she couldn't do it without Holland. And he couldn't do it with someone screwing around in his mind.

She would have a talk with this Nelvandra Kiml. And, thanks to her time at the bureau, she had a reasonable idea of where to find the woman who was supposedly a friend of Holland's.

The bureau liked knowing things more than it liked actually doing anything about them. If something became too much of a nuisance, they would be forced to act, but if it was just a low-grade annoyance, well, it could go on indefinitely.

The resistance was a royal pain in the ass, but to date, they hadn't caused any real harm. So, it stood to reason Ekron would keep close tabs but wait and remain poised to act. The benefit of time travel was the ability to undo nuisances. This was why Brythe was the pinnacle of the three realms—anything they didn't like, with few exceptions, could be undone. The Universe, of course, had a say in the matter too. But by and large Bureau Ekron would have its way.

Of course, doing that issued in a whole slew of other issues from a temporal mechanics standpoint—even, possibly, convoluting streams of reality if you followed the director's mad ravings on the topic. Knowing what Maddie knew now, he was more intimately aware of some of those concepts than anyone else could have possibly guessed. It would be a travesty of science to kill him. That was a price she was willing to pay...

Maddie dressed, applied a light layer of makeup accentuating all the wrong things, broadening her nose, making her eyes look smaller, and then pulled her hair up beneath a dark blue dockworker's beanie. The modification was slight, but more than adequate. She made her way to the town center.

The resistance headquarters, as loose a term as that was, was located below street level. In actuality, it was a sealed-off and reinforced section of catacombs spanning a dozen or so shops. Or at least that's what the intel suggested.

Maddie knew it was going to be dangerous snooping around in ToobRaiders' headquarters, especially in her weakened state. But if she could get face-to-face with Nelv, she felt like she could work out the details from there. Generally, she preferred to operate with a better plan than "work it out from there," but it was all she had and, frankly, she was sick of sitting around.

Her information suggested entry through a back alley basement behind a shop named Smoog's Nick-knack Emporium. A little disarming to break into a shop with a name like that. Maddie made sure not to slip into complacency. She walked the alley to scope it out.

One side benefit of being injured was her somewhat feeble gait fit right in with the general Dustbin population, being it was impoverished and mostly driven by industry. People with injuries here were the norm.

She saw from her initial pass the exterior access had a large padlock on it, but that bothered her. It meant anyone inside wouldn't be able to exit that way. She wondered if it was just for decoration.

After a while she made another pass through the alleyway, this time holding a bag of scones from a shop farther on that was part of the catacomb complex and an unconfirmed co-conspirator. She'd scoped out the shop while she was there and saw no exit to a lower area from the front-of-house and so had effectively struck out yet again. However, on this pass, she noticed the hinges on the left side of the angled basement access had no pins in them. *Bingo.* She cringed at the realization she'd actually internally vocalized the word as a celebratory slogan.

It was possible the double door had been reinforced internally to create a single door that opened to one side. That's what she would do. The lock and the weight of the door were likely enough to deter most would-be thieves. Others might know its purpose and know enough to stay away. It could also be boobie-trapped.

That's also what Maddie would have done. But if it was a trap, why would they hide it? She could muse on the topic all day and get nowhere. So, she walked over and lifted gently at the edge of the door. It didn't budge, but, as she felt under the lip of the sheet metal cladding, she found a well-concealed slide latch.

Taking a quick look around, she slid the latch and the double door swung up to the side as one piece, just as she had suspected. It was on a counterweight and pulley mechanism which, shockingly, didn't make a sound as the door lifted up. She fought the urge to say bingo again.

Maddie stepped over the lip and onto a set of wooden stairs leading down to the basement. The first step creaked softly but was not horribly loud. She continued in, fully committed now, and pulled the door closed behind her. She slid the latch, which had an internal handle that matched the external one, back into place. And that was it; she was in.

Seconds ticked by as she waited for a full minute before continuing farther, ready to bend time and try again if she was discovered. Still, no one came, but it was dark in there. She did have the foresight to bring a flashlight, a nicety people in Vellem and Brythe had, but that many in Kirksfold forewent opting to spend their hard-earned money on other niceties. Such as food.

Maddie moved slowly down the stairs until she reached the stone floor of the cellar. Still no surprises. She checked her bandage. There was a growing blob of bright red. She applied pressure with her fingers against it and moved across the room.

As she drew near the lone corridor, she saw what she'd expected to see—a tripwire. Her heart skipped a beat as, mid-stride, her foot had drawn frighteningly close to the line. She followed what she could of it. To the wall, up and then along with the ceiling of the tunnel, off into the distance. That suggested an audible alarm rather than a nasty one, like a grenade or kinetic or deadfall type of trap. *Good.*

She stepped over and continued on down the narrow, stone-lined hall. She realized this, too, was a type of trap. Essentially the hallway acted as a sally port. If she was caught here, she was dead—nowhere to hide. She moved forward with more haste. She may not have tripped the wire, but she could be caught as easily by unlucky timing.

She drew near to the corner and again, a tripwire. Tied to the same line running along the ceiling. *Either one would ring the bell*, she imagined. The good news here was she could follow that line to where it terminated, and she would be in one of two places; either a sentry station or the command center. Maddie allowed herself a fleeting smile as she continued on. *So far, so good.* She kept pressure on her side and kept going.

The hallway tunnel offset a few yards, changed from rounded river rock to coarse brick, and then carried on past a handful of doors. The return line for the tripwire carried on until it hit an eye-lag in the ceiling, turned sharply left, and disappeared through a hole bored through the wall above a nondescript wooden door.

She traded her flashlight for the Brenner, then gently twisted the handle. It turned freely to reveal a small office space with a cheap wooden desk, an aging personal-sized refrigerator, and some cabinetry with layers upon layers of paint on them. The current color was baby blue, but it didn't look hopeful or cheery, it just looked sad.

There was also a closed-circuit TV monitor on the far wall. Maddie was standing in the middle of one of the viewports. A short woman with short, dark hair was seated facing the screen with her back to the door.

Maddie had her pistol low, but still aimed at the woman's back.

"I assumed I'd see you sooner than later. Sooner, I guess," said Nelv as she turned around slowly to face the newcomer.

"Nelvandra Coggins? Or do you go by Kiml?" Maddie asked.

"Kiml, these days. And for quite a few years now. You Ekron types ought to be a little more current on your resistance leaders."

Maddie shrugged.

"And... I go by Nelv. For the record, I know you pretty well, Miss Timms. Or do you prefer Special Agent Harbinger? A bit maudlin, don't you think?"

"Yeah, well, I didn't get to pick it exactly." She casually inspected the room as she talked. "You'd be a pretty good villain, you know... if you were one," Maddie said, holstering her sidearm and crossing the three paces to a nearby chair. The image on the screen betrayed her compromised state. She sighed and sat down, still holding her side. Maddie leaned back with a grimace and then continued, "At least you've got the monologuing thing pretty buttoned down. You may have surmised with that evil genius intellect that I'm not here on bureau business."

"If you had been, you wouldn't have made it out of the alley," Nelv said with a dark smile.

"And I wouldn't have come alone either. Of course, I could just keep trying this again and again until I get it right."

"You mean like you did with Holland?"

Maddie's nostrils flared, but other than that, she left no indication of just how on the mark that comment had been. She smiled. "Yeah, about Holland..."

"Of course, he's why you're here, so let's get on with it. What do you want?"

"Someone is screwing around with his mind."

Nelv burst out in abrupt laughter and then tried to look serious, motioning with her hand to keep coming. "Please, tell me more," she said, wiping a tiny tear from the corner of her eye.

Maddie's gaze was frosty. "I mean that quite literally. It could be that the implant you had put in him is going wrong or it could be something much, much more sinister than that."

Nelv said nothing.

"Look. What I did was screwed up. I'm not here to beg forgiveness for what I did to your friend in another stream of reality—or several—I'm here to help someone we both love, in the here and now. What I need to know is, did you do something to Holland's chip? Or have something done?" She searched Nelv's eyes. "Holland's abilities, if fallen into the wrong hands, or even if he's just being manipulated for some petty purpose... it could kill him. Or at the very least, turn him into a vegetable."

"The man's a killer. Don't let the dreamy blue eyes fool you. He can take care of himself."

"I watched it happen. He acted like someone shoved a wire hanger through his eye socket. He could barely stand,

and that wasn't the first time. Someone is torturing him through that implant."

The pixie-haired woman sat motionless—the silence, palpable. Her eyes dropped. "What's going on? Tell me about it."

Maddie explained the symptoms Holland was having and what he was trying to do. Nelv confirmed it was Prator who'd done the work, but that she'd never heard of a backdoor before or that implants could be used against someone. She did go on to say she thought it unlikely Karnal knew about that mechanism. But if he did, she was absolutely certain he would have no qualms about using it. She was also deeply concerned the mob boss knew the extent of Holland's gift.

That was one thing Maddie agreed with her on. Power like that in the hands of a criminal organization... That sounded like the worst possible scenario.

"Do you know what Karnal might try to use something like that for?" Maddie asked, shifting again in her seat. She slid her hand through the buttons of her blouse and came away with blood on her fingertips. All the walking and skulking around wasn't faring well with her stitches. *Cloak and dagger...*, she thought. She looked around for something to wipe her hands off on.

Nelv didn't comment, but stood up and offered her a handkerchief.

"You sure you're good to be up and about?" she asked.

"No. Does it matter?" Maddie replied, wiping the blood off her hands.

Nelv nodded skeptically, then continued, "I wouldn't have the slightest idea of what Karnal would want to use him for, but it's most likely a whole host of things. Karnal's got his hands in a lot of different pies these days, as I'm sure you're aware. But if he's trafficking kids, who is on the other side of that exchange?"

"That's what Holland is trying to find out. In the meantime, I intend to sort out this situation with his implant. You should have seen him..."

"Well, if it *is* Karnal, only Prator would know. I think he'll be hard to convince to give up *that* information. He'd just as soon give up his own skin. And, honestly, that's likely the truth of it."

"We'll figure something out."

"We?"

"Yes, you're going to take me to him."

Nelv rolled her eyes and then shook her head. "You've a very large set of balls, Madam Harbinger. You're upending the entire Kirksfold underground, myself included. All while you're sitting foremost atop that list of very prominent criminals, by the way. Balls indeed..." She smiled and slipped a long, double-sided blade into a sheath in her DDF-issue boot. "But, I like me a scrapper," she said with a convincing smile and stood up, reaching out a hand to help Maddie out of her chair, which she accepted.

Holland had transited directly into the holding area he'd investigated before, and just as he'd imagined, the pens were occupied. All but one. None of the kids noticed him. He imagined they might already be drugged. Some may have been under the influence to begin with. Such was street life in the Dustbin. It dawned on him that may have been part of the scheme. Karnal was most likely responsible for the drugs getting into the kids' hands to begin with. Maybe there was an even more nefarious aspect to it all.

His thugs knew who their clients were already and picked them up at will. Were Karnal's hooks so deep into Dain Burrough's underbelly? If so, he could be just as involved with the brothels and orphanages, turning the whole thing into a proper industry. Holland's blood churned with cold fire.

The sound of shuffling from down the hallway came to him, and he realized the last occupant was probably on their way now. He needed to get gone before anyone saw the flare from his passing.

He transited out to an alley nearby, one accessed from the old granary forming the back entrance of the warehouse. If they were taking the kids to the Hall of Ways for transit, then they'd most likely go through there. He'd stake it out for an hour. If there was no movement, he'd have to risk another entry and figure out if they just hadn't moved yet or if they'd left by other means. He fretted that might be the case, but had to go with his gut.

Holland looked around at his surroundings, typical Dustbin—trash and drizzle. Brick walls of industrial buildings were made dark by the perpetual moisture in the air. Cramped, slick streets, with trash piled in some areas and scattered haphazardly elsewhere crisscrossed this section of town. There was no one around, at least. The buildings in this area were two and three stories tall, which made it pretty dim, too.

He moved around a stand of pipes and ventured toward the warehouse's intersecting alley. His breath was visible in the chill air, so he kept his chin down so as not to flag his position as he stood near the corner of the building. Looking on toward the granary loading docks, tall, green doors stood imposingly in the recesses of the landing. But they appeared to be unattended. Probably not many people breaking into mob headquarters these days. Holland, of course, being the outlier.

He began to wonder at his plan. Was this just a waste of time? Were the kids being carted out some other way and he was missing it—even now scuttling his only chance at finding the boy? He cursed under his breath, rubbing his hands together to keep them warm. But he was committed now. He could just as easily miss the moment by bouncing around all over the place. And he'd be ten times more likely to get caught doing so. This was the most likely. He settled his mind and then settled in to wait.

Thirty minutes passed, and he'd convinced himself to do something idiotic when he heard a noise down the way. It was the clunking and grating of metal on a slide. The dock doors began to slide apart. Darkness within.

Holland slipped back a little farther around the corner but kept a line of sight on what was going on. And then a man with a wheeled cart carrying a good-sized crate appeared from within. Holland wasn't able to see it all that well at this distance, but it was more than large enough to fit a kid, maybe even a full-sized man.

He watched longer, as one by one, the crate was accompanied by five more of similar size, and then the man walked back into the warehouse, whistling as he went. Holland seethed at the disgusting lack of empathy. The soullessness of Dain Burrough exemplified.

After a while, a flatbed truck rattled up the side street and Holland was forced to scramble back into the depths of the alley where he'd been staking out the scene. He wasn't too worried about being outpaced by the truck once it departed.

The going was slow downtown, not so much for bustling activity as for the general obliviousness or obstinance of its residents. A traffic incident, of which there were plenty, might take an hour to sort out. Clusters of carts, mule-drawn or human-powered, stood still equally often as they ventured to their destination. Same too for the rarer internal combustion-powered variety.

As such, Holland kept pace easily. He jogged occasionally but ofttimes passed by the vehicle, slowing down before reaching the next block. When the truck made a turn while he was ahead of it, he'd just parallel the rig for a block or two, and either it or he would reconvene courses somewhere along the line.

It helped that he'd grown up in the Dustbin, spent his whole life trodding its cobble-lined streets, breathing the cloying, peat, and coal-choked air. He was intimately aware of its nuances and anticipated the driver's path as often as he followed it.

The truck made one last turn toward the Hall of Ways and made its way right up to the main loading docks as if its cargo were nothing more exotic than, well, than children apparently. Holland walked into the main pedestrian entrance. He looked a little out of place wearing the clean denim and cardigan ensemble Maddie had reunited him with. Shiny black boots didn't help either, but he'd always found knowing what you were about was a great sort of camouflage, regardless of how you were dressed.

He walked casually but with purpose through the long, high-ceilinged hall—the windows of the atrium doing little to illuminate the floor below.

Unlike Vellem and Brythe, there were no other portals than the main cargo zone, so Holland made certain the crates made their way to the queue and then stepped out for a bit so as to not draw attention by loitering too long. This was the one place in Dain Burrough where things operated pretty tidily. The flow from here to Vellem was constant. There were rushes, of course, but not at 10 and 34 O'12.

When he came back from Drummirsbank and the Cafe on the Corner, caffeinated and with the clarity brought on by feeding his belly half a bagel with egg, he realized he was excited, even hopeful. All that went to hell when he saw four of the six crates were already gone and the waysmith, was pushing the fifth into position for transit.

He broke into a brisk stride, bumping into more than a few people along the way. Light bloomed further on as he reached the remaining crate. The other waysmiths were preoccupied and so didn't see him right away. He quickly scanned the outside of the last crate for its bill of lading and saw the contents were specified simply as "live cargo." But it was the destination that puzzled him most: *Private Residence*.

He couldn't fathom that. How? Who had a portal in their private residence? He was just concluding the only person he could think of was the Operatrix herself when he heard a quiet scuff behind him, and then things went black.

Prentiss pushed bits of stewed turnip and celery around on his plate with a chunk of stale pumpernickel bread. He'd eaten some, just because his well-honed street survival instincts wouldn't allow him to not eat *anything*, which was what he'd been inclined to do.

A scuff of a foot on stone from the direction of the tunnels perked his ear, but he didn't react to it. Instead, he slid his plate over to the edge of the cage near the back wall, where he expected the foot's owner to come along if they grew so bold.

He'd seen that odd purple flash earlier. Knew that his meal was likely as much a trap for this other person as it was any sort of gift of sustenance bestowed upon himself. Odds were on the former. It was a lot of food. More than enough for his 65-pound frame. He didn't blame this anonymous cave-dweller for their hesitance around the holding area at all.

He hadn't seen the person who had transited out, but what kind of person could they be, that trafficked children, locked them up in cages, and skulked about creepy caverns? The man with the driver's cap seemed to just be doing his daily work, as despicable as it was. He didn't seem to Prentiss to be the kind to be creeping around, hiding in the shadows.

There were several other cages here, too. And enough room for more crates than just the one he'd come in, which was gone now. To Prentiss, this had the look of an operation. For what purpose? He looked down at the meal just in time to see a slender hand with scabby fingers and dirty nails grabbing the piece of bread from a now clean plate. He and a blonde girl met eyes. She quickly brought one of those fingers to her lips and then darted back into the dark of the tunnel, her feet padding softly in the distance after the image of her had gone away.

So, this was the cave-dweller. An escapee? Or a survivor? The fact she would continue to hang around after whatever happened didn't bode well for him ever getting out of the caves alive. He'd likely have to leave the same way he came in, which didn't seem likely in the least.

Prentiss sat back against the bars of his cage. His butt was cold and instantly started going numb again. He thought about asking Maker to help him get out of the cage, but was concerned about where he'd go from there. The last time was from box to cage. That seemed less like an answer to prayer than a cruel joke.

Maybe he was doing it wrong. Maybe he wasn't being specific enough. He didn't see any other great opportunities presenting themselves, so he figured he'd give it a try.

"Maker? If you're there, and you've got a break in yer schedule, and if it wouldn't be too much of a trouble, would you mind breaking me outta this cage? But don't bother yerself with it, if it's just going to make matters worse. To say it in plain terms, I'm asking to *improve* my situation, and frankly, the last time was a bit of a disappointment. So, to summarize, out of the cage and not into worse trouble. Do you think you can do that?" he asked into the cold dark.

Silence followed. Except for the intermittent, yet interminable dripping of water somewhere in the distance.

"Kinda figured…"

He pulled his legs up close and rested his chin on his knees. He let out a deep sigh and thought again about the blonde girl hiding somewhere off in the tunnels. She was on the outside of the cage, yet she seemed as much a prisoner as himself. He thought of Holland and realized how much he truly missed the grumpy old bastard.

How strange he'd acted in that last bit of time they were together. He thought about the woman and wondered if she was any better or if she had, like had always seemed a high probability, succumbed to her infirmities. He'd probably never know now.

He took a rock and started etching stick people into the floor of his cell. What he drew looked strangely like a family. There were four of them: a man, a woman, a boy, and a girl. And there was a dog. Even the sun was out. What an imagination he had…

Marceline's stomach hurt. She thought eating would make her feel better but in fact, the cramping in her stomach had only grown worse with the addition of celery and turnips, and a few bits of carrot. It had taken every ounce of willpower she had to save the piece of bread. She didn't know when she'd eat again, but having something to put in her stomach when she woke up in the morning would be truly wonderful and she wanted to give herself that little gift. The thought stirred something. A gift...

What the boy had done, giving her some of his meal, that was a gift. That was a level of selflessness she hadn't experienced since her sister left with that waste of a human being, Bruni. To that point in her life, she'd never met anyone more incompetent and cruel. A truly remarkable combination and what her sister saw in him was completely outside of her ability to comprehend.

She didn't fool herself, though. She was young, but she was sure it was about what all men and women seemed to care about—what they did when they were alone. Maybe it was that part that she couldn't understand. How it was that fooling around made people stupid. If that's what happened to you, then she wanted nothing to do with it.

Her thoughts drifted back to the boy, so small, so lonely, and afraid. He didn't have a chance on his own. But she told herself she would survive and do whatever it took. It was just that letting the boy get eaten by the lady had sounded so much easier when she'd said it in her head than now when it was likely to happen in real life.

She sat up, the infinite gray out beyond the pitted iron bars unchanging, making it impossible to tell if the fog was near or far—it filled every bit of sky. *It'll be here when I get back*, she thought. A foghorn groaned loudly. The noise was everywhere, but she felt like its source was somewhere to the right, beyond where she could see. Somewhere farther toward the end of the cliffs. When the sound faded, all that was left was the squawking of gulls and the dull roar of waves below.

She looked one last time but knew she had already made up her mind to talk to him. No time like the present.

Marceline had made the trek back in minutes. She was getting very good at picking through the tunnels in the dark, just by feel. She was sure it was only a couple hundred yards away, but in the perpetual gloom, it felt like miles... like an eternity. Plus, the tunnels crisscrossed one another, so it was almost impossible not to get lost.

But after enough tries, one could pick out one tunnel from another by where this rock would catch a foot, or that wall crumbled into stone rabble, how close the tunnels were to each other in one area, or the slope of that one versus another. Marceline had learned all their tricks, and it turned out the tunnels didn't go on forever and ever after all. It was a maze, but not an unknowable one.

She'd stood at the edge of the light for near on twenty minutes, by her reckoning. There was no movement, no sound of shuffling feet, so she snuck along the edge of the rock wall until she was near the boy's cage.

"I'm Marceline. What's your name?" she whispered, knowing the boy knew she was there.

"Prentiss," he whispered back, not moving from his curled-up position against the back wall of the cage.

"Thank you," she said, meaning for the food.

He nodded.

"They're going to lift the cage, and when they do, you need to run—straight away. The lady will be coming, and you don't want any of that."

"A lady? What lady?" he asked in his small voice.

"The mean lady. Only, she's not really a lady, she's a monster. A for-real monster. You have to run away. Down this tunnel. All the way to the end, but before that, there's a little cubby, a ways down on the right. It's just a ledge in the rocks behind some boulders. You have to get there quick and stay there, real quiet. I'd wait thirty minutes at least. And that's *after* you think she's gone."

"Who is she? Won't she see me? I mean, with a flashlight or something," he asked, his voice getting louder and more concerned.

"No. She likes to do her hunting in the dark. And the more you roll around in the dirt down here. The harder it is for her to smell you."

"Smell me?!?" he gasped out loud. Then quickly backed down to a whisper, "Smell me? You can't leave me in here. You gotta get me out." He was looking around frantically. She was concerned he might go hysterical.

"Prentiss! Focus," she scolded, feeling much like her older sister before she'd left. "You have to run for it. It's the only way."

She could tell he understood. He was smarter than she'd assumed he would be, but she could see it in his eyes. He was just scared. And why shouldn't he be?

"Okay. Tell it to me like I told it to you. It could be any time."

And he repeated it to her, and they made their plans to reconnect and then she was gone again, into the darkness like a wraith, a ghost girl.

CHAPTER 10

Trapped

Nelv had not wanted to take Maddie directly to Prator's workshop. Her suggested alternatives were to wear a blindfold or be drugged. Both of which were completely off the table. Besides, Maddie assured her, she'd just bend time until she got her wishes, anyway. If not now while she was in her weakened state, then later when she was stronger.

The resistance leader reluctantly agreed, but was firm on using a blindfold for the last part of the journey. This made walking problematic, but it was their only option, as Nelv had staunchly resolved never to learn how to drive a Bulger and detested animals in all forms, particularly mules. And also kittens, according to her dossier, which Maddie had thought was an odd fact to include when she'd read it.

Maddie stubbed her toe again. She was certain she'd tripped on every uneven cobble along the way, which played hell with her side and made the walk feel like a death march. When it happened once more, she burst out, "For Gadd's beloved mother, Nelv! If we have to do this with a blindfold, can you at least give me a heads-up?"

"I'm trying," Nelv hissed back. "This area's less than desirable and I'd prefer not to bump into any Klan goons. Now, watch your head," she scolded and pushed Maddie's head down none-to-gently. Her hair brushed through what felt like creeping vines. She heard the rustle of dry leaves and the soft snapping of spiderwebs, and her skin crawled. She couldn't be over with this soon enough.

"Besides, we're almost there. Just steering past this pile of trash and then around this vagabond. Oh, hey Jovik," she said to someone else, apparently to the vagabond in question. And then back to Maddie, "Watch your step."

Maddie was anything but thankful for the heightened sense of smell the blindfold afforded her. Hearing as well. A loud skittering of glass on stone made her jump as Nelv kicked away what she had to assume was an empty liquor bottle from her path. *Just get this done. One step at a time. Just get this done. For Holland,* she told herself.

Soon, they arrived and she could make out the glow of an overhead lamp from around the edges of the blindfold.

"Okay, can I take this off now?" Maddie asked, reaching for the blindfold. Nelv slapped her hand.

"No! Prator doesn't like change, and he especially doesn't like strangers. If he somehow figures out who you *are*, we're both dead. So mostly just don't speak. In fact, don't do anything. Let me handle this."

With that, Nelv rapped on the wooden door and proceeded to wait. A minute or two later, a low, gruff voice from inside issued through, "Yah. What is it?"

"We need to talk. About a mutual friend. A recent friend."

A small circular hole opened in the middle of the door and movement flickered behind it.

"Who's she?"

"She knows about what happened to him. He's in bad shape."

"Who, the old man? Finnery? And you think it's *my* work? Probably sleet."

"He doesn't do drugs, you know that."

"Who knows what a man does? Grumpy old bastard…" Prator grumbled.

"Just listen," Nelv scolded. "You and I both know it's this updated chip. Now, you need to help him."

"Why'd you bring her instead of him?"

"We're afraid to move him. He looks like death and then he'll start screaming," she lied. "You want me to bring him here like that?"

"I suppose you're right. Best you take me to him," Prator replied and started to unlock the door.

"No, you're right," Nelv said quickly. Maddie detected a trace of panic in her voice and hoped Prator didn't pick up on it.

Maddie ran out of patience. "Look," she butted in. "Is this a chip thing or something else? Is he being manipulated? Is there a backdoor into the device you gave him?"

"I'm not talking to this new friend of yours, Nelv. I don't know her… And I don't like her."

"Tell me about it…" Nelv grumped.

Maddie's blood was beginning to boil. "You don't have to like me, but if you're screwing with Holland, I'm going to return the favor, and you will certainly not like that."

Maddie reached for her blindfold.

"No, no, no, no… don't do that Mad," Nelv said, reaching for Maddie's hand. And then to Maddie and Prator both, "Let's back this down a bit… step away from the ledge. Okay?" And then to Prator, "Now, you don't want *her* kind of trouble.

It's like the clap—it's a terrible nuisance and if you get it bad enough, it keeps coming back. Do you get my meaning?"

There was silence. And then the sliding of a heavy bolt echoed through the vacant alley. Maddie was losing her mind, having to wear the blindfold during all of this.

"The blindfold never comes off. Ya understand?" Prator warned.

Maddie didn't nod her understanding right away, but when it was clear they would go no further without her agreement, she finally conceded. But the hairs on the back of her neck were starting to tingle with concern. *This is not going to end well*, she thought to herself while listening intently for movement from within.

The door swung inward and the short, wide man with a bushy beard and leather apron known as Prator stepped aside to let in two women; the short, angry-looking one Karnal recognized as Nelv, leader of the resistance group that called themselves the Toobraiders—a ridiculous name for a ridiculous organization. The other woman was tall, with a nice figure and he was sure he hadn't seen her before. The blindfold did little to hide her beauty. Or her contempt. In fact, with the way she carried herself, he reckoned her for a Brythienne, maybe Vellem aristocracy.

As planned, Bigg Baby and the skinny, rat-looking guy they called Pickle jumped into action. Baby smacked the tall one over the head with a sap while Pickle grabbed Nelv.

Karnal smiled darkly. Hurting people was just part of the business. It wasn't his fault most people were weak and pathetic, and he was not.

He was about to address Nelv when suddenly she thrust her head back and split Pickle's face open and then stomped on his foot before bolting out the door. Karnal's eyebrows lifted in bemusement. Before he could issue a command to run her down, she barreled back through the door with a broken two-by-four. This was turning out to be good fun after all…

Nelv's last stand was cut short by a meaty hook from Baby just as she reared back to clobber Pickle. Her feet flew up, and she landed flat on her back. It looked like she'd run into a half-lowered garage door and actually caused Karnal to wince a little. He stifled a nervous laugh as he scratched at the days' growth of black stubble on his jaw. He did not envy the headache the woman would have when she woke up.

Prator, the proprietor of the workshop and resident mad scientist, closed the door. Looking down at the two unconscious women and then up at Karnal questioningly he asked, "Now what? She's Ekron. That's what Nelv was implying, anyway. Kill her, right?"

"Ekron, huh?" Karnal cocked his head, ideas and scenarios started careening through his head like a crash-up derby the way they did when new and exciting opportunities presented themselves amidst high levels of risk. He's always had a higher threshold for such things than most. "Kinda weird for her to pop up here… And what's she doing with one of the resistance honchos? That's an odd pairing."

Prator's face was screwed up in concentration and then his head lifted. "What if she's the one they're talking about in the papers?"

"The one on the wanted list? A diabolical serial killer … in a blindfold? Yeah, that doesn't smell right. But, if she's Ekron just the same…"

Karnal squinted his one good eye in concentration as he rubbed his temple. "Drug her. And then chip her. If we have the old man controlling transit *and* we got her to do Time..." He smiled broadly, liking the sound of it. The chaos of the crash-up derby was beginning to settle out. All the possibilities laid out before him. *This* was the beginning of an empire.

"Boss. What do you wanna do with the small, feisty lady?" Baby asked.

"Kill her. Feed her to the pigs. No one that matters is gonna miss one pain-in-the-ass bitch. The authorities, least of all. Damn nuisance, the resistance is, anyway. ToobRaiders..." he said derisively. "Nice distraction, though. But we don't need that anymore. Not with the old man and this Ekron lady," he said, standing over Maddie and eyeing her speculatively. "Kill the pint-sized pain in the ass ... and ditch the body."

Bigg Baby turned to his next in command, the pale, sickly fellow with his eye patch flipped up. Apparently, his right eye wasn't all that good to begin with, and Clan Karnal thugs all wore theirs on the left.

"Pickle. You heard him. You've got clean up. And do something about that eye patch. It's a disgrace. We got one piece of equipment we all gotta wear. Figure it out," the mountain of a man chided.

"But, if I keep it down, I can't see," the other man whined in a nasally, highly unattractive tone.

"Maybe a screen over the middle bit, so you can see through it," Prator provided helpfully, as if explaining arithmetic to a kindergartner.

"Oh, yeah. This guy really is smart," Pickle said to Bigg Baby, not realizing that no one in the room took his opinions seriously, or that Prator was patronizing him.

"So, body first. Then eyepatch. Got it?" Bigg Baby asked.

Pickle nodded to his superior and gathered up the sub-hundred-pound Nelv, who twitched and then moaned softly.

Prator spoke up, "Just a second. Nobody gets killed in my shop. I've only got the one rule and you guys show up and wanna break it." After rummaging in a cabinet, he stepped over to where Nelv was and administered an injection of something or other. Pickle nodded cheerfully then walked out the door with her draped over his shoulder like a sack of potatoes.

Karnal walked across the room and sat down casually on a waiting lounge to think. The room was comfortably sized by Dustbin standards. It had a coffee table, a large round rug in the middle, and a hanging, stained glass lamp. The light was low but near the back, a bright overhead lamp cast a cone around a raised, reclining chair. It looked somewhat like a tattoo parlor that way.

Bigg Baby had the woman from Bureau Ekron bound and gagged in that chair within minutes. There was dark, drying blood in her blonde hair, but the blood from a previous wound on her stomach was fresh and seeping through her blouse.

She began to stir and Prator practically dove for the chair, stabbing the needle into her neck and pushing the plunger to the stops.

He stepped back and wiped his brow with relief. She settled, her head lolling to the side. Prator pushed her head up and flipped a strap made for the purpose across her forehead and secured it. She was asleep, but she looked anything but peaceful. He turned to Karnal.

"This isn't sustainable and, to be honest, I don't know that a chip will do it either. At *any* time in the future, she could decide to undo it all. But... in the short-term, at least until we figure it out, I think I have an idea."

"I'm listening." Karnal cast a scrutinizing eye in his direction.

"Have you ever heard of magnetic flux ... interfering with temporals, I mean?"

"No. I didn't think anything could disrupt that. Gadd's goat if it's true."

"Well, I don't know about any celestial livestock, but there's a story anyway, about a Bureau raid that went wrong. It was the Deadlies—their hideout at the old sardine packing plant on Duinn St."

"Before my time, but I remember hearing something about it. What do sardines have to do with magnetic ... flux, was it?" Karnal asked, looking up while he searched his memory for the term and then returned his attention to Prator.

"Well, nothing really. Except all that packing and processing equipment takes a big electric room. They were holed up in the main electric room, the substation, and something went wrong. Ekron agents screwed up, tried to redo the moment, but it didn't work. Not once, not twice... nothing. No one knew why. Assumed it was some sort of anomaly.

"I've been puzzling on it for a long while. My hypothesis is that it has to do with electromagnetic flux. That place had big, loud, high-voltage transformers. Vintage stuff. Fed the whole block though. I think that's what did it."

"That place burned down."

"Yeah, coincidence? Most likely, the bureau clockies burned it down just to obfuscate the reality of the situation. Make it seem like it could be some strange happenstance, or something about the place. But anyway, all I'm saying is it's not the only game in town. There are plenty of other manufacturing facilities but, ones with really big electrical equipment like that? With dense fields of mag-flux? The best bet is the hydroelectric plant south of town. You don't get much more magnetic flux than that. Plus, it's out of the way."

"Prator, you really gotta read the room," Karnal stated, looking around. "Obfuscate? Really? What is it about Big Baby and I that makes you think we spend our free time with our nose in a thesaurus?" he asked, shaking his head. "Anyway. Hydro-plant. Got it. How long 'til she wakes up?"

"Nelv got half a mule's worth of tranqs in her. This one got the rest. It'll be an hour or two. And even when they do wake up, they're gonna be pretty well muddled for a while. I'd say you've got a good two- or three-hour window. If you get her down there, right in the middle of the big turbine room, we can figure out how to test this theory. Besides, every agency between here and Brythe is looking for her. So, best to keep her well out of the way. Win-win, I think."

"You weren't thrilled to help out with the old man. Why's she different?"

"Well, for one, it's way more interesting than doing chips all day. Or even memplants. Beyond that... Ekron agent? In my house? That's not how I do business. Plus, my neck's on the line along with yours. If she wakes up and is able to shift time, sooner or later, we'll both be in a mess of trouble. Ekron agents have a way of getting their recompense." He darted a look at Bigg Baby. "Means payback."

Bigg Baby nodded understanding, seeming not to take offense at the explanation.

Prator looked again at the woman in the reclining chair and added, "I'd rather avoid that."

Karnal nodded, contemplative. He strode over to where Maddie was, grabbed her face with one hand to look at her in the light, and then let her head flop back over.

"She's not going to die on us, is she?"

Prator strolled over, looked at the wound in her hairline, felt her temperature, and then pulled up her blouse enough to take a look at the wound beneath. It'd been seeping considerably but seemed to have coagulated in the meantime. He poked around the stitches and dried blood.

"This isn't bad work. It's not infected. That was a pretty nasty wound. Whoever gave her this probably thought she was dead, but I doubt this work was done local. Maybe Cloates, in Vellem. Though, his hand isn't what it used to be. Could be Smythe. If she was on the run... that'd make a certain amount of sense. Though, a bit of an odd pairing, an Ekron agent and a deviant like him. Obviously, she had help." Prator looked toward the door. "What's the connection between her and a ToobRaider? Especially a higher-up like Nelv Kiml? Obviously, something to do with the old man, but... that seems quite an oddity. Makes me uncomfortable," he said, fidgeting with the way his leather apron rested on his belly.

"Fair point. Maybe I'll send an associate to Vellem to poke around. Antipole Sur?" He looked at Prator for acknowledgment and when the man nodded yes, he continued, "Meanwhile, you believe that horseshit about the old man bordering on vegetable status?"

"Nah. Nelv was bluffing. Holland has had a chip for years and the product I gave him is stable. I think they thought they could lean on me to get information. Obviously, they think they know something about a backdoor on this generation of implants, but they don't. What I do is my own special mod, just for situations like this..."

"Well, turn up the heat on that old bastard. I want him strapped to that chair with his eyes floating in mule tranqs before she wakes up." Karnal stood up and adjusted his jacket and then turned to his new lieutenant. "Baby. You heard the man. Prepare a space in the turbine room at the hydro plant and get this Ekron bitch down there. Bound and gagged. I want a gun to her head on every zero and five until I get there."

"Sure enough, Boss," the man, the only one broader than Karnal himself, replied and started for the door.

"Baby... the body?"

"Yeah, Boss. I got it. I'm just grabbing one of them little three-wheeled jobbies with the truck bed. It'll be quicker that way."

"You even fit in one of those?" Karnal asked with a look of amusement on his face.

"Oh yeah, I did Vichi DiVangelese in one of them." He smiled broadly. "I can manage."

Karnal shook his head, unable to get the vision of the two 300-pounders fogging the windows in a micro-compact truck cab. A miracle they hadn't rolled the thing.

Prator looked skeptical, obviously wondering at the same thing.

Holland kicked involuntarily and realized he'd been asleep or unconscious. He blinked away a bleary pseudo-reality which ushered in a scathing new one. He preferred the other. This one felt like a supernova, burning away the skin and sinew from his bones. Stars exploded again through his mind and he clutched his head. Writhing on the floor of the cramped wooden box, he kicked the walls again and again involuntarily.

"Shut up over there," a man growled from several yards away. "You'll throw the lady off her hunt. An' you don't want that..."

The swell of pulsing, blinding agony began to fade. Slightly. Holland braced his head against the side of the box and breathed. The pain was measurably less, but still so intense he was surprised he hadn't thrown up or pissed himself. It was creeping off of twelve on a ten scale. Slowly. Almost imperceptibly. He would give anything to just be at an eight. And then the pain faded, leaving what felt like a raw, echoing emptiness inside his being.

Thank Maker.

But, wait... What hunt? What did he mean by hunt? Holland struggled to take in these new surroundings. Light trickled into the box through breather holes near the top, but just from one side. He could hear someone shuffling around, prying nails from wood, shuffling off into the near distance, and then there was a ratcheting mechanism, clack-clack-clack-clack as something large and heavy was either being lifted or lowered. Then he felt and heard a loud thud as whatever it was hit the floor. It was definitely heavy and metallic. But what could it be?

Then he heard the man shuffling closer, working at another one of the crates, huffing as he picked up something heavy. Holland remembered where he had been, the Hall of Ways. And then came the realization of where he most likely was now—wherever they'd taken Prentiss.

With that realization, his heart leaped in his chest. He pushed himself against the wall of the box and slid himself up to try to see out of the air holes, but it was no use. They were too close to the top of the box and what he could see was just a shadow. Instead, he sat back to listen again. His head swimming from the rapid movement. Too soon, but he wasn't likely to get the rest his head demanded.

The man outside whistled some work song or another in a raspy shrill. Holland didn't recognize it. Then, off in the distance, an echo of a scream. It sounded like that of a young boy.

"Prentiss!" Holland bolted up to the air holes, pressing his face to the wood. "Prentiss! Is that you, boy?" he bellowed, though he doubted the boy could hear him.

The man came over and banged on the box with a crowbar.

"I said that's enough!"

Before he realized what he'd done, Holland transited out of the box and behind the man standing there. He grabbed him around the neck, but before Holland could get a firm chokehold, the man kicked off the crate, slamming the pair hard into a wall of hewn rock.

Holland took the brunt of the impact, air bursting from his lungs. The man swung down hard at his leg. He managed to shift his weight, moving his leg just before the crowbar clanged and sparked off the rock. He cinched his arms tighter around the man's neck. His opponent slapped at Holland's forearm but couldn't get a firm grip, so he transited them both.

Suddenly they were in a residence Holland had never seen before. He glanced quickly at his surroundings as the man struggled even more desperately in his hold. The room they were in was large, well-lit, with oil and electric lamps, lavishly appointed with a broad staircase flowing down along an arcing wall. A manor of some sort.

The man took advantage of Holland's distraction, bending sharply at the waist, and throwing Holland's considerable frame over the top. He landed flat on his back, thudding loudly on the wooden floor. He stared up to see the crowbar arcing down at his head, and rolled out of the way, but barely.

The other man cursed. Holland clambered to his feet. Already the man was charging. Holland caught him by the wrists, but his momentum carried them back toward the stairs and they tumbled back. Holland tried to roll with the motion, something ingrained in muscle memory, but not all that muscle was there anymore. It'd been thirty-odd years since he'd needed to move like that.

Instead, the two rolled awkwardly backward and over the edge of the set of stairs, tumbling head over heels to the next landing. The man's crowbar flew up and shattered an oil lamp and fire quickly spread across the velvet-papered wall and an oil painting of a fox hunt.

The two men tumbled in a knot down the broad, carpeted stairs, throwing punches and elbows as they went until they hit another landing.

Holland was just gaining his feet when the man pulled him into the wooden slats of the banister, which didn't give, knocking him momentarily senseless. Holland's attacker pushed him down the next set of stairs and the world spun chaotically until Holland hit the bottom and sprawled out.

His vision swam, but he knew instinctively that the man would be at him any second. But he couldn't see where he was or think of anything that could help. He heard something up on the stairs and thought it was the man's footsteps. He rolled to his feet and charged up the steps, catching the man mid-step, and driving him back before slamming him hard onto the stairs. The man's breath exploded from his chest and he groaned, grabbing feebly at Holland.

The fighting turned desperate and sloppy as they grew more and more exhausted. Holland grabbed him by his vest, hauled him off the stairs, and hurtled the man the five or six feet to the wood floor below.

He bounced hard. Moaning as he slid to a stop. It was Holland's turn to stomp down the steps to finish off his opponent. But shockingly, the man scrambled to his feet. This wasn't some ginned-up bar fight over someone ogling someone else's girl. This was a fight to the death. They both knew it.

The man in the green vest stumbled around the corner, pulling over a pedestal with the bust of some long-dead patron. Holland clambered over it, but was careful not to follow too closely around the blind corner. He didn't hear footsteps heading down the hall. Just as he peeked around it, a heavy brass fire poker clanged off the wall, close to where he would've been if he'd not been cautious. Holland spotted his opponent standing near a fireplace a dozen paces away.

He chucked another brass implement at him and then, defying any perceived harm he'd taken, leaped over a couch and tore down the adjoining hall at a full sprint. Holland jogged over to the hall and saw at the end of it a large, round, floor-to-ceiling window.

Through it, not far off, Holland could see the shadow of a lighthouse, its beacon shrouded from this angle, light spilling first from one side and then the other. The man, still sprinting, drew near the end of the corridor and was just turning the corner when Holland leaped forward and transited the full distance, piledriving right into him.

The man hit the wall hard, bounced off, and stumbled to the floor. Holland grabbed him, and, in another blue flash, transited again. This time, out in the distance to the top catwalk of that lighthouse.

The wind was fierce and cold, thick with moisture, and the catwalk was slick with it. Below, waves off the Grand Marchioness crashed against slick, black boulders. Holland pushed the man against the railing so that he was leaning out over the rocks and thrashing surf. The henchman's eyes grew round with terror even as both men struggled to keep their footing. Holland pushed further—the man struggled to stay upright and not plummet to his death.

"Who do you work for?" Holland growled.

The man didn't respond, but continued to struggle against him and try to squirm out of the way.

"Who do you work for?" he growled again, louder, pushing him even farther past the tipping point.

Then the man smiled suddenly, maniacally in the stark white light of the beacon. "She's going to take her time with you," he said, an evil glint in his eye. And then a blade flashed in the bright wash from the lighthouse's rotating beam. Holland reared back from it, but at that moment, with the strain of the struggling men, the railing snapped and the two fell—Holland back onto the catwalk, the henchman, out into the darkness.

Holland scrambled back from the edge, his back against the lantern room wall, safe from the exposed ledge.

He heard only the wind and the low, grating rumble of the beacon rotating in its housing. And then the foghorn blasted, filling the air with its mournful wail. It felt like it went on forever. Holland's ears were dull from the intensity of the noise, even more so in its absence.

When he pulled his wits together, he crawled to the edge and ventured a look over it. Far below, he could just make out the body of the man, sandwiched between two of the larger rocks. *It was a good thing I had never been on the interrogation side of things in the war*, he thought. If this was any indicator, he wouldn't have been any good at it.

Now, he had nothing to go on. No clue why they were taking children off the streets. But at least he knew where Prentiss was at. Well, at least he kind of did. It was obvious now that this was the Selsby Lighthouse. And that was the late shipping magnate's manor. On the other side of the promontory rock it was built on would be the hydro-plant and the road back to Dain Burrough.

Holland looked out over the wind-whipped surf as it crashed into the cliffs below the manor. Pretty big waves for a lake, he mused. Although it did connect to the sea, it was via a few miles of river now, so no one called it a bay anymore.

Holland needed to get back to the manor to follow the man's transit path. That's where they'd been taking the kids. That's where he'd find Prentiss, he hoped.

His chest burned. He looked down, and, for the first time, realized he was bleeding. He had a gash from shoulder to chest from the man's knife.

It wasn't a lot of blood, but his frame of reference came from his time in the war, where they were lucky if they found someone's missing appendage and could send it back with them to a triage unit. He pressed his hand against the wound, gritting his teeth against the fresh pain that it elicited. Then he transited back to the manor.

It was bright inside the manor compared to outside. He blinked against the glare, but more so, he realized, against the smoke. The smell of fire was heavy. He coughed, choking on the hot, thick air.

He made his way past the sitting room with the fireplace. Flames were everywhere on the second floor and going up the stairs. The ceiling was invisible but for thick black smoke and flames barely visible within it. Long yards of floor-to-ceiling curtains looked like waterfalls of fire.

Holland tried to orient himself so he could follow the man's transit path when he was hit again by the searing light inside his mind. "Not ... now," he gritted out, but it was lost in the crackle and roar of the flames. He gripped his head in his hands and stumbled as he tried to press forward against the blinding pain.

The corrupted implant burned at the base of his skull. His legs buckled as he was crushed under the wilting surge of pain yet again. He didn't know how much more of this he could take. Already he felt like he was grasping at sanity, his eyes feeling like they were being burned out from inside his skull. And then, in one searing starlight burst of agony, he blacked out.

Prentiss woke slowly. It was dark out still, but then, incrementally he began to realize that it wasn't nighttime, or even heavy overcast. He was literally *in* the dark. Terror crept up from somewhere inside and he remembered something about some creepy caves. And a cage. But then, as his eyes struggled to focus on a light somewhere across the room, he realized something else—the cage was gone.

He bolted upright, rubbing his ankle where the manacles hid bitten into the skin, and a jolt of adrenalin shot through him again. The manacles. There had been manacles and now they were gone, too. He shook his head to clear the cobwebs. *Why couldn't he think straight?* Something was very important, and he just couldn't remember what it was.

He smacked his lips thickly, trying to get the taste of metal out of his mouth, and realized that was what he'd felt like when he was brought here. He'd been drugged. And now he'd been drugged again. He saw the empty plate a couple of feet away. *Stupid, stupid,* he cursed himself for not being smarter than that.

Prentiss rolled over on his hands and knees and tried to stand on wobbly legs. Then something else came to him. The girl. There'd been a girl. What had she told him? When the cage went up ... run. Prentiss's mind snapped into the moment.

Run, she'd said. Or the mean lady would get him. He swung his head around drunkenly, scanning every inch of what he could see. The light at the far end of the room. Four crates that hadn't been there before. He looked everywhere. No one was around. He stumbled forward, toward the darkness. Into the tunnels the girl had told him about.

What else had she said? Halfway down, on the right, there was a hiding place. He tripped on a rock sticking out of the floor and then the floor sloped away, further catching him off balance. He fell and skinned his knees and hands. And then he heard something. In the dark, somewhere behind him. How far had he walked? His brain was too fuzzy, couldn't think straight.

"Oh. I like this one. Brave..." a matronly voice crooned in the darkness. "Where are you going, little one? Where are you wandering off to, in the dark?" the voice asked, syrupy sweet. Those were the worst kind, Prentiss knew. The ones who pretended to care about your predicament. They never did, though. They didn't want to help. Those were the kind that only wanted to hurt. To prey on the weak. The innocent. The small...

Prentiss felt fear trying to stop him. It was a cold, icy hand on his spine. Then gripping his heart, his stomach, his throat. He moved through it. Pushed past the intensifying terror. Walking softly... oh so quietly. He knew how to be small and quiet.

"Not the talkative type? I understand," the voice purred from somewhere alarmingly close. Maybe only twenty paces back. Prentiss pushed forward, still taking small, smooth steps, heel first, rolling to the outside edge of the sole and then to the ball of the foot, like a cat thief. Careful not to grind the sand beneath his foot. Then the next, and the next after that. In the distance, the dripping of water.

In his ears, the rushing of blood with each heartbeat. He heard each of his shallow breaths. They sounded loud as kids stomping through puddles. Like banging pans. Like an over-revving Bulger stuck on an uphill road.

Prentiss's foot found resistance. He reached down and found a large rock, and then another next to it. That rattled something loose in his mind. *A bunch of rocks, halfway down on the right.* Was he on the right? He didn't know. He reached his hand out, and it brushed against something. His heart stopped. But then he felt the cool, rough surface beneath his fingertips.

"I hear you ... little boy."

His heart pumped faster, but the voice wasn't closer. It was, maybe the same distance away but echoed strangely, as if the lady had turned to face another tunnel. One that Prentiss hadn't seen or even known was there. He moved forward on hands and feet now. Just past the boulders, she'd said. He moved a little bit farther. Feeling with both hands, but as quietly as he could, his hand swept through empty air.

Down close to the ground, tight to the boulders, there was a void. He knew it would make a lot of racket if he tried to wiggle in there now. He didn't know where the woman was either. So, he waited until she spoke.

"Where are you?" she asked, into the dark. Her voice echoing down halls in what sounded like a dozen different directions. "Come out, come out, wherever you are."

And just like that, Prentiss was in. Pressed in close to the mountain. Tucked in tight. And then he waited.

The woman hunted. Tried to taunt him. Tried to tempt him with treats. Threaten him with impossible terrors. She passed within feet of him, twice. And then she was quiet, waiting in the darkness.

To a nine-year-old boy, the waiting would seem like forever. To Prentiss, fearing for his life, hiding in a dark cavern from a doppelgänger masquerading as the creepiest middle-aged woman ever, it felt like forever times eternity, and that times infinity as well.

Finally, a purple light flared in the distance, and Prentiss let out a relieved breath. But then... he wasn't sure how, he felt the presence of someone else. Very close.

"Shhh," came the barely audible whisper of a young girl. "Just a little while longer..."

He nodded quietly, though he knew she couldn't see him because he couldn't see a thing. He couldn't actually believe she was here. Had almost begun to think that their encounter had been a dream. The two waited in silence. He wished he could see her face just to reassure himself that she was really there. And then, after a very long time, he heard a small rustle and felt cold lips pressed against his forehead.

"Good luck," she whispered, and then she was gone. Seconds later, a purple light flashed brightly, but this time ... from only yards away. The woman had been waiting all that time. He had seen her tan stockings and the hem of her dress between the rocks before she'd vanished. She had only transited out earlier in order to fool him. She may have materialized right there and been waiting the whole time...

Prentiss shuddered and then realized that he shouldn't have been able to see the woman at all. Marceline should have been in the way, but she wasn't there... The boy swallowed hard, his stomach doing nervous flips. He just wanted to be out of these caves, to breathe the comfortingly foul Dustbin air, feel its mist on his face.

He longed to feel the heat from the old man's wood stove, the warm, powdery smell of burned flux wire from his workbench, the ink and pulp of wet newspaper drying by the fire. Truth be told, he just wanted to be anywhere but here. But there was nothing that could be done. He was going to have to just keep pushing.

At least his brain felt a little clearer than it had at first. *Fear of your own mortality will do that for you*, he thought. That, plus it'd been nearly an hour, he reckoned since he'd woken on what had been the floor of his cell, but was actually just a floor of the greater holding room at that point.

He waited another minute, just to be sure she was really gone. That they both were really gone and then he shimmied out of the hidey-hole and started working his way in the dark, deeper into the tunnels.

Now, what had she told him? *All the way down to the end and then left and left again after twenty feet?* There'd be a dip in the floor and at the dip, he'd be just a few feet away from a column of rock. The rock had steps in it, but barely. He didn't know what to make of Marceline, but forced himself not to think about it. She'd been right about the hiding place past the rocks. And she had kept him from making a noise when the mean lady was just a few feet away.

He shivered involuntarily. He'd heard people talked to shrinks when they were having a hard time coping with life. He had no idea who Shrinks was, but he had a hard time thinking of when life had not been throwing hard stuff at him. This situation was definitely on the weirder side—even for him.

Prentiss couldn't believe how long it took him to navigate the second half of the tunnel in the complete dark. It helped that the floor was mostly flat, which led him to believe that this place had been used for some purpose or another, whether mine or cavern or something of both, it had been used by people in the past. That made the passage easier.

Then there was a dip in the floor and suddenly the air smelled different. Not quite as stale or musty. He couldn't place it though. It didn't smell clean exactly, not that he'd know what that smelled like. It smelled like something else. The air was heavy.

Prentiss felt around with both hands until he got the sense of the rock wall arcing away from him. He hoped this was the spot. The wall wasn't completely vertical. It sloped a little bit toward his feet. He moved his hands around, finding hand- and footholds. This could be it. He felt to the right, and the footholds drew closer to the floor. He stepped up on the sloping rock and then felt around with a foot for another and his foot nestled into the small depression.

He kept going, one after the other, until after a minute he was certain that he was quite a bit off the cavern floor, maybe ten or twelve feet.

He heard tiny pebbles as they fell, bouncing off the rock, making ticking sounds as they were drawn by gravity to the hard rock below.

Prentiss's foot went out, probed for a rock shelf, but there was nothing there. He squeezed in close to the wall to keep himself from falling. She'd said it was there, and Prentiss believed her. He stretched out again, farther than he knew he could without falling, farther still, and just as he was certain he was going over; his foot came down on a flat edge of rock.

His heart was pounding. He thought that was all it ever did anymore. He felt around for a handhold and, after a moment, found a sloping knob. Not a great handhold, but it provided enough friction for him to pull himself toward his foot and get his body weight over and onto the ledge.

When he was standing with both feet on a level surface, he breathed a quiet sigh of relief. Now, it should just be a little ways farther. Already the scent of cleaner, fresher air was growing stronger. It was colder too, which he wasn't thankful for.

He pressed forward, with safe, tentative steps, and then there was a skinny section. There was a breeze coming through there. This section was easy for him to navigate, but it'd be near impossible for anyone much bigger, he thought. He imagined the girl could make it, but just.

Prentiss slipped through the pinch-point and came into a small chamber. It was a natural-looking opening in the rock. He could barely make out some of it through moonlight coming in through a hole in the wall, like a window. He rushed to it but then saw that there were bars on it. They'd been hard to see in the dark, but they were clear as day to him now.

"No, no, no, no..." He grabbed them with both hands, not trusting what his eyes were showing him, in vivid, up-close detail. And then, as he shook, one of the bars moved. He looked at it more closely. Someone had been working at the cement around the bottom. What's more, the iron itself seemed to be near to rusting through.

He started working at it himself, pushing and pulling on the metal, moving it incrementally at first and then a little bit more. He yanked and pushed and yanked some more and then stepped on something that crackled underfoot.

Looking down, he saw a stale piece of bread in the pale light, ground down to dust. And then he saw something that looked like a bleached-out chicken bone before he realized there was another attached to it. In fact, a whole hand was attached to that, and that's when he yelled out loud. He hadn't meant to, but there was an entire skeletonized body there on the floor with him. A body not much larger than his own. He dared another glance down and there was hair. Long, blonde wisps of hair on the skeleton's scalp.

Prentiss didn't realize it, but he was backed against the far side of the cramped space, on the floor, hands around his knees, shaking his head, just saying "no" quietly to himself over and over and over. He was waiting for Marceline to jump out of the shadows at any moment and yell, "Gotcha!" but he knew that wouldn't be happening. He touched his forehead, where he'd felt her kiss. He felt sick. Was sure he was going to be sick and then he heard yelling, or some sort of commotion from way back in the tunnels.

Sparing a glance from the skeleton, he looked back toward the opening that he'd come through. The commotion from farther on had been brief and far away. He wasn't even sure that he'd heard it. But then, for the briefest second, he'd almost thought that he'd heard ... his name.

Prentiss swallowed, pushing down his fear. He stood up, still watching the skeleton, and then he stepped over to the bars again. He could get that one bar out, at least. Then, if he *did* go back down there, at least he'd have a weapon.

CHAPTER 11

THE HYDRO

Maddie was surrounded by the sounds of big machinery. She'd been sitting for a while now, trying to figure out where she was and what she was doing there. That had happened more than a couple of times lately. She even felt like she had the hangover that should accompany that sort of behavior, only this was like no hangover she'd ever had before.

Her limbs felt like jelly. Like there were no bones in her body at all. And then there was a nagging feeling... like she ought to *know* something of great import.

That lasted for a little bit and then she remembered Nelv. *What a strange, angry little person.* She remembered being blindfolded. She *didn't* remember being clubbed over the head, but the soreness on the side of her skull and the prickly stickiness of her hair told her that she'd suffered some sort of head trauma. It could have been a fall, but she was leaning toward the former. Just a hunch.

But, still, things were not quite right. That made her think of drugs. She thought about them, how she felt about them, what it would feel like to be on them. And that felt right. Yes, that felt like what was going on. She was on drugs.

So, her summation was that she'd been clubbed over the head, probably by... there was a bad man in there somewhere. Something with a C, no, no... a K! She felt the thrill of triumph at that revelation. And then there was another guy. Sciency. She was certain that someone sciency was involved ... somehow. But then, they'd figured out who she was. Otherwise, they'd have killed her and not bothered drugging her at all.

That part didn't quite track. Wouldn't they have wanted to kill her so that she couldn't just undo the whole thing? That's what she would have done if she were in their shoes. Killed her, that is. Unless there were some other nefarious intentions at play. Those men seemed the type to have them.

It was always about nefarious intentions, she opined. She existed because ... so did they. That made her the *opposite* of nefarious. And she quite liked that. For some reason, she had been feeling very much *not* like the opposite of nefarious lately. She'd been feeling guilty, and that was an uncomfortable feeling and a sad one. But now... where was she again?

Wherever it was, it was loud. She realized that she was still blindfolded.

"Really? Still with the blindfold?" she asked out loud, through wooden lips and a stubborn tongue.

She could just see under the edges of the blindfold. She cocked her head back to see more clearly and nearly passed out from the pain and nausea that swept over her. She didn't want to repeat that feeling, but tried again after a moment, anyway. Just not quite so fast this time.

To her right was a big machine with piping running through and around it. It looked like it was the size of a truck. A real truck, not the little three-wheeled jobbers they drove in Dain Burrough. *What a shit hole*, she thought absentmindedly. *So, lost...* But there was *something* about the place. Some redeeming quality, but she couldn't quite put her mind on what it was.

A burst of steam from somewhere and a whine as a pressure relief valve closed caught her attention. That brought her back to the line of reasoning she'd been working on, unspectacularly. Through the clamor, there was an underlying roar. Definitely water or high-pressure gas noises going on. She carefully turned her head to the other side and saw a similar contraption as before. Not similar. Identical. And beyond that, a couple more. *They aren't boilers*, she thought.

Now that she had a sense of what she was hearing, she could distinguish them a little better from the din assaulting her. There were maybe six or eight of the contraptions. They were behind her as well.

So, big machinery, rushing water or gas. A big echoey room. Yeah, that narrowed it down not at all. This is where being a guy would have been really handy. Knowledge about stuff like this seemed to be provided at birth for them.

She had no desire to make that trade, but she was sure it had its perks. Never having to wait in line for a restroom being pretty high on that list. Seeming to instinctively know how to operate any firearm was a close second. Okay, maybe not *that* close. She did okay with firearms as it was. But she could definitely use a restroom right about now.

She wanted to shift time, just do a big do-over, but felt like it was important to understand where her captors had taken her. And more importantly, why. It was a rookie mistake to just punt when things got tough. Here was where the answers were. If she went back now, she'd be just as clueless as before.

She also needed to find out what they'd done with Nelv. Her thoughts wandered to how Holland was faring. That thought was bittersweet. How was he holding up with all this going on? Had he found the boy? Or did... What was his name? Colonel? No... Karnal! Did Karnal get him, too? And where were they taking the kids? What did this have to do with Director Turnbull and the Operatrix? *And what is he—or she—anyway*, she wondered.

She'd never heard of anyone who could bend time and space. But then there was the aspect of his dual personalities. She couldn't even begin to imagine how he'd pulled that off. There was nothing in any of the histories that she knew that could explain his powers. She wondered how much of the history and science that she'd come to take as fact was missing or altered by the person—or thing—she'd called her boss for near on a decade at least. Though time, as an occupational hazard, was somewhat nebulous for her. Hard to keep straight.

Then a hard, metallic object pressed into her temple, which she could only assume was a gun. She tried to bend time, but nothing happened. Maddie's pulse spiked, pounding in her head as she tried again, but with the same result.

"Don't try it, lady. This place is s'posed to make it so you can't slip time. But I don't feel like finding out."

"Can you see the ghosts?" she asked. "The images of other streams of time superimposed on our own?"

The man stiffened. She smirked; she could tell he was looking around. That's when she would have struck if she'd been prepared for the moment or not bound to a chair. Instead, he struck her, and she gasped in pain with the force of the blow. Stars shot around inside of her head. Her head itself felt like a smashed pumpkin held together with baling wire—like it could just fall apart if she moved the wrong way.

At least the blow had knocked the blindfold off a little more. She forced herself not to look around, to not give away the deception.

"Smart one, huh? Let's see how smart you are with your brains painting the machinery."

Then Maddie had the barrel of a snub-nosed revolver shoved into her mouth and pulled up so that she was facing her attacker. It was a face she didn't recognize. But then someone far off to the right spoke up.

"That's enough, Townie," a deep voice boomed over the roaring din of machinery.

The man turned to look, a sneer cutting across his bony face. He had a large, hawkish nose and coarse black eyebrows that made him look almost comical, if not for the intensity of malice she saw in his eyes. Here was a man who hated everything, including himself. A set of dark-framed glasses might have completed the comic look, but did nothing to hide the villain beneath.

He turned back to Maddie and made a feint of smacking her with the back of his hand, but she just stuck out her jaw. Daring him to do it. He reared back farther, as if committing to the act, when the newcomer seized his hand, bending the wrist forward so that the man dropped to his knees in pain.

The new guy quickly slipped the revolver out of the thug's free hand and backhanded him with it. The man called Townie sprawled across the concrete but to his credit, picked himself up and skulked off to the other side of the room and out the door without a word.

The new guy turned to face Maddie. He looked at her as if appraising her worth, or possibly just seeing if she'd been damaged and whether he was going to be in trouble with the higher-ups.

"Guy's a low-life. Even for one of Karnal's goons. He won't be around long. You hurt?"

"All kinds. But if you're talking about the face... I've had worse."

"Yeah, I get that sense."

Maddie looked at him again. She recognized him. If it wasn't for the drugs, she felt like she would have figured it out already. She strained at the memory of it and then her thoughts shot back thirty-five years. But to her, it was less than half that time. The tunnels. It was Mansignol, but fuller in the face. Broader for sure. This one looked like a house.

"I know you."

"Yeah? Am I on some sorta sheet or something?"

"No. You're Tommie? Mansignol... I knew your dad."

"Well, that makes one of us anyway..."

He dragged over a chair, presumably left by the man watching her earlier. He spun it around backward and sat down with his arms crossed on its back. Maddie could read black lettering tattooed across his knuckles; Bigg on his right. Baby on the left.

Malphius poured himself a cup of coffee from a battered thermos and screwed the cap back on. He leaned back, the chair squealing with displeasure as he did so, and then something gave. The chair dropped and jolted to a sudden stop—scalding coffee flew everywhere. His face, his chest, his crotch. "Jonnes balls!" he gasped, jumping up and leaning over with his arms and cup outstretched. It was a vain attempt at trying to get the hot liquid soaking through his grungy coveralls off his sensitive skin.

Coopernall, the scrawny new kid who'd been wheedling his way up the ranks, was on the floor laughing so hard Malph thought he'd soil himself.

"Ahh, shaddup, will ya? Now I gotta go change outta these clothes and you're stuck manning the console 'til I'm back." Malph swung a lazy kick in the kid's direction, but Coopernall scampered out of the way and rested back against a metal cabinet, still struggling to breathe for laughing so hard. He rubbed the tears from his eyes.

"Jonnes balls..." Coopernall repeated, laughing and shaking his head.

Malph cracked a little, too. A grin sidled up his unshaven, age-sagging jowls, but then something on one of the antiquated black and white monitors caught his eye. The shape of a man carrying something over his shoulder past camera five. His smile evaporated. A couple of seconds later, the same shape passed by camera twelve going down the adjacent corridor, toward the livestock pens. It was clear he was carrying a body. Another one...

"Coop. Cut the feed to cameras fourteen and fifteen," he rasped and swallowed, his smile replaced with a dour grimace. "I'm going on break." He paused, his eyes shifting nervously. "Uh... to change," he said, nodding as if to convince himself, and strode out of the slaughterhouse security booth, leaving the younger man to stare after him uncertainly.

Malph was not going to change his clothes. He only had the one set of coveralls to anyone's knowledge. And he was not known to care much about how dirty they got. The frequent rains on his walks to and from the slaughterhouse and Cillers' Still was as much of a wash cycle as he required. But, even if nothing else changed, in Malphius's mind, *he* had.

The Harbinger Broken

He was finally fed up. Fed up with lying. Fed up with how he felt after taking the meager cash Karnal's goons doled out for his silence. Fed up with the general shittiness of his world.

Maybe it was seeing Holland after all these years. Not even Ciller's aviation fuel could numb his conscience after seeing that ghost from his past. Besides, he knew someone would just take his place. Some other apathetic low-life looking for a payout.

Probably Coopernall. Maybe somebody new. But it wouldn't matter. Dain Burrough, the Dustbin, was the dregs of humanity and he just couldn't stomach being part of it anymore. A miserable man, perpetuating a cycle of misery.

What did it matter? He wasn't even saving anyone, right? Not even himself? So what if the mob erased another body? So, the scud, what? Malph pondered this even as he made his way past the five cameras and turned down the next hallway toward the livestock pens. He ran thickly calloused fingers along the painted plywood wall, over the imperfections in the wood, nail-pops covered over by years and years of dingy white paint. Maybe the other guys could do it, but he couldn't. Not anymore.

Malph's stomach churned like ulcers to the day's first shot of 90 proof. He belched and blew out a long, low breath and kept moving. Past camera twelve, through the pale brown plastic curtains that used to be clear at the end of the hall. The fresh smell of manure, disease, and rotting slop hit him, assaulted his senses, dull as they were.

So, what was he going to do? Face off with some hopped-up kid, thirty, forty years younger? He knew exactly what he was doing. He'd just be another body disappearing beneath the shitty hooves of a drove of hogs. Malph's dead eyes failed to register emotion with that thought. He realized he wished he had a shot in his hand, one last warm rush of courage.

He unconsciously licked parched lips. He entered another room. The ceiling was low. Suspended fixtures cast anemic light along the long rows of pens. The stench, cloying, palpable, gaggingly intimate. This area was the breeding pens, where they kept the sows and the piglets. He saw but didn't see the sows languishing in filth, small bodies jostling for position, stepping on each other, squeezing in to edge the others out.

The main area was down below, but you had to take a small flight of stairs to get to it. There, the covered holding yards extended out in staggered levels on down the street. Up the stairs was the old, unused hayloft. That was where Karnals' goons dumped the bodies. It was high up, impossible to see from the structure's street-side entrances. And there was the added bonus that they could watch the pigs' frenzy over the corpses.

Malph didn't have a plan, but cracked his knuckles as he walked. He grabbed the medallion around his neck, dangling in his greasy salt-and-pepper chest hair, brought it to his lips, and kissed it. It wasn't a religious relic; it was just something Nelv had given him years ago on a vacation the two had taken. Nothing special, just an excursion up to a hunting cabin his uncle had out in the hills. But she'd given it to him, and he had precious little else in the world. So, it was his last act. To remember the happiness they'd shared for a little while. She'd probably curse his stupidity for being so rash and reckless when she heard of this. Good. She'd be right ... as usual.

Malph trudged past camera fourteen, rounded a corner, and caught sight of the man's shoes just as he disappeared up the wooden set of stairs leading to the loft. He smoothly closed the distance, waited at the bottom, out of the way. *Still got it after all these years*, he congratulated himself. And then he scooted up the stairs with renewed vigor, energized by his new conviction.

That buoyant feeling was short-lived. He cringed at the creaking of a loose board near the top. Luckily, the man didn't seem to hear. The rustling and snorting and chomping of hundreds of pigs below was dull but surprisingly loud, even up here.

The man in dark, tight-fitting trousers and a short dark jacket dropped his load on the floor of the loft and then stepped over to the railing, nodding exaggeratedly in approval at what he was about to do. On sleet, most like.

"Sooie, pig, pig, pig!" the man hooted down to the horde below. Malph slid toward the back of the space, sneaking in directly behind him but a few paces back. He looked down at the thug's victim sprawled on the floor and stopped cold. He recognized the person; the pixie-cut hair, elfish features, the small frame. Malph swallowed. Red rage descended like a fog. His hands flexed, balled into fists. He looked up, and the man was staring back, smiling with a wolf-like grin.

"Someone you know?" he asked gleefully, savoring the deliciousness of the moment and what was sure to follow. Two for the price of one. Lover's leap maybe...?

Malph charged and a wicked blade materialized in the man's hands, but he didn't care. They collided, slamming into the wooden railing. It groaned with the impact. The man's hand flashed, and bright swatches of crimson blossomed all over Malphius's coveralls, but he didn't... *couldn't* stop. With two meaty hands, he grasped the man's head and began to press with all his strength, trying to squeeze his skull into a pulpy mess like a rotten cantaloupe. He pushed his thumbs into the man's eyes and lifted him up. The man's feet began to scramble on the floor, his toes scrabbling wild designs in the straw and dirt.

He dropped the blade and grabbed Malphius's wrists, vainly trying to pry away the growing pressure, groaning with the pain even as Malph growled in psychotic rage. And then there was a whimper from somewhere down near Malphius's boots. Stunned, he cast the man aside and stared at the now twitching body of the woman on the floor. He made to reach down, to hold her, but then, blinding pain shot through his shoulder as the other man plunged the recovered blade down into his clavicle.

Malphius howled and stumbled back, clutching at the shiny black handle of the blade embedded deep in his shoulder. His adversary rushed in, driving a straight kick into his solar plexus that sent him crashing into the wall. He slid to the floor, unable to breathe, and then the man drove his knee into Malphius's face over and over again until Malph could no longer ward off his blows.

The Clan Karnal thug smiled evilly, exultant, his face streaked with snot, sweat, and dirt from the fight. He turned to the body of the woman on the floor and began pulling her at first and then pushing her toward the edge.

Malphius's face was a bloody mess. His coveralls were slick with blood from the knife still embedded in his shoulder. His hands lay limply at either side. He watched as if in a movie as the man maneuvered Nelv's body. Her head rolled side to side with each movement. It seemed like she was trying to protest. Her mouth moved, but no words came out. And then she saw Malphius, and she grew suddenly still.

The thug stepped back, exhausted, still shaken from the altercation with Malphius. He fumbled with her jacket, twisting it in his fists to get a better grip, and drug her to within a foot or two of the ledge before stepping over to the other side once more to give her the final kick.

Malph stared at that beautiful face. Remembered so many mornings waking to it nestled up beside him, staring at him as he blinked away the remnants of the previous night's dreams. Remembered it screaming at him, crying as she threw empty bottles at him from across the room. Remembered it solemn, stoic as he closed the door for the last time.

He didn't know how it happened, but he found himself standing, teetering on the edge of the platform, the man raised over his head. And then he threw him down, thirty-five feet to the muck-covered ground below. The man didn't die but writhed slowly in pain, broken, one leg bent wrongly behind him. And then the pigs crowded in. Muffled cries escaped the frenzy, but only for a moment or two. Then the sound of feeding was uninterrupted. Chomping and snuffling and the rustle of thick bodies in the dozens roiled on.

Malphius collapsed against the railing and then back down to the dust and straw of the hayloft floor. But that was okay. He was staring into the face of his one true love. He reached out for her hand. He'd promised once to never let her go. That was good. That was good...

The bar broke free. Prentiss could almost get his whole body through the space if it weren't for his head. No squeezing that through. Some of the kids said he looked like a gutted fish—just a head and a bunch of bones. He supposed they were right.

He looked down at his thin frame and then back to the pitted and rusted bars. These other bars were a little bit loose, too. With the one he'd managed to bend over and then work back and forth until it finally prized free of its upper pocket, he would likely be able to loosen the others or dig away at the concrete that filled the holes where they were set into the native rock.

But that would be for later. Right now... he needed to do something. He hated to admit it, but the noise down the tunnels probably meant that there were more kids, just like him. Kidnapped, caged down here, just to be set loose, and hunted.

He shook his head, teeth on edge, a grim purpose in his heart. Someone needed to pay for this. If he were only bigger, he could do something about it. But if there were kids down here, they needed to be free. He didn't know if you could kill whatever the lady was, but he could at least do this.

The first thing was to see what was going on. He'd thought he'd heard his name. That was weird. Admittedly, he was a little bit preoccupied at the moment when he'd heard it. Couldn't be certain. But still...

Prentiss squeezed his body through the crack and entered complete darkness. His heart started pounding again as his pupils grew wide, struggling vainly to draw in light that wasn't there. He knew it was a long way to go in the dark. And he still needed to get down. In the far distance, he heard voices. Small, some louder than others, some barely audible, as if muffled by something.

The crates. He'd been drugged, but he hadn't thought that it was possible that the crates had been occupied. His stomach sank. He'd left them there. How many were there? He couldn't remember. Not many at the time. But the voices he was hearing now. There were more than a couple. *The mean lady could be here any moment*, he realized. *She could be here now, wandering the tunnels in the darkness.*

Prentiss felt himself shaking, but he resolved to not let the fear take over. He scooted to the side of the ledge where he knew the rock column to be and reached out with the bar, probing with it, trying to feel where the foothold was.

It was far. Really far for him. Maybe it had been easy for the girl, Marceline. She was taller. Plus, girls had longer legs anyway. At least the ones he'd seen. But boys... they were strong. And fearless. At least the older ones, anyway.

He slid the bar into the back of his belt. He'd made the belt from a discarded bridle from a mule whose heart had burst while pulling a wagon up Offerman's Sloughway grade. It had only hit the dirt, and he'd nicked the parts he needed—throat latch, browband, cheekpiece. He knew the names because he'd sit and watch the men training the younger fellows with fitting the team.

Prentiss had been very interested in work during his days on the streets. He'd watched boilermakers, team crews, hide tanners, wheelwrights, just about every blue-collar job in Dain Burrough, on account of the fact that they got paid daily and had coin on hand.

He leaned against the wall and reached out with his foot. Farther, farther than he felt comfortable and then farther still... and there it was. His heartbeat settled. He shifted his weight out onto the new foothold and began to work his way back down.

Step by step, he made his way down and around the column. And then, step by step, he made his way back down the tunnel. Right and then right and then straight on to the dip in the path and then straight some more. The dirt and grit crunched underfoot. Water dripped in the distance. His breathing was his only companion as he walked. Well, maybe not his only companion. He looked around for the spectral image of the girl, but saw nothing. He wasn't sure if he felt better or worse for that.

It took him twenty minutes by his estimation and as he drew closer to the holding room. The light grew brighter and brighter. He felt more and more exposed. For the first time in his life, he realized he felt more comfortable in the dark than in the light.

He breathed a deep, ragged breath to calm his nerves. Listening intently for any sign of the woman, but he heard none. He saw nothing to indicate that she was there, either. Three of the cages were down. He didn't recall hearing that happen, but then, he had his mind on other things when he first went into the tunnels. Well, the whole time in the tunnels, actually.

Within the cages, there were more kids. Two in the first, one each in the others. Pounding and a muffled cry came from the one unopened box. The other boxes all sat with one sidewall removed and propped up against them. Prentiss jumped at the sound of the pounding when it started again.

"Okay, Prentiss. Now what?" he asked himself under his breath. He hadn't had to do anything to get out of his cell. He had just woken up, and it was gone. And then he remembered the ratcheting noise. What had the man done? Was there a mechanism? What if the man came back? Where was he now?

"You, over there. What are you doing?" one of the kids asked from their place in the closest cage. It was a boy. Prentiss recognized him. He was from the area around Barkor's Foundry, the other side of the slough way hill. The kid looked rough, like he was still pretty schnockered from whatever they'd given him.

"Ay, yeah, what're you doing," came another slurring voice. This one was from the far cage with the two occupants. This kid, Prentiss didn't recognize.

"I'm going to get you out. But you need to be quiet. And patient. And if the mean lady comes, well, you better hope she doesn't, but if she does, you yell really loud so's I know. You got it?"

"Whaddaya mean? Jus' get us out now."

"Yeah, do me first. Open up this cage, little buddy. I got sleet. You can have it. All of it."

"Shhhh! Just shut up and let me think." Prentiss waved his hands as if warding away gnats or evil thoughts. The clamoring continued.

A muffled cry came again from the box, followed by a couple of weak thumps. He could get the box open at least. And then he'd work on the cage mechanism. He might need help after all.

As he stepped forward to get a closer look, he saw something glint on the ground near the far box. Keys. Those would come in handy. Prentiss darted across the remaining fifteen or so feet and snatched them up. He slipped them into his pocket, but then thought better of it.

He whispered loudly, "Incoming!" and chucked them across the room where they slid between the bars of the first cage. The boy grabbed them and frantically got to work on his manacles, not needing any further instructions from Prentiss to figure out what to do.

"Pass them along!" Prentiss whispered loudly again. The boy nodded and, once freed from the ankle cuff, threw them to a girl in the next cage over. Prentiss turned to the crate, dug the end of the bar into the edge, and started prying. He'd seen it done before, down at the foundry loading docks. He worked it side to side and then jammed it in again. Repeating the process over and over until a tiny gap finally appeared, and he saw thin fingers appear in the space.

"Thank you," a voice whispered from inside. It was a voice he recognized. His heart jumped in his chest.

Prentiss worked the bar frantically back and forth until, with help from the girl inside, they were able to pull the wall wide enough for her to escape. She was taller than Prentiss, and as she exited the crate, the light caught her blonde locks. Prentiss couldn't speak. She went to say something, but when she saw him, she came up short. She was clearly still struggling to recover from whatever they'd given her, but the cogs were turning slowly.

She stumbled forward and crushed him with a hug, crying and whispering over and over again, "I'm sorry. I'm so sorry, Prentiss."

"Barrett? What happened?" he asked, not knowing what to do but pat her back as she cried.

"I'm so sorry. You were right. You were... You were just trying to protect me and I treated you so poorly." She shook her head and then pulled back, wiping snot and tears from her face with her sleeve. She smiled timidly and shook her head again. "What is this place? What are you doing here?" And then she took in the other crates and saw the rest of the kids in their cells. Her hands went to her mouth. "Gadd's ghost! What's going on here?"

"Nothing good."

She turned back to Prentiss and looked him up and down. "Are you okay? What are you doing here?"

"Some guys came to the shop. They were pressing the old man about something and he wouldn't tell 'em. But then they took me and told him to come and fess up. Only, before he could show, they gave me to this other guy, Gurlish. He's the one I seen kill that guy at the Hall of Ways and he was taking kids. This is where they take them, Barrett. We have to get out of here."

"Yeah. Pretty scudding obvious that. But what are they taking kids for? And if they've been taking them here, where are they all at?"

"That's the thing. Kids go in. None come out."

"What do you mean?" she asked, her face going slack as she looked intently at him. "What do you mean 'None come out'?"

He didn't know where to start. Didn't think she'd believe him even if he told her the truth.

"I don't have time to explain. But there's a bad lady and that guy Gurlish is no prize, neither. We need to get the others out of their cages. Will you help me?"

She nodded yes, wiped her nose again, and wrapped her arms around herself.

"Okay. There are some sort of levers and stuff, I think. That's how they raise and lower the cages. We just need to lift them up a little. Just enough for them to squeeze underneath. Do you think you can help with that?"

Barrett nodded again.

"Okay, but for right now, I just need you to keep an eye out for the lady. She looks normal, but she ain't."

"What do you mean?"

He didn't mean to go down this road, but now it was too late.

"I mean, she's a monster. A for-real monster. You see her. You yell, okay?"

Barrett looked at him like he was speaking another language.

"Barrett." He grabbed her shoulders and looked into her eyes. They were beginning to tear up again, but she was keeping her composure. "Barrett, you just need to tell me if you see her. She'll just show up. She's a waysmith. In fact, she's the Operatrix I think, but she's... well, she ain't altogether human. That's all you need to know. You see her, you scream."

She nodded, the tears welling up for real this time. But she stayed firm and nodded once more. *Good*, he thought. *She gets it.* He turned to the back wall to find the row of levers he'd heard being operated before.

CHAPTER 12

Fire and Ash

Selby Manor Lighthouse,
Lake Grand Marchioness

Holland groaned, his face pressed against the parquet floor. He coughed and couldn't stop coughing. His body shuddered, felt weak. Through bleary eyes, he saw light and smoke and his ears were filled with the roar of fire from every side. And the heat, it felt like a weight pushing down on him. Flaming bits of wallpaper or drapery fluttered down and he smacked them away, patting away the embers threatening to ignite his dried-out and scorched clothing. Embers landed on his neck, and he swatted them, finally coming to the realization that he needed to go and right now.

In a rush, he remembered why he was there, remembered the man who'd attacked him, or more accurately, who he'd attacked. He remembered that he needed to get back down to the caves and the kids down there. To Prentiss, he hoped beyond all hope. Holland took a quick mental inventory, preparing to bend space, and realized what had happened, that he'd been incapacitated by his implant. *I'll be having a word with Prator*, he thought darkly. First things first, though. If he could manage it.

Holland transited, following the path of the man, back to where he'd been in the caverns. They were bare. Empty crates, cages hovering off the floor a foot or two. They were swaying gently, though there wasn't a breeze down there. He took in the scene. Thought about all the pain, the tears, the terror that these kids must have felt. How long had this been going on? His gut twisted in rage, and he thought about Prentiss again. What had the henchman said? The lady... he'd throw her off her hunt.

Ice burned in his stomach and throat. Hunt, huh? Holland didn't know who this lady was, but he was starting to suspect that this had something to do with the Operatrix. Who else would have a lair that you could only get to by transiting in and out of?

Maddie had said that Turnbull was the Operatrix. That made no sense, but... the people, the Ephemera, had told him about a devil. Could this devil have the power to shapeshift? To transit and bend time and change bodies as well? If so, that was something on a whole new level. And terrifying.

Or was it some kind of doppelgänger, taking over bodies and using their powers, like in stories he'd heard growing up? That seemed clumsy. How could it keep up with two different lives, seamlessly flowing between the two? Well, with the power to transit and bend time, it was possible then.

What if there were more? Were there other compromised persons? In the entirety of the three realms, did you need more than the heads of Bureau Ekron and the Guild of Ways? So, could there be other doppelgängers? The Ephemera spoke of a devil. One. One man or being. If so, who, or what, was he? Every question answered nothing and instead seemed to water a garden filled with further ones.

Holland stepped forward, looking around the crates to find any signs that the kids had escaped, rather than what he was most afraid of. That they were already gone. Or worse.

He could see no signs of a struggle. No blood. Then he spotted the keys on the ground beneath the last cage. He jogged stiffly over, his knees, back, and ribs aching. His lungs were still raw from the smoke and heat of the fire. His throat actually felt burned. He tried to swallow, but it stuck, and he just gave up, breathing through his nose, though his nasal passages were inflamed as well.

Circling the cage to the far side, he reached down to pick up the keys when suddenly the cage dropped unexpectedly. He pulled his arm back as it thudded to the ground with an echoing boom. Holland spun to look back across the room to where he'd earlier spotted a battery of levers.

At first, there didn't seem to be anyone there, but then he heard the shuffling of shoes on grit. A short, primly dressed woman with cow-like features stepped from behind the crates.

"Oooh, almost. That was close. Could have lost your little fingies," she chortled, her eyes bright with amusement as if it were a fun game, the maiming of another person.

Holland looked on coolly.

"Oh, don't be such a sourpuss. You are here, after all, in my rumpus room."

"Yeah, well, you should fire your interior designer. Looks like a dungeon to me."

She laughed, her voice lilting as she paused, taking in the man who'd broken into her domicile, burned her house down, and killed her henchman, though she might not know about that just yet.

"So, you look like you've got a story about you. Who are you? What are you doing here? You must be a pretty good waysmith to find this place. Tell me, have you seen the other places? The Elsewhere?"

Holland again refrained from response.

"Ooh, a man of mystery. Tall, handsome, if a bit old... Dangerous?"

Her dark eyes flashed with curiosity, but then she somehow morphed into the form of a man. He, too, was tall, but thin and with an air of authority and deference.

"Perhaps we should talk, man to man," he suggested, in a rich timbre. "I'm intrigued. Do you know who I am?"

Holland cast about nervously, looking for any possible leverage, any fatal pitfall he'd need to avoid if this came to an altercation.

"No. I wouldn't be too hasty, my good man. And don't bother transiting out. I'll either find you or replay the moment until I get the desired result. You're really quite ... trapped."

Holland transited out anyway.

– / –

Holland cast about nervously, looking for any possible leverage, any fatal pitfall he'd need to avoid if this came to an altercation.

"How many times do you want to do this? I've literally, all the time in the world..." the man said, gesturing expansively, his voice echoing off the walls luxuriously.

"So, we've done this moment?" Holland asked.

"Mmhmm," the man provided with a disarming smile.

"Have I died already and you're just playing with me, or are we still working out the details?"

"Oh, I like your thinking... you have verve. You remind me of someone. A real feist. Maybe you know her?" the man hazarded.

The blood drained from Holland's face, though it was probably hard to tell for the soot and ash smeared all over it. He swallowed, but forced his face to remain neutral.

Suddenly chimes tickled the air, and the man held up a finger.

"Hold on, I should get this..."

He pulled out a short, polished wood cylinder from his pocket. Twisting the top, a thin antenna extended from its base and the ringing stopped. He held it up to the side of his head like a telephone handset.

"Mmm. Yes. I see. That is good news."

Holland stood in stunned amazement. Not at the device—which was beyond his imagination, having never even heard of a telephonic instrument that one could speak and hear through freely without a wire cord—but the casual arrogance of the man. It was a foregone conclusion that matters would resolve just as he wished them to be, and then he'd go on about his business.

Holland thought about trying to transit out—again, apparently—but realized that the only way to stop the man's ability to bend time was to stop the man himself.

He charged and dove for him, but the tall man, not flexing so much as a muscle in response, shifted away. He appeared several yards on the other side of the room and continued his conversation.

Holland flew through empty space, landing flat and sliding across the rock floor. He wheezed painfully from the impact and was reminded of the nasty gash across his shoulder and chest as he felt a fresh flow of blood from the wound.

The man covered the receiver of his phone device.

"Do you mind...?" he hissed in mild annoyance. "I have terrible reception down here." Then, turned his attention back to the phone conversation. "Right. Let them know I'll be there forthwith, though the location seems a little melodramatic. But what are you going to do? Mobsters, always so serious. Never with a sense of ... cognizance? Awareness? Not a self-aware bunch, as a whole really," he said, shaking his head and clicking his tongue as he slipped the device back into his pocket. He turned to Holland.

"Well, friend. Lucky day." He smiled again.

Holland stood up, looking on questioningly, but just as he rose fully, the man appeared before him, dropping a sledgehammer of a fist into his solar plexus and whispering into his ear, "See you soon." He disappeared in a burst of purple light.

Air exploded from Holland's lungs as he dropped to his knees, struggling to breathe and wheezing pathetically with his face in the dust.

Well, that seemed to answer some of my questions at least, he thought as he pressed his face into the ground to get his hands underneath him. Now he was left with a new question—where could they run?

The man called Bigg Baby, Tommie Mansignol, cracked his neck side to side and resumed his conversation.

"...so they sent me up to St. Marduke's after that—may it rest in hell. You know, it was the kids that burned it down? Allegedly," he said with a sly smile.

Maddie's recollection was that dozens of those same kids died in that fire, as well as most of the clergy, administrators, and attendants.

The fact that this man, Tommie, remembered it as something other than the massacre it was, was telling. She refrained from comment, wondering how much of her actions in the past were responsible for the tormented person that sat before her. If that was something that could even be quantified. It was a class she'd had to take in Academie, Ethics, and Morality in Temporal Restructuring. It'd been her worst class by far.

"Anyhow, sooner or later, you all end up working for the big man. Whoever that may be at the time. Or sometimes there's a couple of them and you're on one side or the other. Killing old friends, just cause they're taking a paycheck from the wrong employer. You know how it is…"

No. She didn't.

"So, tell me 'bout yourself, Miss Clockie. You been at it long… fixin'? Ever done anything I'd know about? I mean, 'sides the war obviously, seein' as you knew my old man. That's what you meant by you knew my old man, right? From the war?"

Maddie nodded. "I'm not at liberty to provide details…"

Bigg cocked his head, leveling a gaze that suggested he may or may not be at liberty to ensure that she kept breathing.

She revised her strategy. "So, like I was saying, um, yes. I spent some time in and around certain conspicuous events that proved to be instrumental in the turning of what was most certainly going to be a resounding defeat upon the forces being managed by the wise and valiant General Crum, who was not in any way a pompous, lecherous, gasbag," she said with no little sarcasm. Then Maddie paused to think, searching the air for another example the man might know or like. Most assignments of Ekron resources were preemptives, issued well in advance of the actual altercation. If there was a smooth period of history, it was best to assume it had been heavily altered, riddled with Ekron activity.

"I did the Battle at Roy," she offered proudly.

"Never heard of it."

"Exactly. That's why I can speak of it. It didn't happen."

"Now you're just shittin' me."

"No. It's true. And there may have been an election or two in there."

"Oh, now you're into politics. Sounds like Ekron is up to their eyeballs in treason."

"It's never treason if you're on the winning side," she chided.

"Kinda like, 'No body, no crime.'"

"Something like that, I guess." Maddie squirmed a little at the parallel and how closely it fit.

"So, what do you have to do with the old man? Lady like you's not hard to look at. Seems like you could do better. Not saying the old man's not, well, he's got a set of balls on him, anyway. Killed Straightz as easy as tying his shoes. Ratchit, too. Then threatened Karnal himself. That was something…" That seemed to dislodge a thought. "You ever heard about something called a priapism?"

Maddie's face must have betrayed her surprise. He shook his head. "Never mind… mixed company."

"Mr. Baby… or Bigg, Tom? Can I call you Tom?"

The massive thug shrugged.

"Tom, the old man and I, we're currently on a mission. Unsanctioned, admittedly. But there's a very, very bad individual out there. He's erasing history and anybody that gets in his way. He's the one taking the children, I think. I haven't put all the details together yet but, it's him and even the

Operatrix herself. Does that sound like someone you want to have anything to do with? He's not human. I mean, really not human."

"Not my problem."

"Children, Tommie. Just like you when you were sent off to that hellhole, St. Marduke's."

"Not my problem."

Maddie flared. "You mean just like those dozens of other kids that died in that fire? Not your problem. Like that?"

"I said, it's not my problem," he growled, clearly not liking the direction things were heading. Baby stood up, looked down at Maddie, and snorted. "Well, I guess Prator was right about this place messing with your ability to bend time. Guess you'll just be doing it when we want you to from now on. That, plus your boyfriend who can transit to just about any place he feels like. With the two of you, we won't have to work for anybody. We'll own the place." He laughed and wandered off toward the door that the thug named Townie had left through.

And then looked over his shoulder. "Have fun when Karnal gets here. I'm sure he'll have some interesting ideas on how to get you to play along," he said before walking out and leaving her alone in the echoing din of machinery.

Maddie looked around. This was the first time she'd ever been caught and tied to a chair. Seemed like a thing that Ekron agents should be used to, but they were really more about not letting that kind of thing happen, bending time to undo crap like this.

No luck this time. To be honest, she was floored that these bottom feeders had figured out how to thwart her powers. She'd heard of one such instance, but no one knew what had happened, just that there was some fluke that interrupted a raid. Some random, cosmic anomaly according to the whiz kids in R&D, but now, it was clear that it was something to do with the place itself.

It was imperative that she get out of there, immediately. Before Karnal showed up. Or worse, the Operatrix or Turnbull, whatever it was. She didn't know how things worked, but it was likely that there was at least some cooperation between the Operatrix and Karnal.

Maddie's previous investigations had pointed to a significant outflow of illicit goods from Kirksfold to Vellem. She had, at the time, no inkling that there was human trafficking on a significant scale going on as well.

No children were showing up in Vellem and no one was clamoring about a bunch of missing homeless kids in Kirksfold. But, once she'd made the connection between the director and the head of the Guild of Ways, it opened up all sorts of terrifying eventualities. This was a takeover of sorts. And on at least one level of it, there were children being used as a commodity. But for what purpose, she hadn't divined.

She would have to ponder that at another time. Right now, she needed to get out of here and circle the wagons with Holland. She pushed her chair with her feet, working her way closer and closer to one of the large contraptions behind her. She'd spotted a manifold with sharper edges on it and thought that she might be able to work her ropes against it. They were only about a 1/4" or 3/8" thick, from what she could tell. She scooted around, lined up, and tipped precariously backward.

Her head swam again, but she got stable and found that she was perfectly balanced. The manifold was cold against her skin. She could hear the rushing water loudly there. Feel it vibrating through the piping. Maddie worked the knot against the sharp edge. It rubbed her wrists in the worst way. She was going to have deep blisters before she was done.

She kept working, nonetheless, and occupied herself by scrutinizing the machine ahead of her. There were large pipes, and they circled and changed diameter like a flugelhorn. Additionally, there was a large dial-like object at the front end. From this angle, she could see copper coils. Massive copper coils on a radial arm. This wasn't just about water; it was about electricity.

There were large electric fields being generated here and from her studies, that was exactly the sort of thing that could complicate temporal alignments. Not that you would feel time differently here, but navigating streams would be near impossible. Nothing would show up where it ought to. That's why they waited for the zeroes and fives. Time streams in the matrix showed up where they were expected. In here? Not even close.

She tried to focus now but found that the rushing noises she was hearing in the room were almost mimicked in her mind. The way she sorted the pathways, aligned the streams; they were there, but vaguely. Skewed, backward, upside down; so many ways it was like trying to navigate a funhouse maze of mirrors.

She might be able to do it, but not with any certainty. She could end up hundreds of years in the past. Or future. She might never be able to return to this exact time-place. Suddenly, she was glad she'd been unsuccessful earlier.

The knot started to fray, her wrists and hands were slick and raw but she kept working on it. Within a minute or two, she cut through. Of course, the ropes didn't just fall away. She had to move them around to create slack, each small motion biting into the raw flesh beneath.

The muscles in her neck and shoulders twinged from the prolonged, awkward angle. The tension wrapped around her ear as if pinned with a spike in her temple. Every jostling movement not only hurt her brain but the stitches in her side.

She'd seen worse, she told herself, but knew it was a lie. This was the hardest, most painful moment, the most desperate she could remember. *With the exception of that day in the command center when I lost the entire Bramble Pigs squad*, she corrected. But the memory of that had dulled with time. This was now.

Her hands slid free, the ropes giving one last lick at the wounds on her wrists. Now it was time for her feet. The sound of muffled laughter came to her, barely audible through the sounds of machinery and rushing water in her ears. They were close. Just on the other side of the door.

She rocked down to all four feet and pushed back with her toes once more, just trying to get out of the line of sight. Reaching down, she fumbled furiously at the knotted ropes in an attempt to untie them before realizing she could just lift the chair legs out now that her hands were free.

With all caution she lifted the chair, just as the door squealed on its hinges. The voices booming in now were the man, Tommie Mansignol, and another man. She'd not heard his voice but read the cruelty, the arrogance in it. This was the mob boss, Karnal, she was sure.

Maddie skirted around the chair quickly, still feeling wobbly, her butt and thighs numb from sitting for what must have been a couple hours. She moved back behind the machinery stiffly, waiting for the two to draw closer so she could skirt around the back and closer to the main door. The sounds of the machinery and water were a surprising comfort as she tried to remain undetected.

"Where's she at, Bigg?"

"Gotta be around here somewhere. There's just the one way in. We blocked the other exits," Bigg Baby replied.

"I explicitly told you she was not to be left alone until we figured out if Prator's mag-flux idea was going to work," Karnal reminded him.

"And we did. She woke up, couldn't slip, that was that. That's when I came to get you cuz it seemed pointless to wait any longer."

"Well, your stupidity may have just cost us our lives. Now find her. That pompous asshole from Ekron will be here any minute."

Maddie was circling around behind the equipment when another man entered the room, and she was forced to dart back around the corner. She was pinned down now.

"I hope you don't mind, I let myself in," Director Turnbull said as he strode across the floor, polished brown wingtips clacking crisply over the noise. He had the fluid grace of a dancer and looked at ease in his navy slacks, button-up shirt, and thin leather suspenders, even here amidst all the piping and racket of industrial equipment.

"Turnbull. You came. I think I lost money on that bet."

"Looks like you lost more than just money, good man," he said, looking around searchingly. "Where's the girl?"

"She's around here somewhere's," provided Baby.

Turnbull burst forward, transiting the few remaining yards between them, delivering a vicious blade-handed strike to Baby's trachea. He stumbled back, clutching his throat, tripped on his own feet, and hit the ground on his back, writhing in pain and struggling to breathe.

"I don't think I asked you, now did I?" Turnbull said curtly. Turning back to Karnal, he smiled. "So... she's missing, then? You drag me out, from important business mind you, to show me an empty room where my missing agent used to be. Disappointing Karnal. What kind of operation are you running, anyway?"

Baby flopped into Maddie's line of sight from where she was hiding. He kicked over a folding chair as he thrashed about wildly gasping for air. Their eyes locked. It was hard to feel sorry for him, but seeing anyone suffering in that way was hard to watch.

Maddie shifted around the turbine so that she could just see the other two through some of the piping. Karnal stepped forward but paused, seeming to think better of it.

"I mean, I give you five regards for the cleverness of your plan, holding her here where her powers are muddled up. Luring me here as well. But I'm not in the habit of being caught unawares and, as you can see, I'm quite capable of defending myself." In that instance, Turnbull was no longer Turnbull. He was the spitting image of the man now suffering from acute hypoxia on the floor. The broad, mountain of a man known as Bigg Baby was standing across from Karnal, now. His twin, now lifeless on the floor. He cracked his fingers and rolled his neck, looking ready for a brawl.

"A very special thing happens, you see, when I kill a man... I become him." He smiled darkly. "But only in appearance." He took a step forward. Karnal looked on, fear reflecting in his eyes, though he held his ground.

The clone of Bigg Baby stepped forward once more. "In appearance... but not in nature," he said as his arms began to stretch out, bending at odd angles and in too many places. His chest swelled outward and split from chin to waist into a slavering maw filled with razor-sharp teeth.

Karnal stood there, stammering, eyes wide, feet locked in place by terror. The creature burst forward, taking the upper half of the hulking man into its mouth and crunching down with a sickening snap of bone and cartilage.

It chomped down repeatedly. Blood poured down the man's belly, hands, pants, and boots as the doppelgänger, now in true form, lifted the body off the floor, tipping back to take it foot by foot into its eviscerating jaws.

It'd seemed like hours, the street kids all holding hands, creeping through the darkness, all of them trusting the scrawny nine-year-old Prentiss to lead them away to safety. Barrett was first in line, then the other girl, Dorne, she was called. Followed by Brevo, Cheel, and last, Duxton, the boy from Barkor's Foundry, brought up the rear. *Brave one that*, Prentiss thought. Even so, they'd made it to the worn-smooth stairs around the rock column in record time. Even managed to navigate it successfully without anyone falling. Much.

Street kids made a way. If there was one to be made. Prentiss felt a swell of joy and a little bit of pride when they'd all made it up safely to the ledge. And then there was the skinny bit in the rock. Brevo, Barrett, and Dorne had made it through easy enough, screaming in surprise at Marceline's bones on the other side. *Oops. Coulda mentioned that bit*, Prentiss realized at the time.

Duxton had been farthest back, waiting on Cheel. Cheel, however, while seeming okay with the dark, was not okay with confined spaces. He was crying and likely had pissed himself and was unwilling to move a step farther once the others had disappeared and he felt the crevice he was meant to navigate.

"I won't do it, I won't do it," he squealed. Duxton punched him hard in the stomach, dropping the boy to the ground where he wheezed pathetically. He shoved the kid into the crevice and the rest of them pulled Cheel the remainder of the way through. Brutal, but effective. Street kids made a way...

The bigger boys had worked on the remaining bars and removed them in short order. Then it was the cliff, the dark waters of the big lake slapping the rocks with bone-white fingers below.

They'd navigated the wall well enough in the night, moonlight illuminating small trails in the near-vertical rock. Small, cliff-dwelling white-sock ferrets peered at the oddity of the group but would scamper away as they drew close.

The near-vertical slope lessened as they worked their way higher and then, under the amber glow of low-hanging clouds, they saw the first licks of flame rising from the house on fire.

In fact, it was much more than a house, it was an estate manor with several buildings and its own water tower. All were engulfed in flame. The group of children, cold, shivering on one side, felt the press of heat from the other. There was no way around.

It looked as though there had been, but one of the supports on a skeleton-like lookout structure had burned and buckled much more quickly than the rest and collapsed across what would have been a straight shot to the mainland.

Beyond, a long jetty angled toward the base of a town on two levels. One at the base of the quarter-mile wide falls known imaginatively as Marchioness Falls. The buildings at the top were mills and textile factories mostly. At the bottom, a large power plant and its ancillaries were interspersed between building-sized boulders and white, feathery trains of water flowing from the river above.

Prentiss's heart swelled as he realized that they were just a few miles from town. Now they just had to figure out how to get there. And he needed to find Holland, to let him know that he was alright. He was afraid of what the old man might have done or agreed to with that snake, Karnal. The old man didn't say much, but Prentiss knew, deep down inside, he cared. And he wasn't a man that let things go.

"Now what?" Cheel grumbled, still holding his belly though it'd been at least an hour since the incident in the caves. Barrett's hand slipped into Prentiss's as she drew up next to him, looking down at him with eyes that reflected the flames from the structures beyond. He looked up at her and then at the others flanking them on either side.

"We go through. There's a little bit of a gap between the big building and the outbuilding there. There's less trees. I think we can make it through right there," he said, pointing the way.

"You gotta death wish, kid? I say we let the whole thing burn and cut through the ashes in the morning," offered Brevo shrugging off any urgency to get away to safety, likely since he'd not seen the danger for himself. Prentiss had only seen tan socks, really. But he was still terrified to his core about that woman and what she might do if she found them.

"Brevo. You can stay if you want, but I'm putting as much distance between me and that woman as I can get. She eats kids. Kids go into the tunnels, and they don't come out. This might be her house, I don't know, but I would rather face fire and flame, and cliffs and darkness and anything else, than be hunted by that thing again. So you can stay, but you'll be doing it alone."

With that, he looked at the others, who were standing in various states of stupor at what he'd just described and what he was intending to do.

"Did it really ... hunt you?" Barrett asked.

Prentiss swallowed and nodded, a haunted look in his eye. "I would have died, but for I had help. Another kid. She didn't make it," he offered vaguely, not wanting to get into the details of exactly how that had all worked out. That a ghost had told him where to hide and how to find the exact spot he'd led them to in order for them to escape. Monsters apparently could be real, but ghosts... that was a bridge too far for most, it seemed.

"And because of her, I'm here to help you," he said and started walking toward the burning complex. To a person, they followed. Brevo, notably last.

It was easy at first, the burning building was ahead to the left, and there was a courtyard that led from the solarium attached to the three-story structure across to another building with lots and lots of glass in it. Nearly the whole roof was glass. It was one of the few buildings not on fire.

Trees on its left side were alight, but those on the far side, closest to the cliff, not so much. Then a huge palm tree fell like a giant's torch, blocking their way and crashing into the glass roof of the building. Their only way forward was now through the glass building.

It seemed daft, but there was no other way and no choice but to go fast and find another way out. What Prentiss found inside was both lucky and unlucky. The flaming tree had crashed through the roof and would have caught the inside of the building on fire, except for what the building actually held within it, was a huge swimming pool. That was lucky.

What wasn't lucky was the fact that Prentiss couldn't swim and there was no way around the tree since it was still on fire and was blocking both the near and far sides of the pool. They would have to swim under the trunk to get to the other side, and they needed to do it right now.

"Who can swim?"

"I can," Barrett said, raising her hand. So did the other girl, Dorne.

Cheel was quite proud of his aquatic prowess. Brevo, too. They'd both frequented the mill pond and would do trick dives for coins, or at least they said as much. Duxton could doggie paddle.

"I don't know how to swim," Prentiss confessed. "You guys go on. I'll find another way around."

Brevo spoke up, "Look, you're scrawny and cocky and I don't like you very much, but we're in this together. So you're just gonna have to hold on to my neck and when we go under the tree, you just hold your breath and kick."

Prentiss looked at the boy waiting for the punchline, but none came.

"You're serious," he said.

"As a heart attack."

Prentiss thought that sounded ominous, but he had no choice.

"Okay. We all go in. Cheel, you lead the way."

The dark-skinned boy flashed a mirthful smile, ran, and cannonballed in. After that was a splashing frenzy as he made his way toward the tree and under it, presumably to the other side.

Next were Dorne and the other boys. Dorne stopped to wait for Barrett, who followed seconds later. The two frog-kicked, hand in hand until they got to the tree. One and then the other ducked under and disappeared.

Brevo turned around and stooped so Prentiss could grab hold of his neck. Neither said a word. When Prentiss was good and snug on his back, Brevo took two big steps and plunged into the dark waters.

They immediately went under and Prentiss had to fight the urge to claw and scratch his way to the surface, standing on Brevo's head if he had to for air. He fought it, but only just. Instead, he cinched his hold tight around Brevo's neck.

They broke the surface,

"Hey! You trying to choke me to death?" Brevo sputtered.

"Sorry," Prentiss said, as he forced himself to relax his hold.

True to his word, the older, bigger boy was a strong swimmer. The two glided toward the fallen tree as it crackled with fire along its entire length. Flames, too, were climbing the walls to either side. They really needed to speed things up.

"Okay, squirt. Here we go. Just hold on and don't screw this up. If you fall off, I ain't coming back for you."

Prentiss didn't need any encouragement to hold on tight, but something in the boy's voice raised the wet hairs on the back of his neck. If Prentiss had any misgivings about trusting Brevo with his life, it was too late to do anything about it as they tipped forward and slid into the darkness below.

Prentiss struggled to hold on. Water went up his nose and caused him to panic a little and so he started kicking, just like the boy had said. Something about the downward angle and the way Brevo was swimming caused him to slide forward. Before he knew it, he was floating free and could just feel the swishing of water as the boy kicked on.

"Nooo!" Prentiss yelled in a flurry of bubbles before he could help it. He started thrashing, surrounded by darkness, before realizing his eyes were closed. He opened them to find firelight above and to either side, but nothing he did could get him there. His lungs burned. He just wanted to open his mouth for air and finally, the panic took over. He drew in lungs full of water, gagged, thrashed, and fought desperately but for nothing.

And then he was sputtering and coughing on a cold, wet concrete floor. Flames were blazing beyond a group of shadows. They slowly resolved into the silhouettes of his companions.

"Prentiss!" someone was yelling and slapping him.

"Prentiss! There he is!"

It was Brevo, smiling down at him.

"I'm ... okay," Prentiss gasped out. "You can stop ... beating me ... now." He rolled over as more water and snot spilled out of him.

"Come on. We gotta go. Cheel's found a way out," Brevo said as he hauled Prentiss to his feet. Barrett came around the other side and helped to guide him toward the open door with farther darkness beyond.

Prentiss looked back at the burning pool room and the dark waters where he was sure he'd died. He patted Brevo's back as the three of them scampered for the door.

"Thanks. For coming back for me," he said and then coughed some more.

"This one threatened to beat me up if I didn't," he said, nodding toward Barrett at Prentiss's hip, who was glowering in his direction. "And I believed her. Plus, you done alright by us back there. You'd already found the exit. You didn't have to come back."

Barrett's look of menace melted into a broad smile. The three of them slipped through the door to the freezing cold outside and the darkness that ensured the path ahead was fire-free. Now, if they could just manage not to fall down any cliffs, they might just survive the night.

Behind them, a section of roof on the main building collapsed in a huff, sending flame and fireflies of cinder high into the night sky.

CHAPTER 13

THE GRAND MARCHIONESS

Holland stood up on unsteady legs and brushed himself off. The slice across his chest was oozing again, some of it sticking to his shirt when he moved the wrong way. It stung like hell, too. It would need to be cleaned and was going to take a boatload of stitches, he was sure. *Best if I got back and checked on Maddie, anyway.*

This lead was a dead end now. He'd killed the henchman, burned down the mansion, and the kids were gone. The only thing he could do now to find Prentiss was to find the Operatrix or Director Turnbull, which seemed ... problematic.

There was no way he could compete with that. In their brief encounter, the man, Turnbull had toyed with him. He wasn't even trying. Even made a show of it.

Holland could possibly re-do the moment, he thought. If Maddie was well enough, go back to before those thugs had come for Prentiss, just like Nelv suggested. At least now they knew what they were dealing with. Humiliating as it was, he was lucky he hadn't made himself a big enough threat for

Turnbull to shift back and undo everything they'd learned. He hoped, anyway.

So, that's the plan, he thought as he dusted himself off, gingerly. Get back to the flat, formulate a game plan with Maddie, and get stitched up.

They would hide out, bide their time, and then save Prentiss by never losing him to begin with. He breathed in, nodding to himself. *That could work. It's probably the best bet.*

Holland fixed the place in his mind, and before transiting out, was struck by an odd thought: the dream about the Elsewhere and the Ephemera. What was that about? Why did it happen then, after all these years? Something nagged at the back of his mind, a detail begging to be remembered. Though, he couldn't think for the life of him what it was.

He shook his head gingerly. The burns on his back and arms, the bleeding slash across his chest, the beating he'd taken, every inch of his body throbbed with pain. Now wasn't the time for speculation. He honestly doubted his body could take any more punishment. He needed to get to safety before Turnbull came back. And, he realized, he needed to see Maddie.

Holland transited, but right at that moment, he remembered what it was about the dream.

Oddly, he didn't end up at the flat. Instead, he found himself in a solitary space. He hadn't been there in decades. Not since that day as a child when his powers had failed him and Maddie, then as agent Timms, had been so disappointed in him. He realized now that Turnbull must have had something to do with it at the time. Her plan to catch the killers off their guard by coming at them off-time and out-of-place had been clever but failed to anticipate Turnbull could do both. It hadn't been Holland's fault at all. Huh, the thought had never occurred to him...

Thinking of the man caused Holland to grow anxious. He scanned the space again; afraid he'd find either Turnbull or the Operatrix or some other incarnation of him standing there, ready to strike. Or more likely to taunt him some more before killing him once and for all. But the space was empty.

The whole place was so still, but the silence was a creature all its own. The emptiness, alive with hidden possibilities. It felt electric and grounded all at once, if that made any sense. Like it was the center of an energetic vortex, the eye of a cosmic storm.

He let himself relax a little, but was still on alert. The Elsewhere was exactly as he remembered it—a large plaza surrounded by stone columns. The natural color of the stone, if it was stone, was white with hints of blue, red, green, and amber within it. Not a composition he'd ever seen in nature.

The columns bore an angular fluting pattern that ran in irregular swirls down their length. He doubted anything so exquisite existed in the three realms, or even in Brythe.

The outer circle of columns supported a viaduct. The contents spilled into long, spoke-like pools extending to the inner circle where the transparent, golden liquid spilled upward into a smaller viaduct supported by the inner columns.

Holland shook his head. He didn't remember it quite like this. He wondered if it was different now. Or if he experienced it differently now that he was older, or possibly more powerful as a waysmith?

As he studied the grounds, he realized the inner circle held a raised dais. Why had he never come here to explore? He knew the answer. He felt unworthy, small. This was a cosmic way place. What right did he have to be here? It was like suddenly finding one's self in Maker's mud room. What now? Kick off your shoes and go check what's in the fridge?

He knew somehow that it was right to have left it alone. But the dream ... had that been an invitation of sorts?

He felt himself drawn again to the dais inside the circle. He crossed the courtyard, paused at the steps, and then, taking a deep breath, began to climb.

As he reached the area contained within the columns, he found the dais empty. Something like a chime rang out, but barely audible. So much so that he almost questioned whether he'd heard anything at all. He turned to search for the source of the noise and there, in the middle of the alabaster floor, was a small object. He looked around to confirm he was still alone and then walked over to it.

Resting on the floor was what looked like an ornate key with a crimson ribbon. The key was large. It would take up most of the palm of his hand. It was formed from a metal that looked like brass but pale. It almost had the appearance of tarnished silver, only there was a deep luster. Holland stared at it as it rested at his feet. Not knowing what else to do, he bent over and picked it up.

No sooner had he placed it in his palm to inspect the intricate scrollwork than he began to notice it growing warm. It started to vibrate slowly at first, and then more and more erratically. He looked closer at the phenomenon and it lost its shape, melting into molten liquid, like quicksilver.

Before he could react, it slithered up his arm, wrapping underneath his bicep. It was hot, almost to the point of burning. It whipped behind his shoulder and sank into the implant behind his ear. He swatted at it frantically, but it was too late.

Burning white light seared his vision. A torrent rushed through his mind like an avalanche of noise and numbers, like a kaleidoscopic, symphonic crescendo. When the rush was over, he felt the thin husk of his implant fall to the floor, looking much like a metallic scab. And then the scene around him melted away. He felt the movement but hadn't initiated the transit this time.

No longer was he in the Elsewhere. He wasn't in the caverns below the Operatrix's mansion either. He wasn't even at Maddie's flat at Badbriar's. Instead, he found himself in an empty gravel lot between the lapping waves of a shoreline and a shabby macadamized road. It was barely that. The road was little more than asphalt patches filling random pockets in the slabs of basalt rock stretching between a handful of utility buildings.

Beyond that stood a large facility with a scaffold tower supporting massive tubes running down a 60- or 70-foot cliff wall. Above that, industrial-looking buildings perched along the edge of a precipice hundreds of yards long in either direction. The whole thing was maybe a quarter or third of a mile wide, with the two- and three-story buildings dotted along its entirety.

He didn't know what happened, or how he'd come to be here, of all places. But he recognized it. It was the town of Marchioness Falls. At the base was the hydro plant feeding Dain Burrough and the surrounding area.

Stretching out behind him, beyond the thin umbilical line of a low jetty, was the nob of rock known as Selby Point and atop it, the glowing inferno of the estate complex he'd been inside fewer than thirty minutes prior. Beyond that stood the lighthouse where he'd accidentally killed the child-trafficking waysmith. Not that he wouldn't have, just not until after he found out what he needed to know.

That's one hell of a fast fire, he thought in awe at the spectacle of the whole of the mount on fire.

"Good. Let the place burn," he said to an audience of rocks.

He turned his back on the mansion. The buildings of the split-level town were nestled into the broad falls like ticks in a hound's hide. He was still trying to understand the reasoning behind his detour to Elsewhere—and now here—when he saw a tall, well-dressed man appear from nothing and then enter the hydroelectric facility.

Holland's heart skipped. What was *he* doing here? What could the Director of Bureau Ekron possibly need to do in an industrial plant in the middle of nowhere and in the middle of the night? Holland imagined that Turnbull assumed an identity for a specific purpose, but maybe he just favored that body?

Still, he had a bad feeling. He realized he was shaking his head slowly, not sure what to do even as he was moving forward, shifting space to cover the two hundred or so feet to the facility's entrance. *Not too close*, he warned himself as a waft of whiskey and sandalwood rose through the typical industrial scents of machine oil and diesel.

Slowing his pace, he realized he didn't have a plan. But it was clear he was meant to be here. Was it the Ephemera? They seemed to be shifting things behind the scenes, playing a more active role than he'd ever known them to before.

In his mind was a fresh image of the three beings he'd known as the People throughout his childhood. It was odd. He'd never been able to fully formulate an image in his mind. He hadn't realized it was three distinct beings. Now, he was certain there were three of them and that they weren't exactly human. Too varied in physiology. Very tall, very short, too large a head on too narrow of shoulders. Just shadowy images, but clearer than ever before. It must have been them. But what did they want?

He remembered—the devil. Holland felt an icy chill run through his body. They had warned him of the devil. And now, they'd brought Holland here...

Holland stopped at a gated entrance, his hand resting on the cold, slick post. He looked around one last time and slipped inside. It was a utility corridor. On the ground was the body of a man with an eyepatch and comically large nose and bushy eyebrows. However, those features did nothing to hide the look of someone truly nasty. One of Karnal's thugs. Eyepatches were not all that common. What was going on here? Turnbull and Klan Karnal working together?

Holland heard a door close at the end of the hall and jogged quickly down to the end. He quietly cracked the door so he could see what was happening on the other side before following Turnbull farther.

There were three men standing between two rows of large equipment that looked like they might be hydroelectric generators. Thick black lines spider-webbed the air above them on a trapeze network. Above that was a tall atrium ceiling that ran the full length, dotted with large high-bay lights washing the room in bright, yellow-white light.

The rushing of water and whir of machinery filled the air. He could almost feel the buzz of electricity in the air. His hand unconsciously drifted to the empty spot on the back of his neck where the implant had been. He wondered at the meaning of its absence.

The three men only spoke for a moment before Turnbull shot forward, impossibly fast, incapacitating the man who was just as tall but easily twice his weight. *The behemoth known as Bigg Baby*, Holland realized. The man who'd hauled off Prentiss that day that seemed so long ago now.

Holland felt an immense sense of satisfaction seeing him drop to the floor like that. As the man writhed on the floor, clutching his throat, he did feel the smallest pang of sympathy until he thought again about the boy. It didn't much matter, though. Holland's experience told him the man was dead and just didn't know it yet.

He watched as the director turned to the other man, the one Holland recognized as Karnal. His stomach lurched inside him. Jumping at the thought of this man receiving his comeuppance as well. How could such good, such perfect justice be doled out by a man as evil as he knew Turnbull to be?

Of course, he didn't know things would go that way. Likely, Karnal and the director would negotiate some terms and the industrial-scale trafficking of children would continue, but with some other low-life orchestrating the transactions.

But then something else happened. Instead of Turnbull standing before the heavily muscled mob boss, suddenly it was Bigg Baby who was standing there. Holland's eyes went back to the place on the floor where the man's body lay, lifeless now. It was the same. He struggled to get his brain around it, but then things turned even stranger.

The twin of the massive mob enforcer began to morph, to change into something altogether monstrous. His arms stretched out, his chest swelling impossibly large as if to burst forth with millions of baby thugs before his chest burst open into dozens of dagger-sized teeth.

Holland involuntarily averted his eyes, and when he did so, he saw movement behind one of the large pieces of equipment to his left.

Maddie! He couldn't believe his eyes. What was she doing there? She should be in bed back at Badbriar's.

His mind struggled to harmonize all the information assaulting him when his attention was drawn back to the monster now devouring the former mob boss. Karnal's legs flopped lifelessly as the monster jerked and bobbed, taking in the man's body into its own. Crunching bones, devouring it a foot at a time.

Holland wanted to throw up, to run, but he couldn't leave Maddie there. Suddenly a noise from Maddie's location caused both him and the monster to turn. Maddie was standing there, looking down in shock at the chunk of metal she'd inadvertently knocked off the turbine chassis that had clanged loudly to the floor.

The monster crunched down hard on what was left of Karnal's legs, hanging as they were from out of its engorged chest maw. The bloody stumps toppled to the floor as the creature stood fully upright, easily seven or eight feet tall. Then it began to morph back down into the body of the director, Osmius Turnbull.

He dabbed at the corners of his mouth with a kerchief as if from a particularly satisfying morsel of duck confit.

"Oh, excellent!" he exclaimed. "Saves me the trouble of hunting you down. We've much to talk about. Of course, I may have a spot of indigestion but," he said, pounding his chest, "some things can't be helped. Now," he said, leveling his gaze at the woman.

Suddenly, Holland saw the faintest trail of purple light, like dust, whipped up from an empty lot. It whisked between Turnbull and Maddie, and he realized he was seeing the transit path, the way being formed. He was somehow physically observing the pathway taking shape. That was new.

He'd never experienced this before. He didn't know if it was something to do with this place, or maybe his recent detour through the Elsewhere.

In the fraction of a second it took to ponder this, he saw a faint blue wisp dust-up between himself and where Maddie was standing now; a line that intercepted the director's path mere feet before her. He realized he'd already committed to the action.

Suddenly, Turnbull burst forward. Holland's own path yanked him through space, and he collided with the man as he materialized, slamming him into the wall of machinery with a satisfying crunch. Turnbull stumbled to the floor, dazed and dumbfounded by what had happened. His eyes focused on Holland, standing there, also amazed at what he'd just done.

A new trail of purple dusted up between them even as Holland's own pathway washed away to the side, but too late, he realized. Turnbull clipped him as he tried to dodge. He spun wildly and tumbled into Maddie. Her arms came up to catch him or ward off the blow, but the two still crashed into the wall of piping and equipment. Maddie cried out in pain.

Holland tried to grab her but saw the purple traces engulf them both. He just couldn't react in time before Turnbull was on them. They whisked outside to the base of the falls in an instant. Holland was still struggling to orient himself when the wisp of light shot up the cliff to the buildings far above.

Before he could counter, he and the director were standing face to face on a broad corrugated rooftop far above the hydro plant and where he knew Maddie still stood below. Turnbull looked at Holland appraisingly, a wry smile creeping across his face.

"Not bad, for a human." He looked down at a dark patch in the material of his shirt and dabbed at it. Holland must have caught him on the machinery just right when he'd hit him earlier.

"But you're still *so far* out of your depth…"

The faint violet trace brushed out and Holland's own slipped away and back in a loop.

In a burst of light, Turnbull shot forward while Holland's body began its path. Turnbull materialized first, fists extended, torso arched sideways in a two-fisted horse punch meant to crush Holland's throat and solar plexus. A movement that would have launched him off the roof, no doubt impacting the ground within yards of where Maddie stood now.

But Holland wasn't done. His own movements had shifted him away from harm and then around behind the man with a force of his own. He slid forward into a side kick, delivered into Turnbull's exposed ribs with a satisfying crunch as he pitched out over the edge and into the void, arms and legs flailing.

Holland watched him fall, waiting for reprisal. A purple wisp shot out from the tumbling body, arcing up to a point next to him. His own body was engulfed in the faint light as he spun in an instantaneous burst, far faster than he could have on his own. He whipped a shift-augmented fist at the place where Turnbull was materializing, but his hand passed right through. His mind was reeling as his fist returned unconsciously to a boxer's defensive position at his jaw.

Turnbull's blurred-out face congealed back into form as Holland's own twisted in confusion, unable to comprehend what had happened. Faster than humanly possible, Turnbull's hands shot out, twisting Holland's head, the bones in his neck exploding with the force of the movement, his spinal cord shredded. Holland's body thudded to the cold, metallic roof. Eyes staring lifelessly past Turnbull's shoes.

"Hmmph. Impressive, but still so much to learn..." Turnbull snorted. "Still, I like your style..." he said, addressing a twisted cufflink before turning to look down at his former employee and pupil and giving a polite wave.

That was quite satisfying, he thought. To actually have a little dust-up. Turnbull remembered what the man had said in the caverns beneath the mansion. "How many times have I died?" Turnbull mimicked Holland's words with exact timbre and pitch and glanced down at his lifeless body again. "Why not? Let's try that again, shall we?"

- / -

"Not bad, human." He looked down at a dark patch of moisture in the material of his shirt and dabbed at it, his hand shaking slightly. A thin sheen of sweat was cool on his forehead. Holland had caught him on the machinery just right down in the hydro plant. That was unexpected.

"But you're still *so far* out of your depth," he told him, already knowing how this encounter had ended.

To Holland, the fight felt odd. Osmius seemed odd. Like he was going through the motions to get to the good part. It was an errant thought.

A faint purple mist dusted up between the two and Holland's own blue path whisked away to the side and back. The two men transited and found themselves face to face, but Holland was presented with something he couldn't comprehend. He was staring at himself.

Instinctively he transited up and away, positioning himself on the spine of the rooftop yards away. Just a little safe space to figure things out.

"I can't impersonate just anyone, you know," Turnbull told him.

Holland stared back warily, waiting. The director had the air of a showman. He assumed this was either subterfuge or an opportunity to stroke his own ego. Living by deception, he imagined the man had very little opportunity to play to an audience.

"I see you're *dying* to know..." Turnbull said, delight and desire playing across his face. Holland could see the competing urges warring within him—the desire to share how clever and powerful he was, but also the monster within desiring to destroy. Maybe there was more to it. The pure enjoyment of the kill.

He'd struck a nerve in the caverns when he'd mentioned it, much by accident. The chance to kill over and over again, savoring the moment. Holland's stomach turned at the thought. The unknowable depths of depravity, the carnality... He knew there was no way to win, but to be batted around like a plaything, toyed with as he died over and over again. And then what, he'd move on to Maddie?

"You can only impersonate something you kill, is that it?" Holland asked accusingly.

"Mmmm, you are a clever one," Turnbull purred, seeming to relish the moment all the more, his hand trembling a little as he wiped the corner of his mouth, salivary glands overly excited with the heightening stakes. Not that there was a chance of him actually losing...

A flash of violet dust struck up from Turnbull to Holland's position on the roof. At the same moment, a blue trail kicked up to a new spot on a roof just a few paces away and higher up still.

Actual movement followed, with Holland materializing on the metal spine, cringing at a sharp pain in his side.

Turnbull materialized, licking a crimson-dipped talon. The claw-like finger that had been stretched grotesquely long shrank back down to human proportions before his eyes. Holland looked down and saw a fresh flow of blood beneath a long rip in his shirt.

"You know, I don't usually eat mature flesh. So tough and a bit bitter, to be honest. Children really are best. But sometimes … I make exceptions." He smiled.

"So, how many times have we done this? Or should I ask, how many times have I beat you?" Holland taunted, trying to get a rise out of the man-monster.

"Beat me?" he scoffed. "You can't beat me. But I like your swagger."

Holland transited down as the man spoke, threw a shift-augmented punch at his stomach, and flitted away to another rooftop. The ploy nearly worked; he felt the faintest pressure of fist to flesh before it faded. In the fraction of a second it took to go from intention to movement—Holland wondered if Turnbull could use the transiting power to somehow move without moving? He'd seen the man's eyes grow round with surprise, but his fist had just passed through, except for that tiny bit of pressure at the start.

"Ooh, you're a quick study. I haven't had this much fun in, oh I don't know … centuries? Waysmiths tend not to be the sharpest tools. The clockies at Ekron are much smarter, but they lack imagination. If you had the power to bend time, you'd really be something. Why you'd almost be a Thracean like myself," Turnbull mused.

"What is that? Like a doppelgänger, but with powers?"

"Well, yes actually. We absorb what we eat. Three Realms is dominated by people who can either transit space or bend time, both just along the channels, the matrices. What a divinely ordained opportunity for a being such as myself. Being able to do both. Any time and any place I please."

"So that's what you're doing here? Just a cozy place to feed? You're a parasite then?"

"I'm a predator!" he snarled. "With my own private hunting ground." He looked down over the edge of the rooftop to where Maddie had been left. "So, you two seem ... familiar. Lovers, then?" he asked, raising an eyebrow.

"Something like that."

"How cute. For years, I thought about what it would be like to know her in that way. Too dangerous, though, and she served her purpose. Always on the trail, always reporting her progress. Like a loyal hound. Be a silly thing to screw that up, just for a piece of ass. But it was a fun game. Until she finally figured it out. A shame, really. Perhaps, now, I can satisfy that curiosity. I'm sure she'd be more than willing, if it were you, that made those overtures..."

Before he realized what he was doing, Holland burst forth, the faint trace of blue dust whipping up between them. This time, though, Holland materialized just beyond the man, turned, and in one fluid judo-style movement, ripped him over his shoulder as he transited over the edge.

The blue dust trail whooshed down to the roof of a wooden two-story structure. Holland threw the man down with all the speed and power he could generate, even as he whisked away at the last second. He came to rest within feet of where Maddie stood, eyes wide and shivering. Behind him, he heard the shattering of boards as the man's body broke the roof and what sounded like the floor below.

Maddie stood there, eyes wide, shivering in the damp, piercing wind. She cringed against the pain in her side, but muscled through it enough to speak, "Holland, are you okay? What happened?" she asked in weak, breathless tones.

"Can you bend time?" Holland asked, desperation straining his voice.

"No... I don't know ...I must have busted half of these stitches. I'm in no shape." And then wondering what he was getting at, "Why? How far back?"

He looked at her, concern etched on his face as his eyes drew down to where her blouse was soaked through with blood.

"We need to get you somewhere safe," he said, looking around expectantly before grabbing her elbow. The two of them shifted away from the cliffs, out to where the jetty connected to the mainland. Just a quarter-mile beyond, much of the hilltop was consumed in flame.

"What happened there?" she asked in surprise.

"Not sure. Well, actually, that might have been my fault," he provided, shrugging.

Maddie looked at him, surprise, doubt, suspicion all playing through her mind. "What do you mean? What's up there?"

"It's the Selby Manor, but more importantly, it's where the Operatrix lived. That's where they were taking the kids. There are tunnels inside that rock. You could only get there through the ways."

Maddie's hand went up to her mouth. "That's where the kids have been going? And Prentiss, did you find him?"

Something flitted across his expression. *Confusion*, she thought.

"Um, yes. Resilient young fellow," Holland said and cringed ever so slightly. It was odd to her. Out of place and then a cold certainty shot through her mind.

"But you left him there?" Maddie asked incredulously, her tone betraying her skepticism.

Holland stood there for a moment, thoughts flashing back and forth behind his eyes, and then he sighed resignedly. Before her eyes, Holland's body shrank across the shoulders, his skin smoothed out, his face suddenly clean-shaven, his features morphing from strong to aristocratic. He morphed from Holland ... to Turnbull,

"Yes. Yes, I did." He shook his head sadly. "I so hoped that this would work, but sadly, the time for games appears to have passed."

Maddie stumbled back, catching a heel on a proud stone. She crouched low, gasping in pain as she used a hand to keep her from tumbling to the ground. She kept moving backward and shaking her head in disbelief, realizing what must have happened.

She turned, hobbling as fast as her feet would take her, holding her side as she tried to do the only thing she could do. She hazarded a glance back over her shoulder and the man who'd stolen Holland's body—*killed him*, she realized in terror—was striding casually after her.

She pushed faster, not sure where she was going, or where she could go. She had to be anywhere but here. Her mind raced. Ahead was a small shack halfway up the jetty. She pressed on, running as fast as she could manage, the bleeding wound in her side no longer of any importance.

She spared another glance back, only now it was the Operatrix that was following, her wide-set bovine eyes gleaming with excitement. Maddie pushed forward again. Everything in her body wanted to shut down, to collapse, to plead for mercy. A thought that had never in her decades in existence ever crossed her mind before.

She realized that this was how she was going to die. All those other times were just a warm-up.

Turnbull, the Operatrix, was quite literally a monster. She didn't want to look behind her again, but couldn't help herself. But when she did, her pursuer was gone. Maddie spun, her foot catching an edge on the rough walk, and tumbled to her hands and knees. When she looked up, she was staring at a polished pair of brown wingtip shoes.

Her eyes worked their way up to the face, but instead of the look of supreme satisfaction she'd expected, Turnbull seemed shocked, stunned even. His mouth moved, but nothing came out. His arms stretched as they had before when he'd transformed in the machine room but only halfway. His chest began to swell and part, but he couldn't seem to find the strength to open his jaws. A long, viper-like tongue escaped the cavity, lashed at her face dumbly and then the half-formed creature toppled sideways.

Maddie pushed herself aside, clambering painfully to her feet, and was shocked to see a boy, perhaps nine or ten years old, standing there. His expression a mixture of determination and surprise. He looked down at his empty hands and at the long steel bar protruding from the monster's back.

"That's for you, Marceline," he said in a voice, small and barely audible over the wind and the waves splashing against the jetty rocks.

Maddie was speechless. Beyond the boy, hiding near the utility shack, a few kids stepped out of the shadows. They all looked like orphans. The street kids of Dain Burrough. The Dustbin. They trickled from out of the shadows and surrounded the boy. Maddie saw now that they were all covered in black soot and speckled with ash.

"You guys came from up there? From the fire?" she asked, dropping to a knee and holding her side. She felt faint, weak.

The boy nodded. The kids all reached out, putting their hands on his shoulders, except one, a blonde girl who slipped in beside him and pressed her hand into his.

"You're the Harbinger. You don't look well. Is the old man...? Is Holland...?" he asked, not seeming able to finish the question. Where she would have expected to see tears brimming in his eyes, instead there was a hardness. It wasn't callous, it was just ... ready. Ready to accept the harsh reality of the world as it came. Because it always came.

Maddie chewed her lip. The feeling of loss, of lostness at the realization that something that had existed in the world that was truly good, was gone now. It hit her and it was her turn to swallow hard against the overwhelming urge to cry. It always came. Like it had with the Bramble Pigs. Like it had for Twyllis and Lute, Needlesprom, and yes, Mankeer who had been, as Turnbull had suggested, the final piece to fall into place. A moment, but thricely.

Maddie wished she could undo this. Wished she could go back to that time, alone with Holland, and never go back. She cast her gaze back to the scene before her. These children, standing over the corpse of a monster. An actual monster who had destroyed the lives of so many people, so many children. She couldn't redo the moment. A monster as powerful as Turnbull had been? She couldn't chance it. But Holland? She didn't know if she could do it.

Her eyes drifted back to the little industrial town behind her. To the building where Holland had been cast down. And there, impossibly was the shadowy figure of a man. A weak blue flash blossomed in the darkness and the figure appeared again at the base of the jetty. Maddie squinted to see who it was, her stomach clenched tightly. Light bloomed again, and the man was only yards away.

It was him, bleeding, bruised, and broken. And drenching wet. He was standing, but barely. Maddie's heart leaped, but she couldn't help but hesitate. After dealing with the doppelgänger, Turnbull, she couldn't trust what she was seeing anymore. But then she saw his eyes when he looked at the boy. The man's face broke into a huge smile of relief and the street kid rushed to meet him. He threw his arms around him, though it clearly hurt to do so.

"Boy. I was so afraid." The man's eyes filled with tears. "So afraid, when I couldn't find..." he choked on the words. "I'm so glad you're safe."

The boy buried his face in Holland's chest and hugged him as hard as he could. Holland's eyes bulged at the pain of it, but he said nothing and just hugged him back. "I came for you. But you were gone. How did you escape?"

"I had help," Prentiss said and left it at that. "But you really did that? You came for me?" he asked, looking into Holland's eyes, who only nodded. It seemed as though he was trying not to embarrass himself by blubbering like a child and then he looked over at the small crowd of children a few feet away.

"Is this your help, then?" Holland asked, looking at the other kids covered in soot and ash standing a little farther on. Prentiss didn't bother correcting him. "So, this is everyone?"

The kids all nodded, but Prentiss still didn't say anything on the topic.

"Master Finnery—"

"Holland. Just Holland will do, Prentiss," he interrupted, squeezing the boy's shoulder.

"Um, okay... Mr. Holland... I think you need to look after the lady. She looks as though she's in a bad way. To be honest, you both do."

Holland looked up at Maddie. Their eyes met, and nothing more needed to be said.

"To my place ... with everyone," Maddie said, nodding toward Prentiss and the others.

"No, you still need yours until this all blows over with the authorities. With Karnal, Bigg Baby, and Straightz all dead, we should be okay for a little bit at least."

Prentiss's eyes grew round at the news of the thugs' demise. He looked at Holland with a mix of awe and healthy respect.

"Prator's still at large, I think. He betrayed you, Holland," Maddie said through gritted teeth. She could feel herself fading. She thought she'd pass out if she wasn't so cold.

"We'll deal with Prator. But, for now, you need a place to lie down. These ones, well, I may not have enough soap to go around for this lot," he said, breaking into a smile that ended in a pained grimace. "Myself included," he wheezed out.

"Holland. I don't know what happened to Nelv," she said, having to get this last point out. "If they got me, they must have gotten her, too. They wanted me for my abilities. I don't know what they would have done with her."

Holland stared at her for a brief moment before stepping over to where she was struggling to stand and wrapping his arms around her. She leaned into him gingerly, for her sake and his.

"Don't worry," he said. "Nelv always comes out on top. One way or another."

She hoped he was right.

CHAPTER 14

MAKING RIGHT

The creak of a floorboard sounded from the far side of the room. Nelv's attention was drawn to the stairs where she saw a tall, thin young man with sand-colored hair staring slack-jawed. She had pulled Malphius's head up into her lap, was covered in blood, and was stroking his hair while softly singing a lullaby. He still had the knife buried in his shoulder and was unconscious, or maybe worse. She stopped singing. "Coopernall?" she asked.

The kid gulped. "What happened here?" he asked, voice quavering slightly.

"...is unimportant," Nelv finished. "You round up the raiders. Visit Prator and lock him up, tight. I need him for something. Then go down to the warehouse and you kill every last one of those eyepatch-wearing sons of bitches in there. Karnal, Bigg Baby, I don't care... everyone. But, before you do any of that, you get 'Ol Nat and send him here with his kit. You got that?"

"That'll take all of us. Every single person we have. Sleepers and all," Coopernall replied.

"Yes. Yes, it will. Call in everyone who's sworn the oath. I don't care who they are. And it'll take an arsenal, too. Brighton will help you with that. This isn't the battle we've been fighting, but it's the one we should have been. Now get outta here."

Coopernall looked down at Malphius, the man he'd been stationed there to keep an eye on. "He gonna be okay?"

"Not if you stand there jawin' all night," she said, turning to look down at Malph, like a mother would her babe. "Now go. Get it done," she told him, not bothering to look back up.

Nelv resumed stroking Malphius's sweat-soaked hair and started singing again, softly.

BOOK CLUB QUESTIONS

1. The core theme of The Harbinger Broken is redemption. Whose redemption arc do you think is most dramatic, Holland, Maddie, or Malph's?

2. Holland discovers an intimate history with the infamous Madame Harbinger, someone he only remembers from his childhood. How would you feel if you discovered a secret like that? Could you forgive that person?

3. Maddie struggles with and finally gives in to her feelings for Holland after she repeatedly visits him in an alternate time stream. When she goes back, years later, to rekindle things, she finds him happily married. How do you think this disappointment affected Maddie?

4. It wasn't necessary for Maddie to keep all the memories of her interactions with Holland on a memplant. Why do you think she did this? How do you think she felt when she realized that Holland had seen/read them?

5. Why do you think the people of Dain Burrough never thought to question the bay receding and never coming back? What parallels are there to our culture/society?

6. If Holland could transit anywhere at any time, why do you think he stayed in Kirksfold after his wife passed away?

AUTHOR BIO

Eric's base camp is at the foot of the oft-smoldering Sierra Nevada in NorCal where he enjoys surfing, snowboarding, and mountain biking with his wife and three adult sons. He has a hard time keeping his crayons between the lines. His stories are best described as Sci-Fi, Epic Fantasy, Time Travel, Military, and Action-Adventure ... in a blender ... on nitrous ... strapped to a circus monkey in power armor ejected at low orbit.

Discover more at
4HorsemenPublications.com

10% off using HORSEMEN10